Zaira

Zaira

A GIRL BEFORE HER TIME

PATRICIA BORLENGHI

Patrician Press ● Manningtree

Patricia Borlenghi set up the Patrician Press at the end of 2012. She is the author of several children's books including *Chaucer the Cat and the Animal Pilgrims, Dear Aunty* and *The Bloomsbury Nursery Treasury* and has worked in publishing throughout her career. She divides her time between England and Italy. *Zaira* is her first historical novel.

Published by Patrician Press 2014
For more information: www.patricianpress.com

First published as an e-book by Patrician Press 2013
Revised paperback edition and e-book edition published by
Patrician Press 2014

Copyright © Patricia Borlenghi 2013

The right of Patricia Borlenghi to be identified as the author of this
work has been asserted in accordance with the Copyright, Designs
and Patents Act of 1988.

British Library Cataloguing in Publication Data. A catalogue
record for this book is available from the British Library.

ISBN 978-0-9927235-6-9

Printed and bound in Peterborough by Printondemand-worldwide

www.patricianpress.com

For C. J.

Thanks to my husband, Charles Johnson, Tim Roberts, Tilde Borlenghi, Karen Dixey, Jan Turner, Verina Jones and Diego Zancani. I am especially grateful to Sandra Kramer who edited the book.

Thanks to Tim Roberts also for his "Magnox (Pattern Paper)" lino-cut print for the cover illustration.

"ci cuppa Zaira!"

This epigraph is from *Zaira*, a lyrical opera in two acts by Vincenzo Bellini with a libretto by Felice Romani. After its successful debut at the Teatro Ducale in Parma in 1829, it virtually disappeared from operatic programmes. It is taken from Voltaire's *Zaïre* and is based on a moral rather than passionate conflict so this may account for its limited appeal.

1. Zaira

'Why is it always me who has to fetch the water?' Why can't my lazy brothers do it sometimes?' thought Zaira Crespi. Her family had their own spring and well but because of the drought both were virtually dry so during this very hot period the family had to use the public spring instead.

It was indeed unbearably hot. The temperature was nearly 40 degrees – unusual for a place 500 metres above sea level. Sweat was running between her breasts and pouring down the inside of her thighs. She tried hitching her skirt up a little more. She had already discarded her shoes, her dirty toes barely distinguishable in the muddy grass. Her face was hot and shiny, her armpits smelly and her arms and legs glistening in the heat. She undid a couple more buttons on her blouse. But it was no good; even if she stripped off completely, she thought to herself, she would still feel like the inside of a scalding hot bread oven.

She was bending down to place her bucket under the spout when she felt someone pinch her bottom. 'Hey, what's going on?' She spun round and saw Matteo running off and sniggering with his two friends. She threw down her bucket and ran up to him – 'How dare you? You pimply cretin...' and then she pushed him as hard as she could with her outstretched hands against his chest. Matteo staggered back a couple of steps. He was completely stunned to be pushed so violently by a girl in front of his friends. He went bright red and slouched off without saying a word but he wasn't very talkative at the best of times.

Zaira went back to her house, her empty bucket in her hand. Even in summer the house still smelt of stale wood smoke, rising damp and something rancid: butter perhaps or some old meat that she had forgotten to throw away.

'Papa!' she screamed as she came into the kitchen. She tried to keep it clean but it was full of flies, the inevitable fact of living on a farm.

'What do you want, Zaira?' said her father Bartolomeo impatiently, coming down the stairs from his bedroom, his razor still in his hand.

'Papa, tell my brothers that in future if our well dries up they can go and get the water from the *fontana* themselves. I'm never going there again, after what happened today.

'Calm down and tell me then,' Bartolomeo said.

'Well, that horrible boy Matteo pinched my bottom.'

'What! And how did he manage to do that?' asked her father indignantly.

'Well, I was bending down to put my bucket under the tap, and I felt my bottom being pinched, and then I went after him and pushed him.'

Bartolomeo went white and then very suddenly slapped his daughter across her face.

'Never, ever let that happen again.'

'But Papa, it wasn't my fault,' stuttered Zaira, holding her face and trying not to cry.

'No daughter of mine should be in a situation where a man can touch her, let alone pinch her bottom.'

Zaira blew out her cheeks, still holding her chin where her father had slapped her, and stormed out of the room shouting:

'You're so unreasonable; you should be hitting Matteo, not me.'

'Matteo is Delfina's son. You shouldn't have touched him, hmm, retaliated like that. It isn't the kind of behaviour I expect from my daughter.'

Zaira came back into the room, utterly perplexed. 'Oh so it was all my fault and Matteo is completely blameless,' she said sarcastically.

'I'm not saying that – I'm just saying you shouldn't be so – uh – provocative, bending over like that.'

'Oh, Papa, I didn't do anything – I was just getting some water. Why are you so unreasonable, twisting things?'

'Just get on with your chores, Zaira. I have said all I want to say on the subject.'

After Zaira left the kitchen, Bartolomeo felt full of remorse. He had hit his own daughter, his flesh and blood, the flesh and blood of Maria. He never meant to hit her. He was angry with Matteo for not showing his daughter her due respect. But he was irritated that Zaira had not prevented it from happening. And if she were married, no one would have dared touch her.

'I have never struck her before,' he thought to himself. He rehearsed what he would to say to her, 'Zaira, I try and do the best for you, my beautiful, clever daughter, but you are a temptation to every man while you are still a single woman.' But he only said it to himself, not to her.

Surprisingly, he was more liberal than most fathers. Usually, rather than being too strict with her, which was more natural to him, he went the opposite way, always making allowances for Zaira; for her faults, her single-mindedness, her stubbornness.

Maybe that's why his daughter was so different from other girls of her age. It was more his fault than hers.

'Dear God, forgive me, I promise I'll never hit her again.'

*

For a second she had no idea where she was. She had forgotten the time, the day, even what year it was. It would soon be 1900, a new century, but in her dream it was a long time ago. She was in a dress with a crinoline holding a delicate lacy umbrella, and fanning herself in a ladylike manner, tending her little flock of pet sheep. She rubbed her almond-shaped eyes and shook her long wavy hair. Back to reality now: 'No girl like me would ever own such a dress,' said Zaira Crespi to herself.

After the row with her father, Zaira had been on her way to the old rock face where the millstones were cut. She had always loved this spot. In the afternoons the sheer rock faces were in shadow; the sun a lacy imprint over their grey foreboding presence. The atmosphere was dark and mysterious. Some of the huge circular outlines of the millstones were still in place, waiting to be carved out of the rocks with stone saws, and taken to the big mill in Tortello or to smaller mills in the *Cinque Valli*, the Five Valleys, by teams of oxen. Some, too small or irregular in shape were never cut. It was exhausting, backbreaking work, the stonecutters patient and strong like beasts of burden themselves. Once a millstone fell off a cart and rolled all the way down into the village. It was lucky no one was hurt, and the stone was now used as a table top outside Delfina's house.

Zaira had fallen asleep with a book in her lap, under an apricot tree, halfway up to the millstones in the hilly orchard known as 'di Miguel'.

'Whatever made me dream of being a dainty little shepherdess?'

She looked down at her wide hands: 'Me, dainty?'

She laughed at herself.

She was tall, slender, long-legged, and athletic. People said she was beautiful, but she couldn't agree. Her idea of beauty was to be delicate, tiny and fragile. She was none of these things.

She would have to start heading back. Papa would get mad – again. In the distance she could see the familiar shape of Sant'Antonio, the church where she went every Sunday and Holy Day of Obligation. The white conical-shaped bell tower with a cross at its top stood out in perfect contrast to the sky. Dating back to Byzantine times, it stood on a hill in the upper part of the Apennine village of Torretta, overlooking the *Val di Tara*, the valley of the River Tara, which was one of the five rivers of the *Cinque Valli*. The church was indeed a special place, halfway between heaven and earth, as the villagers used to say. Its strategic position ensured that it could be viewed from all around.

*

Torretta was an isolated community, cut off from the lowland towns and cities, its inhabitants barely able to read and write. It was only recently that children were made to go to school. The people of Torretta were contradictory: on one hand hospitable, generous with food and wine, entertaining visitors who passed through the village; yet there was nothing they liked more than gossip or a diverting feud. Property and land were the most important assets they owned and they guarded them with their lives. Nothing else interested them. Although some people had owned their own land for centuries, others had only acquired it recently; they had been *'mezzadri'* working for a local landowner. A decade after unification the feudal laws had been changed and these workers had the opportunity to buy the land they had worked. But owning land was no longer enough to earn a satisfactory living.

Some people in the village were already leaving either for

abroad or to work in the factories in nearby towns or on bigger lowland farms to supplement their incomes.

*

Zaira in her own way was fond of the church and the little cemetery where her mother was buried; the place where she had been baptised and made her First Holy Communion and Confirmation, times for feasting and celebration, when she had been dressed up and was the centre of attention.

She remembered her First Holy Communion dress, long-sleeved white lace, floor length, with an underskirt of white silk. It had been made from her dead mother's wedding dress. She had been so proud and possessed of a strange feeling that her mother was gazing down at her somehow. Zaira did visit her mother in the cemetery and tried to talk to her but she never felt her presence, just the cold grey stone of her monument: Maria Filippi Crespi, beloved wife of Bartolomeo Crespi.

Her father had tears in his eyes at the sight of Zaira in her white dress. She never knew whether they were tears of joy for his daughter, or tears of sadness at the memory of his beloved wife.

For her Confirmation in front of the Bishop of Piacenza, she had worn a plain, white velvet knee-length dress. Her Aunt Elena had bought the material specially and made the dress by hand.

Zaira could still remember the soft feel of the velvet. When she stroked it upwards it felt rough, reluctant, but when she stroked downwards it was smooth, and inviting, like the touch of a fawn's horns.

She remembered the touch – so cold, so hard against her lips – of the stone as she knelt to kiss the Bishop's ring. No one had ever explained to her why she had to kiss his ring.

She felt awkward and clumsy as she balanced on one knee, in front of this old man dressed in golden robes and a tall tapering hat, holding what seemed like a shepherd's staff.

As she walked nimbly down the steep hill, sometimes running, back towards the village, she turned to see the snow-capped Alps in the distance, rising above the blue mists of the Po Valley.

Sometimes the mountains looked just like clouds. On other days she couldn't see them at all. Today, although it was very hot, the sky was clear and she could see them distinctly. She thought they were beckoning, telling her something. Beyond the Alps were cities like Geneva, Paris, London...

'I wish I could go to such places. Make my dreams come true.'

She shrugged her shoulders. She was a young peasant girl, living in the remote village of Torretta with her father and two brothers.

She had been taught that family was everything and nothing else mattered. Her father was a widower, and when her young aunt Elena had recently left with her newly wedded husband for Turin, it was Zaira who had to keep house and look after her father.

Would a girl like her ever be able to leave her village and seek her fortune on the other side of the Alps?

For one thing her father Bartolomeo would never permit such a thing. 'No daughter of mine will leave here and go to dangerous places alone. Never.' She could imagine him saying this in her head, although she would never dare mention it to him.

Italy was going through terrible times. Bartolomeo thought only Torretta was safe.

Bartolomeo and his cronies went to market in Lunano every Friday, dressed in their best hats and jackets. They never tired of discussing politics. 'What a mess it is. A united Italy? Things are worse than ever,' he said repeatedly, even though he admired what Garibaldi and his men had achieved. It was the big cities – Milan, Turin and Rome – that received the political attention. The rural areas had already started to decline and nothing had improved. Still it wasn't Garibaldi's fault. He still remained a true hero.

Zaira had been christened Zaira Rosa Anita – Rosa after her great-grandmother and Anita after Garibaldi's wife.

The Italy that Garibaldi, Mazzini and Cavour had imagined was still not a reality.

Italy was not truly unified. Each region still had its own identity, its own problems. Peasants from the region of Emilia-Romagna mistrusted anybody outside their province, especially those from Tuscany, and there was even rivalry from village to village. The people of Torretta despised those from the next village, Vernazza, and vice versa.

Zaira was used to hearing tall tales about Vernazza: a man with two heads; a man who got the 'moon sickness' and changed into a werewolf at every full moon; the woman with only one eye in the centre of her forehead; and the boy who was in love with his donkey.

'What nonsense!' thought Zaira. Even her own grandmother, Leonora (Bartolomeo's aunt and stepmother), used to rattle on about the people of Vernazza when Zaira was little.

Zaira had since guessed it was really because a boy from Vernazza had jilted her grandmother. Instead Leonora married Bartolomeo's father, safe old Crespi, the widower of her late sister, Elvira. The Crespi, one of the main families of Torretta, gave their name to the upper part of the village, where the church was situated.

Zaira's mother, Maria, apparently had not been so insular or ignorant. She had originated from Poeti, the town further up the mountain, famous for its grand castle and monthly horse fair. She had loved singing and once had persuaded Bartolomeo to take her to the opera house in Parma but the opera was long and too serious and neither of them had enjoyed it. However, they had both loved the name of the heroine: *Zaira*.

Zaira tried to keep a mental picture of her late mother in her head. She was still talked about as being 'very lady-like, very lovely'.

'Why did she leave Poeti and come to Torretta?' Zaira asked herself often but she already knew the answer – a woman always had to live in her husband's house.

Sometimes Zaira had some very unkind thoughts about the mother she had never known, *'Povera Maria'* who had died giving birth to her only daughter.

Zaira was envious of her father and her two brothers who were old enough to have memories of her mother. Zaira did not – she had always been motherless.

'Maybe death was better than being stuck in a place like this, with a grumpy husband, and screaming children,' thought Zaira bitterly.

This hadn't been true. Bartolomeo and Maria had loved each other deeply; connected in body and soul.

Most men in the village beat their wives; it was just another custom. But Bartolomeo had never laid a finger on his wife. After Maria's death, her parents had offered to take in Zaira but Bartolomeo wouldn't hear of it. Occasionally, he visited Poeti and took Zaira to see her maternal grandparents. They had never approved of their son-in-law and thought that he wasn't strict enough with her, that she was allowed far too much freedom for her age. By the time Zaira was thirteen, they had both died, only three months apart: Zaira's grandfather just lost the will to live after his wife departed this life, as he used to say.

Zaira was very upset when she lost her grandparents, mainly because it meant that she wouldn't visit Poeti so often any more. Torretta became even more restricting and claustrophobic.

'I am stuck in this place, surrounded by stupid people and silly boys who tease me and want to pinch my bottom.' Zaira was suffocating...

*

Finally though, Italy was undergoing reforms. There had been many advances, but it was all happening elsewhere, it seemed to Zaira, 'Things are certainly not changing here in Torretta – it's far too remote – it's been the same here for centuries,' she complained to herself.

That wasn't altogether true. Men were now leaving the rural areas in their droves, trying to seek their fortunes elsewhere. Trains and recently built roads meant that they could now leave even the most isolated of villages. Up until then most people had never gone further than Tortello, let alone Piacenza, Parma or Milan. When the men found work abroad, they sent for their wives and children, or their mothers, leaving behind their deserted farms and houses to collapse and decay and generate bitter internecine ownership disputes.

Zaira's Uncle Franco, Bartolomeo's brother, had already left Torretta and was living in London. He had opened a café and it was doing well, by all accounts.

'Maybe I should go and join them,' Zaira often mused to herself.

Emigration from this area was high because farming land in the Apennine hills was not productive enough. Rich farmers in the fertile Po Valley stifled any competition from the local producers. Then there was the crippling taxation and talk about Italy becoming a world power, ridiculous forays into Abyssinia, men being drafted so that Italy could become a colonial power like England or France.

Some were in favour of Italy becoming more involved in world affairs, while others argued: 'We should put our own house in order before getting involved with wars and foreign adventures in Abyssinia.'

'It's all rubbish, you have to walk before you can run,' shouted Bartolomeo to his companions. 'The defeat at Adua in 1896 was a disaster for us, We should leave these countries alone. Italy's attempt at building up an empire in Northern Africa had been a complete failure. Thousands of men had died in the battle at Adua in Abyssinia.

Zaira knew Italy was in a mess. She heard her father and other men arguing about it enough. But why should it concern her? She was only a girl; she wasn't supposed to have ideas. Her role was to help her father and brothers.

'Life is so unfair,' she thought.

'Why couldn't I have been born a man, or live in a manor house, with servants and a carriage?'

With her chestnut, almost red, hair, grey-green eyes, and short slightly upturned nose, Zaira didn't look like a typical peasant girl. She could have been descended from many different races – the vast gene pool of Celts, Goths, Visigoths, Longobards, Germans and even Mongolians who had all invaded the area.

And not that far away the Carthaginian Hannibal and his elephants had crossed the Alps and made camp in the nearby Val di Trebbia.

Yet the Crespi family were proud of their peasant blood. Her father was always telling Zaira that theirs was a family to be reckoned with, the most important one in Torretta.

'But what does it matter now?' she had asked Elena. They were as poor as the next family.

'We are stuck, like pigs in mud. It's more like living in the Middle Ages than the dawn of the twentieth century,' opined Elena who had similar ideas to her niece.

But Zaira had heard rumblings from her teacher that people

were trying to change things closer to home; emigration was not the only solution. There were agricultural strikes in the Po Valley, and the workers were becoming interested in socialism.

A league for labourers had been set up near Cremona, one of the first co-operatives. But. for now, women played no part in these events and Torretta was too isolated, too small and unimportant to be affected.

*

The only pleasure Zaira had in her daily life was her passion for books; she read whenever she had a chance.

'Well, I'd better head off home.' Her father would be wondering where she was. 'Hopefully he will have calmed down by now,' she thought. She reached the house and Berillo the dog was waiting for her. He had followed her on her walk but she had shooed him away. She had wanted to be completely alone – alone with her thoughts and her unhappiness. She stroked him now, trying to put off having to answer her father's questions.

She entered her house through the main double door. It was a three-storey medieval stone building with the Roman system of semi-cylindrical tiles (*coppe*) on the roof, typical of the area. It was larger than it looked. Outside the windows were small and shuttered, but the metre-thick walls opened out on the inside to make the window space much wider. Her father was in the kitchen.

Bartolomeo was looking rather sheepish. He didn't know whether to apologise to his daughter or not. In the end he decided not to. It was better to forget it ever happened.

'Zaira, where have you been all this time?'

'Nowhere, father, just walking in the hills, and reading my book.' Zaira too had decided it was best to forget about the fact that her father had struck her face. She knew it was out of character for him. It was as if they both agreed never to bring it up again.

'You have no time to walk in the hills or read your *book*! Have you fed and watered all the animals, and what about the cooking?'

'Yes, father,' she sighed, 'I have done everything you asked. The soup is on the stove, and we have the polenta from yesterday. Don't worry, I can manage, and have time to walk and read as well,' she said in a singsong voice, as if she had forgotten all about what had happened earlier.

2. **Leonardo**

Leonardo Bertini paced the parquet floor of the library. The sun was pouring through the open beige brocade curtains at the long windows. It was autumn and the start of the hunting season. He was getting impatient.

Armando, his head groom, had announced the shoot would be ready for ten; it was now nearly half an hour later. Leonardo was anxious to get out there and start hunting the wild boar. They were huge, ugly, wiry-haired beasts with long pointed snouts and dangerous, especially the female of the species when she was guarding her young. She would kill you, to protect her young. The male could weigh more than one hundred kilos, and when wounded it would attack. Wild boar were usually black in colour, but they spent a lot of time wallowing in muddy water, and so when they were spotted amongst trees, or by water, they often looked quite elephantine grey with their dried-up coats of mud.

The dogs would pick up the scent of a wild boar or the cloven hoofed imprints could be followed quite easily along muddy tracks. The huntsmen would dismount from their horses and continue the search on foot, normally close to water, a pond or a river. Leonardo loved the challenge of hunting. He had no doubt that he would end up the victor. He could already mentally taste the delicious dinner Margherita, the cook, would make when the meat was ready to eat, a traditional peasant recipe: *cinghiale* with polenta, the rich succulent brown meat contrasting wonderfully with the dry paste of bright corn-yellow maize. The wild boar was cut up into chunks and cooked in a tomato and onion sauce while the maize was boiled in water and stirred continuously until it thickened. Margherita had to be careful not to let it get too hard – the texture had to be just right, soft and melting on the tongue. Leonardo adored it, especially when it was served with a good vintage of Gutturnio, the local red wine.

Leonardo liked to eat good things, but he was not at all interested in organising supper parties for other people. As one of the only surviving members of the Bertini family he was expected to entertain the other gentry and local dignitaries. However, he didn't do this very often. He found it 'intensely boring' and couldn't be bothered with these people:

'They're all so infernally stupid and so utterly provincial.'

He preferred to go to restaurants in Piacenza, or in Milan, where he often stayed the night.

In fact he was going to Piacenza the very next day to collect his latest purchase, a new model of the most important invention of recent years: the motor car. Four of his acquaintances in Piacenza had built their very own five-horsepower motor car – it was called the Orio-Marchand 5hp – in a factory where previously bicycles had been produced. These four pioneers had taught Leonardo to drive this very early, very basic model. It had an open high-backed seat set above the larger back wheels, while in-between the smaller wheels at the front was the exposed engine, the steering stick on a long pole and the gears beside it on another pole. It was more like a cart than an automobile. However Fiat had started production in Turin, and Leonardo was one of the very first

Italians to order his own motor car from them. Only 25 of the same model had been made. It could reach a speed of 35 kilometres an hour, and was produced in a factory of 150 people (in fact where Elena's husband worked).

Leonardo had arranged for it to be transported to Piacenza by train, from where he would drive it back himself to Bertini.

Leonardo smiled to himself or rather smirked. He couldn't wait to drive his new chrome car, with its black leather-padded back seat and its impressive hood – so much more sophisticated than the Orio-Marchand model. He would look imposing in his brown tweeds imported from Scotland, and his black leather cap and spats, steering the car through the roads around Tortello and beyond – wherever the mood took him.

He had a passion for anything new, electricity, telephones, and now cars. He loved things that could move fast. He would never stop riding, he adored his horses, but cars were different. They were made from steel; they symbolised the coming of the new century: speed, power, the new industrialism. He was keen to be involved in any way he could with all that was happening in industry. Milan and Turin, along with Genoa, were the most important industrial cities in Italy, even in Southern Europe some would say. Factories were opening up everywhere, providing new opportunities for work. Leonardo was fascinated by the changes starting to materialise. Italy had always been such a stagnant, conservative state. Now it was finally learning how to progress, to be liberal, to join with other nations of the world, in becoming an industrially important country. Well, he thought, Northern Italy was, at least.

Leonardo twirled his pointed moustache as he looked at himself in one of the huge hall mirrors. He smoothed his velvet jacket and cravat, and stroked his cream woollen trousers tucked into his tall black riding boots. He was dressed for fox hunting, but he found that less interesting than hunting wild boar and, besides, it was difficult to hunt foxes in the local hilly terrain. There was only a point to hunting if one could eat one's prey. Killing for the sake of it did not appeal to him.

He had always loved beautiful clothes, even as a small boy, and was always very particular about what he wore, that the colours and textures matched, that he wore clean linen every day. He adored the big bathroom attached to his bedroom, where he could soak in the bath, shave his smooth dark skin, and splash cologne all over his muscular body. He and his elder brother Claudio had spent a small fortune installing modern plumbing in the house: there were now four bathrooms, each with its own porcelain water closet, marble bath, wash basin and bidet.

He loved the modern furniture he had bought for the house, and his paintings – not that awful rococo ornate stuff from the eighteenth century; he much preferred Art Nouveau. He was also particularly fond of the Impressionists. When Claudio was still here, he had often visited Paris to see the paintings of Cézanne, Monet, Degas, and he was lucky enough to own a small Renoir. Recently he had spotted a painting by the young Matisse.

He was also passionate about poetry, literature and, most of all, the theatre. He attended all the openings of the plays in Milan, even the silly comic ones, but the opera was his favourite and he often went to La Scala, and afterwards mingled with the opera stars. It was said that La Streppona, the mistress of Verdi, had seduced him, but he would neither confirm nor deny the story. He had lost his virginity to an opera singer, it was true, but he never revealed her name. He was intimate with many of the famous leading sopranos of the day, and also the actresses who toured the theatres of the big provincial cities. Not surprisingly, Leonardo's other great passion in life was the pursuit of women, and they never made it difficult for him. He usually got any woman he wanted. He and Claudio had always been spoiled as children, and always had their own way. They led the lives of true hedonists: wine, women and song, and now cars, of course.

Leonardo had everything – good looks, money, clothes, exquisite possessions – and now he was going to buy a motor car. The women would fall for him even more. They would be desperate to ride with him in his fancy new Fiat. How amusing it would be, he smirked to himself. They would be fighting each other to get into that car.

Yet he was not a happy man. Something was missing from his life. Both his parents had died tragically young, when he was only twenty. His beautiful mother had endured a long and painful death. He couldn't bear to recall how much she had suffered. His dear father was heartbroken, quite literally, and died of a seizure quite soon after his wife. Leonardo and Claudio were left orphaned and very wealthy. Claudio inherited his father's titles, both Marchese and Conte, and became known as il Marchese Bertini. Leonardo could also have styled himself 'Conte' if he had wished, but he decided to stick to 'Signor'. Titles were two a penny in Italy. They didn't mean much. For all his conceits, Leonardo was not a snob. He looked forward to the time when every man was equal, regardless of title or position. Things would continue to change, he hoped, and he believed in universal suffrage. He hoped the government would start to introduce reforms soon. Every man *and* woman had a right to vote.

He knew he led a privileged life, but sometimes it would have been more exciting to be someone completely different. He detested the small-town provincial attitudes of the people in Piacenza. He wanted to be less conventional, less concerned with the '*bella figura*' that was so important to petty-minded people. That was why he preferred the Milanese, who at least on the surface had an air of sophistication. He dabbled in politics but was reluctant to become too involved. He was more interested in science, engineering and exploration. Yet somehow he was always too lazy, and, besides, there were many things to sort out on the estate. Claudio had been even lazier than he was and was not interested in acting the lord of the manor. After their parents died, he and Claudio had debated the existence of a God.

'I can't believe in a God who let Mama die such a painful death. She was so lovely, so kind. I wouldn't have inflicted that on one of my dogs. I would have shot it, rather than watch it suffer so much.' For all his debonair appearance, Leonardo was a tormented soul. He had renounced religion when he was still at boarding school – but had found nothing to replace it. His interest in science led him to exclaim:

'Well, if God exists I want proof. I won't accept any idea of God until it is scientifically proven.'

Claudio had laughed at his younger brother:

'How can a foolish notion that exists only in our heads be proven? It's all balderdash!' But since his parents had died, Leonardo felt the need for something, not religion perhaps. 'Something tangible to make sense of my life,' he thought to himself, 'otherwise why are we here?' These thoughts often led him to have quite serious depression. Some days he just wanted to be alone, alone with his confused thoughts. When this happened he thought he would never come out of his dark mood, but then quite suddenly he changed completely and became his usual expansive, entertaining, larger-than-life personality. Occasionally he tried writing poetry, but was never satisfied with his verses.

Leonardo liked to think of himself as an Epicurean. Epicurus was thought to be a dissolute, an atheist and womaniser, but others thought of him as a saint and prophet. Leonardo was amused by this paradox, and at the paradox of himself.

Their only close living relative was their aunt, the Contessa

Camilla Bertini Manzoni, their father's much older sister. The Contessa was firmly entrenched in the old school of thought. She believed in a hierarchical God. 'He created the ruling classes for a reason. Indeed they have a divine right to keep their lands and money. The peasants are here to serve God and their masters. The lower orders should know their place and not upset the apple cart,' she often said to anyone who would listen. She didn't believe in education for the masses, and now there was even talk of the advancement of women! All this new liberalism – it would lead to disharmony and chaos. All that interested her was the Bertini name. After all, they were related to the Visconti, the most important aristocrats in Northern Italy!

Claudio and Leonardo had to start knuckling down. They were in danger of running wild; she had to curb their wayward natures, their restlessness. They were much too free and easy with their friendships, mixing with boys who worked on the estate, even fraternising with other farm labourers in the inns of Tortello. And she had heard all the gossip about their exploits with women. Since their parents' deaths she had tried to guide the boys: to advise them and tell them how to invest their money, but both brothers had simply ignored her.

They were fond of 'the dear old thing', but apart from her interest in the new industries, she was so set in her ways, such a snob, and preoccupied with such petty things. The boys started spending their inheritance without a thought for the future. The grief they felt after losing their beloved parents seem to take the form of a 'live for today for tomorrow we may die' attitude. They spent money on anything they could think of: the latest clothes from Paris, the newest furniture and the latest inventions, and frequenting the most fashionable restaurants of Milan. They travelled around the Riviera to San Remo, or to Venice, Florence, Rome and then to Vienna, Berlin, Paris, London.

Claudio had been keen to see the New World, so he decided to make the trip by boat to New York. It was the only time Leonardo didn't accompany him. He wasn't so enthusiastic, and decided there were more pressing matters to attend to at Bertini. 'Goodness, was Leonardo finally facing up to his obligations?' thought the Contessa when she heard this news.

Claudio had found America to be all that he had imagined, so wonderful, so entertaining, and so different from Italy. In fact, he had decided to stay there. Leonardo was heartbroken. He pretended not to show it, but he missed his only brother terribly. Claudio and Leonardo had always been soul mates, more like twins than brothers, with only a year separating them. They had the same tastes in everything, even women, which had led to some quite amusing escapades *and* arguments. They had always done everything together, even worn the same clothes as children. There were photographs of them at Bertini, arms around each other, their handsome, carefree faces smiling into the camera. The painted portraits of them as younger children showed how alike they were, with long curly still-fair hair flowing past their shoulders, dressed in identical white-lace-collared blue silk suits – just like twins. There was one photograph Leonardo was particularly fond of. It showed him and Claudio on a hill not far from Bertini. They were about fourteen, and had been out collecting rocks and fossils, an interest of theirs in more innocent years. The valleys around Bertini had been covered in seawater millions of years ago. There were a huge variety of fossils and shells dotted around the countryside, in hills and valleys, on the ridges and in the sloping vineyards, everywhere. In fact the skeleton of a whale had been discovered near Tortello quite recently. There was also talk of the remains of a rhinoceros, but nobody knew precisely where it was.

Leonardo looked back fondly to those days when he and

Claudio didn't have a care in the world, and all that mattered was who could find the biggest ammonites.

Claudio dutifully kept in touch with his brother, and wrote him long letters about his latest adventures in New York society, the fashions, and the beautiful young American women who fell in love with him constantly. The New Yorkers thought he was a prince, rather than a mere marquis. Leonardo couldn't help smiling at his brother's letters, but he was hurt that his brother had left him to live in the huge house that was Bertini all on his own with no one to share all the responsibilities and all the worries. He and Claudio had never argued about money, and although Claudio, as the elder son, had inherited the lion's share, he decided that Leonardo should receive exactly half of everything. Now that Claudio had disappeared from Bertini, maybe for good, this had obviously been the honourable thing to do. Leonardo had initially been reluctant to accept his brother's generosity, but Claudio had insisted. Aunt Camilla had been furious at this suggestion, but as usual the brothers had ignored her, and they had documents drawn up so that Leonardo legally owned exactly half of their father's estate.

Claudio had asked Leonardo several times to join him in New York, or just visit him, but there was one thing the brothers didn't have in common: Leonardo absolutely loathed any form of sea travel and this was the real reason Leonardo hadn't gone to America. He couldn't bear the idea of the long journey by ship from Genoa to New York. He would have been violently sick the whole time. What would be the point of that? He despised being ill, out of control. He couldn't bear the idea of having such a weakness. Besides, there really were many things to sort out at Bertini.

Like Leonardo, Claudio also loved cars, and in his letters he was now mentioning flying machines. Various Americans were experimenting with aeronautics. Well maybe one day then, when they made flying machines commercially, like the motor car, then Leonardo would think of *flying* to New York, but not just yet. His point-blank refusal to go was almost as if he wanted to punish Claudio for leaving him in the first place.

Anyway he preferred Italy, and that was that. He actually quite enjoyed the peaceful countryside where he lived – the undulating Apennine hills and the view of the higher mountains in the distance, the valleys, the long winding rivers of the *Cinque Valli*, and Tortello, with its medieval castle and tall towers, the fortresses and fortified houses of the area.

*

Most of Tortello was medieval in character, unspoiled and unchanged – its historic centre still untouched by any later architecture. It had its origins as a Roman camp, later becoming a Byzantine outpost against Lombard attack (like most fortified places in the area). The castle was fourteenth-century and had been built by the Visconti family. It was L-shaped with two rectangular encircling walls, one built at different heights to accommodate the strong slope, and the other perpendicular to the first wall, with the top of the battlements in the shape of swallowtails. The main castle entrance led to the main square which housed the *Pieve* – the Romanesque church and deanery, and other official buildings such as the town hall, the prefecture and prison.

The Visconti dynasty had ruled Milan and the surrounding areas from the thirteenth to fifteenth centuries. After lots of infighting in the family and a game of power ping pong with other families such as the Sforza and Scotti, a certain Gian Galeazzo attempted to carve out a kingdom in Northern Italy. Eventually, no direct heir being apparent, power passed to the Sforza family, Francesco Sforza having married an illegitimate daughter, Bianca

Maria Visconti. The founder of this next dynasty was a peasant farmer who made a fortune as a *'condottiere'*, a mercenary soldier. He named himself Sforza. Eventually Milan and the surrounding area fell to the French, and then the Sforza regained it by right of the Holy Roman Emperor in the sixteenth century. The Sforza family then gave way to the Spanish, and then in the eighteenth century Tortello became part of the Duchy of Parma and Piacenza, when Pope Paul III decided to confer an honour on his illegitimate son, Pier Luigi Farnese, who built the Palazzo Farnese in Piacenza.

*

Leonardo was enthralled by modern inventions, yet he also loved history, the castles in the surrounding countryside a permanent reminder of Italy's turbulent past, so different to the perfect calm of the landscape around Bertini. For him it was an unchanged history, and although he was an advocate of social reform, he was still keen to uphold his family traditions. He had his hunting, and his horses, and now he had the estate to run. His family had been wealthy landowners for generations as his aunt never tired of telling him. It was imperative to uphold the Bertini tradition; it was his duty to continue his family name.

Leonardo was caught in a flux. On the one hand he didn't want to change anything about his life, but an inner voice deep inside him told him that his existence was vacuous, superficial, empty. He needed solidity, something more tangible. His aunt was always badgering him, not with too much subtlety either:

'Leonardo dear, you really must start thinking about finding a wife, especially as it is looking less and less likely that that brother of yours will ever settle down!'

Leonardo had started to think along the same lines. After all he wanted children one day. He was tired of his actress friends, so insincere, so fickle, *'la donna è mobile'* after all. When Claudio had left, he realised he was actually quite lonely. He needed a companion, someone he could confide in, and someone he could love. Maybe a wife to share his life with was what he really desired. Leonardo knew that he gave the impression of being arrogant, aloof, ruthless even. If he did meet someone he could really talk to, who would be his companion, his equal, then maybe it could work, maybe he would feel different. He didn't believe in treating women like property. Women should have rights, should be educated. Only then could men and women really understand each other. Leonardo surprised himself by these progressive thoughts; he hadn't even known he held such opinions. He tried to dismiss them from his mind.

His aunt had already mentioned the name of a local girl, the only child of one of the most successful wine producers in the area. She was not sure about the father's origins, obviously quite lowly when one looked at him, but the mother was very sweet, very dignified, and came from a very well-respected local family.

Leonardo wasn't worried about the girl's pedigree but 'Wine – hmm, that sounds good.' With that he poured himself a glass of cold, medium-sweet white Monterosso. 'Just a little glass before I go out hunting. Where is that confounded groom...?' Just then Armando appeared at the library doors, surrounded by the gun dogs. The dogs rushed over to Leonardo and started licking his hands. He fondled them all behind their long ears, and stroked the creases on their faces.

'Signor, my apologies for keeping you waiting, there was a problem with one of the stable boys. His mother was taken sick.'

'Never mind that, let's get going.'

3. **Zaira**

Zaira hated all her domestic duties: the cooking; the cleaning; looking after the animals; weeding the garden; picking the fruit in the orchards. Every day she mentally planned the best order in which to accomplish her tasks: 'It would be best to prepare the vegetables first and then go and feed the animals, then collect the wood for the stove...'

She despised the housework and farm work in equal measure, and all that washing, ironing and sewing was endless. Yet she managed to work out a routine for herself. She planned the meals daily. On Sunday one of her brothers would kill an old chicken, or sometimes they would shoot a guinea fowl or, on a rare occasion, a pheasant or partridge. All these fowl had to be plucked by hand, the head chopped off and all the innards discarded. She would boil the chicken in cold water and make a *'brod'* – a broth, adding an onion, a few sticks of celery and some carrots to it as well. This would be strained and served with little shapes of pasta, or sometimes with *'burdett'*, balls of egg and bread mixed together, floating in the clear soup. The boiled chicken or whatever would be served after with the vegetables. On special occasions they would have *anolini* or *capelletti, ravioli* or *tortelli* filled with grated cheese, bread, egg and a little tomato sauce.

If Zaira had to make the pasta herself it involved a lot of work, but if it was for a feast day such as St Anthony, all the women from the village would assemble and make the pasta communally, and this was one thing she didn't mind too much. It was like a party. The women would laugh and joke amongst themselves, complaining about their menfolk. One woman in particular, Stella Sartori, nicknamed Stella Tettona because of her large breasts, liked to tease Zaira.

'Zaira, when are you getting married then? How about my son Giuseppe? He likes you – isn't he good enough for you?'

Zaira hated Stella, she was coarse and loud, and very full of herself.

'Stella, I wouldn't marry him if he was the last man on earth!' retorted Zaira.

'So Zaira, what man is going to be good enough for you then? Who will ever get to see your *figa*?'

Zaira despised this kind of talk. 'It's none of your business!' she blushed. 'But God knows why anyone would want to see yours!' She couldn't help herself, even though she knew she was being vulgar. And that made Stella shut up for once. All the women laughed.

Zaira can give as good as she gets,' said one.

But Stella still had the final word:

'Let's hope she does give it to a man one day, and then maybe she won't be so stuck up!' Stella said, sticking her breasts out as far as she could and cursing Zaira under her breath.

Zaira just ignored her, but inside she was thinking: 'Ugly, stupid woman.'

The women sometimes made the pasta in the open air on a long trestle table, made up from spare planks of wood. It was usually Delfina who rolled out the pasta made from flour, water and eggs in great long strips, her hips swaying as she kneaded the dough. While she was doing this others had made the stuffing and started to dot one strip of pasta with it. Then another strip was laid carefully over the top, patted down and cut into shapes around each piece of stuffing, either with the top of a little glass or a metal-spiked wheel.

On feast days there might even be roasted suckling pig served with baked potatoes, all cooked on the *'stufa da legna'* – the wood-burning stove.

The job Zaira hated most was the bread-making, especially on hot summer days. The bread oven, a separate little building, with its own tiled roof, stood some distance from the main house. The spacious cavity of the oven was fitted with a little half-oval metal door. The oven had to be filled with bundles of wooden twigs, lit and kept alight until its brick walls and stone floor had reached the maximum temperature. Zaira became vexed and sweaty from this work, her face always red and swollen from the heat, her hair damp and her clothes sticking to her skin. She muttered under her breath, *'Questa maledetta legna'* – 'This damn wood,' as she tried to build up the fire in the oven, pushing the wood as far back as it would go. When the walls were white with heat and the fire raked out into a metal pail, the oven was ready to use. At this point when she put in the bread dough and closed the door, it all seemed more worthwhile and she looked forward to seeing the risen bread, and imagined its taste and hot, light texture in her mouth. Sometimes other women from the village would come and use the Crespi bread oven, so they donated loaves of bread to Zaira in exchange and Zaira would heave a sigh of relief: 'Thank God, no bread-making this week!'

On Mondays she would do the laundry. Water was a valuable commodity. The well water wasn't as pure or tasty as the spring water so Zaira used this to do the laundry. It was a long job, drawing buckets of water from the well and heating pots of it on the kitchen fire to fill the laundry bath. But it was less hot than the bread-making. The old stone house with its very thick walls was cool and Zaira preferred to do the washing in the kitchen. Some women still washed their clothes in the rivulet running through Torretta. It was just a stream at the beginning of the village but it soon changed into a torrent cascading into the river Tara. The women would beat their washing on the stones and leave it to dry, draping it around the huge boulders surrounding the stream. Zaira didn't care for this communal washing, all the women gossiping about their husbands, the schoolteacher or Don Angelo, the priest in Vernazza. Zaira was not particularly friendly with the women of the village. Apart from her girl cousins, who tolerated her, she had no real friends of her own age. They thought she had ideas above her station. Indeed, she didn't like to be seen doing this menial work and preferred to be in the privacy of her own home. The ironing was the worst, heating up the iron over the fire and trying to press the rough linen sheets. 'It's so silly to iron sheets, they soon get so creased again,' she thought. She tried to get away with just ironing the pillowcases and cotton towels, but her father always insisted that the sheets had to be ironed as well. One of the few luxuries in life that Bartolomeo enjoyed was to feel the soft crispness of freshly ironed sheets when he got into bed. 'I have no woman to keep me warm, but at least I can look forward to fresh sheets.' He never said this to Zaira, but this is what he meant.

In summer she and Elena had always made jam from all the various fruit trees. Zaira enjoyed how the fruit in the watery sugary liquid suddenly thickened and became 'marmellata'. They used all the fruits they could find – apricots, cherries, peaches, plums, pears, apples, figs. Sometimes they experimented and combined fruits such as *amareno* cherries and apricots, or apples and pears. Elena had discovered that if they used lemon the jam would taste even better. So when they could, they bought a few lemons at the market in Lunano and used either the peel or the juice to stir into the jam mixture before it came to the boil, after which they had to stir it constantly to stop it from burning. In winter they made jam from *'cachi'* (a kind of persimmon) seen hanging on the leafless trees. Zaira's favourite was the one made from the unripe green tomatoes at the end of the summer. It was a beautiful crystal green and surprisingly good to eat. Zaira learnt to appreciate the taste of good food, even though she told herself she hated doing all these menial tasks. When she slowly licked a spoon of freshly made jam, and then licked her lips, it was very sensual. She wasn't sure why, but it felt so good, and made her body feel good as well.

In the autumn months Zaira had to help her brothers collect chestnuts from the woods. She hated her fingers getting pricked by their harsh spiky shells. Her brothers used to chide her: 'Zaira, don't use your fingers, crush them with your feet.' But she always had to use her fingers to prise out the closely packed chestnuts from their cases.

Bartolomeo sold most of the chestnuts he gathered at the market, but some were kept and made into chestnut flour or puddings. On special occasions, such as Christmas, the women of the village made *'tortei'*. These consisted of a sweet buttery pastry stuffed with chestnuts, almonds or walnuts, raisins or sultanas, cocoa, honey, jam and *'mostarda di frutta'* – fruit soaked in a mustard syrup and sprinkled with rum, or any other available spirit. The quite large, half-moon shapes had to be deep-fried (although some people preferred baking them in an oven and dipping them in honey and liqueur after they had cooled down) and were very rich in flavour. Zaira wasn't capable of making them but it was her job to peel the chestnuts – which was bad enough. First she had to cook them on the top of the wood-burning stove in a flat-bottomed pan with holes cut out in it so that the heat could penetrate right through to the chestnuts. She had to score the skins first which was supposed to make it easier to peel them. But it never did and peeling a kilo of chestnuts would take her hours. She couldn't bear the feel of the chestnut skins stuck under her fingernails.

She wished she was more like Delfina, her old wet-nurse. Delfina took everything in her stride; she was one of the few women in the village Zaira admired.

'Not like me. I'm just a slave to my family,' she thought to herself. 'I wish dear Elena hadn't got married and left me to do all this, but who can blame her?' Zaira had felt so alone after her aunt and dearest friend had left.

Yet in spite of herself she became quite accomplished at household duties. Things came easily to her, in spite of all her complaining otherwise.

Sometimes when it was a really busy time on the farm, a couple of old cousins of her father came to help out, and Zaira managed to sneak off to read her books. But today she had no help, and had to plan her duties very carefully in order to go for her walk in the hills.

'Maybe one day I will leave this dreadful place,' she muttered under her breath. 'Surely there must be more to life than this.' Zaira couldn't decide whether she should write to her Uncle Franco in London. She always said she was going to, but something always came up, and she found herself too busy to start writing a letter.

Zaira didn't know how she would achieve it, but she desperately wanted to break free from the deeply conservative peasant society of Torretta. She was trapped by her ignorance of the world that lay beyond the immediate parishes of Torretta,

Lunano and Tortello. Even though the wider world had become more accessible, people were still either too afraid or too poor to leave, too crippled by taxation to afford the train fare. Some people literally walked away from the poverty of the countryside. Her Uncle Franco had boasted that he had walked all the way to England. Many emigrants' journeys followed the same route (in reverse) which pilgrims had used for centuries before, the *Via Francigena*. The migrants crossed the Alps from Aosta into Switzerland through the San Bernard Pass, to Lausanne, then into Besançon in France, heading north to Reims near Paris and from there to Calais and across the channel to Dover.

*

'Well, he must have got a boat from Calais to Dover, or did he walk on the sea like Jesus?' Zaira asked herself. Uncle Franco had never mentioned the boat in the barely legible letters he occasionally sent home, sometimes even with some money in them. It had taken him about two months to walk from Italy to England. When he had arrived in London it hadn't been so bad. Lots of Italians from the same area had already settled in a place called Clerkenwell, very close to the city and full of factories and small artisans' workshops for clock-makers and leather workers. Uncle Franco had trained as a blacksmith and in Torretta he and Bartolomeo had reared a few fine horses (a new cross-breed, somewhere between a small cart-horse and an Arab, which were then sold in Poeti), but he chose to open a small restaurant instead.

*

Zaira didn't consider that she was exceptional, yet she was. She could read and write very well which was highly unusual for a girl in a village like Torretta. Normally children only went to primary school for two years. Zaira's education had been encouraged by her aunt Elena, who was more like an older sister to her than an aunt. Elena was Bartolomeo's youngest half-sister.

Leonora had given birth to her when she was 45 and Elena was nine when Bartolomeo lost his wife, so Leonora sent her to her nephew/stepson's house to help look after the baby Zaira and her two brothers. Elena herself had always been determined to leave Torretta when she got older, and she had been the first person to put the same thoughts into Zaira's head:

'Darling little Zaira, you are different from the people here in Torretta. You are like me, you want to change your life. People can do anything they want if they have the will, if they try. I'm going to leave Torretta one day, and you will too!'

When Elena was 26, she finally married a man from Tortello called Angelo. They had been engaged for six years but Angelo was training to be an engineer and had just found a job in Turin as a welder in the steel industry. He then changed jobs and went to work for the newly opened car factory, Fiat (*Fabbrica Italiana di Automobili – Torino*). In fact when Elena married she wanted Zaira to accompany them to Torino as well. 'Uncle Bartolomeo, please let Zaira come with us. You know I will look after her.'

But Bartolomeo had put his foot down. 'Elena, that's impossible.' Zaira was shaking and wringing her hands. This would have been the ideal opportunity for her to leave Torretta.

'Papa, please, please let me go,' she pleaded.

He tried to be less brusque than usual with his daughter: 'Zaira, you can't leave me now. I've been quite, hmm, indulgent with you up till now. You have been quite free to do as you pleased. But now Elena is going, things have changed, your Papa needs you.'

Zaira tried to keep her feelings to herself. She knew her Papa was right. It was her duty to stay, she couldn't leave him. But at nights she cried herself to sleep for many weeks after Elena left for Turin, thinking of the opportunity she had missed.

Instead Zaira had to single-handedly run the house and look

after Bartolomeo and her brothers. Fortunately for Zaira, Elena still continued to be a strong influence. She couldn't read as well as Zaira, but she took great pains to read the newspaper or struggle with the occasional novel. Fiction for women had become fashionable, so she used to send Zaira her old newspapers, magazines and books, even some French novels that Zaira picked up from the post office in Lunano on market days. The dialect contained a few French words and Zaira learned to read in French. Some of the women's magazines were full of the usual conservative propaganda. They promoted old-fashioned womanly virtues: *a true woman should concern herself only with sewing, motherhood and the education of children, and charity work.*

However there were also magazines and newspaper articles about the changing role of women. These were the ones that fascinated her.

Zaira had been taught to read and write at the tiny local school and had ideas about becoming a teacher herself. She had also learnt arithmetic and a little geography and history. Education was given to girls solely to prepare them for marriage and motherhood. At that time, the idea of an intellectual woman was preposterous, as bad as being a prostitute. 'A girl must be educated, but not too much.' They had to be disciplined and taught that, above all, duty was the most essential virtue.

And as for reading, this was utterly unheard of for any young girl, let alone a peasant like Zaira. Besides, as Bartolomeo often stated, there was no time for reading. A girl would be too busy doing sensible things like sewing, cleaning and other household duties. Most importantly, why would a girl want to read? To fill her head with useless thoughts, thoughts that would make her restless? The whole idea of reading a novel was totally frowned upon by provincial society: especially stories which were capable of awakening puzzling feelings about love, or ideas about what happens in the marriage bed. It was just too dreadful to contemplate: 'An honest girl does not read books about love'...

French novels, in particular, were thought to be far too 'racy'. Zaira would normally never have had access to this kind of writing if it hadn't been for her Aunt Elena. She had to disguise them in old newspapers and read them where no one would find her. Zaira also read serialisations of novels from the newspaper called the *Gazetta di Torino* – which her aunt used to send her. When Bartolomeo saw his daughter reading this newspaper, he was rather impressed and proud of her in spite of himself, little realising what effect all this reading was having. Zaira was greatly influenced by what she read. She read voraciously, and very quickly, as if there was no time to waste. She loved the fantastic, the wonderful, the improbable.

Her teacher, Teresa Maestri, tried to warn her: 'Zaira, all this reading you do may give you false hope. You may not realise it yet but life continually fails to live up to one's inflated expectations.' Signorina Maestri was very sympathetic to her favourite pupil, but her philosophy was that one had to accept one's place in life. She had a natural vocation for teaching: she wanted to help poor country children to read and write. It thrilled her more than anything when an illiterate child started reading aloud, hesitantly, pronouncing each syllable, but with clarity and comprehension. But that didn't mean that everyone would go on to improve themselves. Some of her pupils would always remain peasant farmers or factory workers. They would never have the chance of further education.

*

The novel Zaira had been reading under the tree was about the power of an upper-class man over a working-class girl. The girl was a 'victim' consumed by guilt and shame. The man was cruel and sinister. Zaira didn't identify with the heroine at all. She found her contemptuous. Zaira would never allow herself to be treated like this. She thought she possessed the strength *and* the intellectual power to be different, to escape the typical drudgery and downtrodden existence of girls like the 'victims' in her novels. 'I would never behave like that,' she said to herself.

Her teacher nevertheless encouraged Zaira in her ideas. Signorina Maestri had come from a good family in Tortello. She was fine-boned and tall – she and Zaira were the same height. She wore her long wavy hair tied up in plaits and she always looked tidy and trim in her neat blouses and high-waist skirts, wool in winter and calico in summer. When she first arrived in the village, she stayed with the Ruggieri family and taught a few of the local boys and girls in two of the rooms in their house. Some families didn't even bother to send their children to her; they were needed at home or were too busy working on the land. Before that time a few children had gone to the next village of Vernazza to get schooling, but only very spasmodically.

Bartolomeo was very irked when the signorina went to stay with the Ruggieri family, his rivals. He had wanted her to board in his house, but the officials at the local town hall in Lunano had vetoed it: 'A young woman living with a widower, never!' This infuriated Bartolomeo, but he had a plan. Eventually he came to an agreement with the schoolteacher. He owned an old unused house further down the village, and Teresa Maestri consented to lease the property from him, both for living in and for teaching from. The house became the first proper little school in Torretta. It was the main reason Bartolomeo allowed Zaira to stay on at the school for longer than the compulsory two years. It was his way of reminding the village that his house had become the first school and Zaira was honorary 'head girl'. He decided to encourage his daughter to read and write, unlike those other illiterate imbeciles in the village. Even he could write his name – the Crespi had always been a cut above the rest. No daughter of his would be treated any differently. And indeed Zaira loved the little school. As she grew older she started to help teach the other children and enjoyed it thoroughly. 'I want to be a proper teacher one day,' she decided.

[The schoolteacher was to stay in the same house in the village for the rest of her days. Teresa Maestri met a younger man from Vernazza who was training to be a priest in the local seminary. They found they had lots in common, and although it wasn't really a passionate affair, they gradually fell in love. Teresa felt some guilt about this as he lost his vocation and left the priesthood. Eventually they married and he moved into the house with her where they brought up several children. The villagers were both scandalised and enthralled by this: 'A Vernazza boy, shamed out of the seminary and now living with the schoolteacher in Torretta!' they gossiped.]

*

'Times are definitely changing!' Signorina Maestri informed Zaira one day.

'Zaira, do you realise women can now study for a degree in teaching at the Polytechnic in Milan? And did you know that a couple of years ago, for the first time, a girl attended a Technical Institute in Piacenza to study with boys?'

Zaira thought of going to the Polytechnic. A teaching diploma could surely widen her horizons.

She also toyed with the idea of becoming a governess. A governess would be badly paid – *'giovinette poveri'*, they were called. However it would indeed be an adventurous, ambitious solution. It would mean independence from her family and she would be able to travel ... something she could never have done otherwise.

Zaira talked to Teresa Maestri about the possibilities.

'Signorina, do you think I could be a governess? I could try and get a job in Milan!'

Signorina Maestri did her best to educate Zaira but she tried to lower the rather inflated opinion Zaira had of herself. She herself had her feet firmly planted on the ground. She didn't want Zaira to become disillusioned with her lot in life. The signorina believed that God Almighty had a plan for all his children, and that fate played a large part in people's lives. And she was also a typical woman of her class:

'My dear, you are very clever, and I am sure you can achieve many things in your life, but ... how can I say this delicately? Well, I can't. To put it bluntly, you are after all a peasant girl. People will recognise from your speech that you are a 'montanara', a girl from the hills. A governess would normally come from an impoverished aristocratic family or from the bourgeoisie.'

It was true. Zaira, for all her fierce ambition, was still a peasant girl, speaking the somewhat unmusical local dialect. She was a daughter, a 'fieula' rather than a 'figlia'. Bartolomeo used to say to her: 'Mange e taz' – 'eat and keep quiet' – with a French rather than Italian inflection.

She could read and speak Italian but her accent was definitely a country one. Parents from the higher classes would not want a girl like her to teach their children.

Yet she continued to toy with the idea and practised speaking good Italian in front of her little bedroom mirror. 'Ti voglio bene' rather than 'ti veui ben.'

She even mentioned it to her father. 'Father, I know this is impossible, but I would really like to go to Milan to train to be a teacher one day.' She was thinking out loud really. She knew he wouldn't agree.

'What are you talking about?' yelled Bartolomeo. He was furious. 'Milan? Teacher? You're off your head. Your place is here.

Who would do all the cooking, the cleaning, look after the animals when me and your brothers are too busy, eh? The vegetable garden, the orchard, what about them? You can't just leave everything! You have to 'Sta a ca'.'

'Bah, there are plenty of girls in the village that could help you. You're not that poor, you could pay someone to help...' Zaira raised her voice as well, in her normal forthright way – she had never hidden her feelings. She had been encouraged by Bartolomeo to say 'what you think and feel'. Zaira had done this all her life. She wasn't scared to stand up to her father, even though she could still feel the sting of that slap on her face. 'All you want is a servant, after all,' she shouted.

'What, pay someone? How dare you talk back to me? You are my daughter. It is your duty to stay here and help your father. The only time you'll leave here is when you get married, my girl. And you're so choosy, God knows when that will be. You might be here for the rest of your life!'

'But...' She stopped talking, pursed her lips, screwed up her eyes, and stamped her foot. Her father was right, there was no point arguing about it. She would always be stuck in this terrible place, so far from the big cities, with nothing but smelly animals to look at. And she would never marry – he was right about that too.

Of the young men in the village, one or two were tolerably good looking, and they all seemed to like her but she had never even noticed them. They didn't interest her a bit. She wanted other things. She wanted a career, adventure, excitement – she didn't want to be a wife, a servant to a husband rather than to a father. Nothing would change.

'I certainly won't find a man of my liking here, that's for sure!'

Bartolomeo was right about that. He knew his daughter. And

even though he wanted Zaira to find a husband, it quite suited him if she didn't.

'Who would look after me if she got married?' he thought to himself.

4. **Livietta**

Livietta Ruggieri was sitting in the drawing room, embroidering a small tablecloth. She had long, straight, black hair tied tightly back in a pony-tail, and an olive complexion, and looked younger than her age. Her eyes were deep brown, darting around here, there and everywhere. She had a nervous, almost hunted expression. Yet she was content. She was her parents' only offspring, cherished and adored. Her mother had lost many children in childbirth so Livietta was very precious. She didn't act like the typically spoilt only daughter. She was a demure, docile girl, and happy to comply with her parents' wishes, to fit in with whatever they wanted. She had no ambitions, no desires. She liked her quiet life: she was learning French, played the piano and sewed. Sewing was her greatest passion and she was always knitting, crocheting, embroidering, or cross-stitching a piece of cloth. She liked to keep her hands occupied. Sewing soothed her, kept her thoughts in order.

She wanted to stay with her parents for ever, living her simple, innocent life. She had no intention of leaving them, of getting married – had never even thought about it, unlike most young girls of her age. She read romantic novels but she never identified with the heroines. She felt so separate from them, just as she felt completely separate from members of the opposite sex; her father was the only man she could ever love. She had read somewhere that an honest girl should not read books about love. Livietta did read about love but it was all too complicated for her liking. These stories did not affect her.

The Ruggieri family owned the Azienda Castellengo, the biggest wine-producing establishment in the Val Chiara, one of the *Cinque Valli*. Livietta's grandfather, Rodolfo Ruggieri, had bought the vineyards and the rest of the Castellengo estate from its original owners. The castle itself was a beautiful brick construction with apertures on the corbels, and built on a square design with two rounded towers to the west and two towers to the east, one square and the other rounded. The chapel and its bell tower were situated next to the eastern rounded tower. In the fourteenth century it had been owned by the Sforza family and then seized by Visconti troops soon after. At that time the Sforza and the Visconti were in continual battle to take over one another's castles and estates.

The views from the house were greatly cherished by Livietta. She could see the Apennines on one side of the house and, when the sky was clear, the Alps on the other, stretching a huge distance from west to east until they became the Dolomites. The sunsets towards the Alps in summer months were very special, the sky changing constantly from pink to scarlet to purple, interspersed with splashes of yellow or green, while the long avenues of vines around the castle shone and shimmered in the soft breeze.

Livietta's grandfather, Rodolfo, and latterly her father, also named Rodolfo, ran the vineyards very efficiently, using modern methods and machinery, and had managed to increase the wine production to an unprecedented level. Their wines proved extremely successful and included local ones such as the red

Gutturnio (sparkling or still) made from a combination of the Bonarda and Barbera grapes, and the white wines such as the dry Ortrugo and the sweeter Monterosso. There was little competition; the other smaller growers knew nothing of foreign tastes or how to maintain a constant standard. This is where the present Rodolfo excelled. He was an expert at the modern methods, and his wines had an excellent reputation both in the immediate area and further afield, to Milan and beyond.

Most landowners in the area made their own wine but not enough for mass production. Even peasant farmers up in the hills in places like Torretta, where the Ruggieri family had actually originated, produced their own wine but it was 'disgusting – like vinegar', according to Livietta's father, Rodolfo.

He felt utter contempt for the relatives his father had left behind in Torretta, the cousins who had never made a success of anything. Rodolfo's father had settled in Tortello. He had left Torretta because he was ambitious and knew he would never accomplish anything there. Then there were the endless feuds; his family was always at loggerheads with the Crespi. What a waste of time and energy! Instead of doing something positive, they argued the whole time about the smallest thing. He couldn't bear all that sniping, all their stupid gossip. He sold all the land he had inherited and left for good.

He went to work at the Azienda Castellengo for the Perdoni family, related by marriage to the Taverna, a well-known aristocratic family of the area. Quite soon he was managing all the vineyards, and experimenting with his own wine-making methods in his spare time. Rodolfo knew that wine-makers had to force themselves into the modern world. The strength and colour of Italian wines made them suitable for blending. He worked twenty-four hours a day on various blendings, which he then sold separately under his own name. With careful planning and economy, he was able to save enough money to think about taking over the entire estate. He made the Conte Perdoni an offer he couldn't refuse:

'My dear Conte,' he started. This was the most important transaction he had ever attempted in this life.

'I propose that I lease the estate for a period of five years, with an option to buy the whole property and contents after that time, at a price to be mutually agreed.' Apart from the vineyards, the rest of the estate was run down and expensive to run, especially the castle, and without Rodolfo managing things, the financial situation would have been far, far worse. The Count and his wife much preferred their house in Chiavari on the Ligurian coast. They liked the sea views, the more equable climate, the orange and lemon trees growing outside their town house. They were getting old; it was time for a change. When Livietta's grandfather made his offer, the Count didn't need long to think it over; the vineyards had ceased to give him much pleasure. He remembered when the vines had fallen victim to phylloxera, and he had never really recovered from this. One had to be conversant with all the new techniques these days. Rodolfo was much better suited to the job in hand. He no longer had the enthusiasm for wine-making, and his children certainly weren't interested in the place. They all lived in Milan or Genoa now. He was happy to let the place go. He would be pleased not to endure the harsh winters any longer as he and his wife both suffered from rheumatism.

'Yes, why not?'

It was the sensible thing to do.

'I am happy to agree to your suggestion. It will be interesting to see if you can make money out of the place. I know I never have, but you are still young, you have the energy.'

So Livietta's grandfather had taken over the beautiful castle and the vineyards. Within five short years he had bought the estate outright, and with the help of unusually clement weather, the vines produced massive yields and the Azienda Castellengo became very successful and renowned throughout the area. When the younger Rodolfo took over from his late father, he inherited a very attractive business concern. He had even exhibited his wines in Paris this year. Things couldn't have been better. He made a very good marriage to a young woman called Rina, from a well-to-do family, distant relatives of the Perdoni, and they lived very happily at the Azienda together with their daughter, Livietta. The only problem on the horizon: whom would their precious daughter marry?

Livietta was sitting in the tall drawing room with its large heavily-draped windows. She got up from the big crimson velvet armchair and noticed the antimacassar was crooked. She straightened it almost subconsciously. She didn't like anything to be untidy or out of place in the cocoon of her little world.

She loved the simple routine of the Azienda. Every morning she and her parents would rise on the dot of seven. They breakfasted punctually at eight, with only a small black coffee and a sweet biscuit. Then Livietta helped her mother with minor household duties, writing letters to tradespeople, or ordering books from Piacenza and clothes from Milan. Then she and her mother sat and sewed, or sometimes they visited neighbours or went to the shops in Tortello in their covered carriage. At other times they took the train via Tortello to Milan to look at the latest fashions. Livietta was interested in the latest sewing techniques, but never once bought any of the elaborate creations they saw in the Milanese fashion houses. She preferred her clothes to be simple in style but well cut in fine expensive cloth. Livietta and Rina were more like sisters than mother and daughter and enjoyed every minute of each other's company. When they went out together they both looked very elegant in their fitted costumes and large-brimmed hats trimmed with ostrich feathers and silk flowers. On their jackets they often wore corsages of roses or gardenias.

Livietta had no interest in meeting young men. Her mother did try to bring up the subject of possible suitors with her but Livietta always said, 'You and Papa are all I need, Mama – *vi voglio tanto bene*, I love you both so much, I don't want to meet any young men.'

Every day Livietta sat down with her parents to a big lunch on the stroke of noon. The menu didn't vary much. Their cook wasn't very imaginative, nor were they. Antipasto with Parma ham (*prosciutto crudo di Parma*), salami, maybe a few pickles, followed by pasta *in brodo* or *pisarei fasù*, the local speciality – small potato *gnocchi* with *borlotti* beans cooked in a tomato sauce – then usually some veal, lamb or pork, and maybe some fruit. The dark red Gutturnio wine, the still variety of course, always accompanied the meal, followed by a small cup of coffee. Livietta was always very careful to accept only one glass of wine but she loved sweet strong coffee.

In the afternoons Livietta helped her father in the office or read one of the latest books sent to her from the bookshop in Piacenza, but usually she sewed, either embroidering a cloth or stitching a tapestry.

In the evening they always dined at eight, usually a '*pastasciutta*', home-made pasta in either a tomato or mushroom sauce (never both) or simply in butter and sage, and then some cold beef or chicken. All three members of the family usually retired to bed at ten unless they had visitors. If they were having the neighbours or business acquaintances around for supper, this was usually followed by a short recital by Livietta on her boudoir grand piano, trying out some of the latest tunes in her sweet soprano voice. Rodolfo had ordered the Gaveau especially from

Paris for his only daughter. Sometimes they dined at friends' houses and very occasionally they stayed in Milan overnight to go to the theatre or opera. Rodolfo always fidgeted when they sat in the stalls in the theatre, uneasy in his over-starched collar and squeezed into his cramped seat. Opera bored him and he had trouble keeping his eyes open, but he was pleased that Livietta and his wife enjoyed these trips. When they were younger they had seen the première of Giuseppe Verdi's 'Otello' at La Scala. Verdi was everyone's hero. He embodied the unified Italy.

'Va, Pensiero' from 'Nabucco' was like the national anthem. Livietta had been so excited to see the lavish sets and costumes and hear the dramatic story of the jealous Othello and his ill-fated wife, Desdemona. And Rodolfo had loved to see his quiet, usually subdued daughter so animated.

However Livietta was quite pleased when the three of them stayed at home, as she liked to get to bed early. As a small child, she was already yawning at five in the afternoon, and used to ask her parents politely:

'Mama, Papa, can I go to bed soon, please?'

Even her Mama remarked on this: 'Livietta, it is so unusual for a child to ask to go to bed!'

Now she was older, she loved curling up in her big white feathery bed to read a French novel. She took great pains to understand the French language, without quite comprehending the subtleties of meaning or idioms in the text. Madame Bovary was a thoroughly nasty character, as far as she was concerned. The moral writings of Italian authors such as Neera and Carolina Invernizio were easier. The heroines in these novels were also tempted to leave their husbands, to commit adultery, but they never did. They always acted selflessly. The rare ones who did leave their families were punished, often dying of a terrible illness.

Livietta shivered when she thought about these things. She

felt so safe at Castellengo and had no desire for anything to change.

'Livietta, *cara*, can you come down to the office in ten minutes?' shouted Rodolfo through the open office door to the drawing room across the courtyard. He wasn't sure she was there, but he knew she could hear him. Although they lived in an old castle, the actual living area separated from the small courtyard was quite small. 'I need some help with these entries.'

Livietta always spoke very formally, and called both her mother and father '*Voi*', the polite form, rather than '*tu*': '*Si, Papa, non vi preoccupate, vengo subito*' – Yes, father, don't worry, I'll be there soon,' she trilled eagerly. She worshipped her father and would do anything he asked. She skipped across the courtyard to the office, which adjoined the larger room where the wine-tasting occurred. The larger room was tall and arched, decorated with original frescoes. The curly-haired god Bacchus was depicted on one wall holding bunches of grapes and a gold goblet of wine. Livietta had often wondered if this had been painted apropos of the wine-tasting or if it was a coincidence. Would wine production already have started here at the castle in the *cinquecento* – sixteenth century, or was the Bacchus theme a common decoration?

As she crossed the courtyard she decided to make a quick trip to the chapel, her very favourite place. She was so proud that they had their very own little place to worship in. It had been built slightly later than the castle. Livietta adored its simplicity. It was lit naturally by the high, rectangular, plain-glass windows and there were two rows of candelabra hanging from the tall vaulted ceiling. The candles were lit every Sunday when the local priest came to say mass. Yet Livietta preferred the slightly gloomy, mysterious atmosphere when the candles remained unlit. The altar was ornately carved and had the crest of the Perdoni family attached to it, a lion and a griffin over a castle. In front of the altar was a single rope, peeking out of a hole in the ceiling, attached to the single bell in the bell house – quite a crude arrangement really but Livietta loved this rope. It was her job to pull the rope every Sunday. Rudolfo had given her this task when she was still a small child, and she continued to this day to ring the bell to alert everyone on the estate that it was time for mass.

Absent-mindedly she gave the rope a little tug, and then realised what she was doing. Luckily she managed to stop the bell ringing. Three long peals would have signified someone had died. That was the only time the bell was ever rung on a weekday unless it was a mass or a holy day of obligation. But Livietta never performed this duty for the dead, one of the estate workers did. It would have been too upsetting for the little girl. Oh dear, she prayed she wouldn't get into trouble, 'I hope Papa didn't hear.' She shivered. She hated to do anything wrong or out of the ordinary. Once she had dropped a porcelain clock off her bedside table. She was so upset she couldn't stop sobbing for a whole day.

Every Sunday when the parish priest, Don Alberto, came to the estate at nine in the morning Livietta rang the bell fifteen minutes early so that the family, the servants and the estate workers would be ready in time. Livietta took this responsibility very seriously; she had to make sure she got it exactly right, and had to watch the grandfather clock very carefully. Thankfully she was always on time.

5. **Zaira**

Zaira liked to walk – walking clarified her thoughts. She could walk for miles, uphill, downhill, along the riverbanks. She took nature for granted. The blue skies, the shapes of the hills, the hues of the leaves on the trees, she never really noticed them. She knew the landscape was beautiful, sometimes breathtakingly so: the sunlight in the midst of a shaded hill, the contours of the mountains, their peaks capped with brilliant-white snow. The skies of so many different colours – pink, purple, yellow, green, but usually that intense blue, so bright, so piercing. But nature never really affected her; it did not move her. She was too intent on her own thoughts, her feelings, her plans. She noticed various animal tracks in the mud or the snow – hares, wild boars, foxes, dogs, cats, herons, crows – but it was just a question of recognition; it wasn't inspiring or interesting to her. She was too wrapped up in herself to notice the environment. Little did she care about the beauty of the place. It was the countryside that was trapping her, enclosing her, like a prison. And, yes, it was a beautiful place but the people who lived there were poor, they struggled to make ends meet, trying to grow things on the impoverished land while in the plains the wealthy landowners got richer every day. 'What good beauty and nature then?' She thought to herself.

One day Zaira decided to make the trip to Poeti on foot. She got up very early and set off at the crack of dawn. The air was calm and still, and fluffy low clouds were hovering in the valleys below, almost as if they were undecided about whether to disperse or not. The colours were muted, subtle shades of purple, pink and grey. As she walked out of Crespi, the sun started to shine. It was still winter so she had wrapped up well in a long black cloak, one of Elena's cast-offs, with a huge woollen shawl wrapped round her shoulders, an old felt hat pulled down over her unruly hair, and woollen crocheted mittens on her hands. They didn't look very adequate, but they were surprisingly good at keeping her warm.

She climbed the unmade-up road past Vernazza and Tedo, and headed towards Il Passo Pelligrinaggio. There had been a few snowflakes in Torretta the day before but here the snow was thick and heavy on the ground – no sign of where the track ended. The snow was blue-white and virgin. How Zaira enjoyed plunging her boots into the deep snow cover. Luckily she was very fit and didn't tire easily, as it was quite arduous dragging one's legs out of the snow. The sun was brilliant overhead and she could feel it hot on her face. She didn't realise then that her complexion would soon become red and rough. If her mother had been alive, she might have advised her to put some olive oil on her face before walking in the scorching blind-white sun.

The view was spectacular because from the Passo you could see all the mountains: the Alps to the north and some of the tallest Apennines to the west, beyond which was the Mediterranean Sea. Zaira couldn't see the sea but she knew it was there. She had never ever seen it. Bartolomeo always promised he would take her to the sea, but somehow it had never happened. 'How long would it take me to walk all the way to the sea?' she mused. 'It must be at least 100 kilometres – so could I do it in a day?' She thought not.

Getting to Poeti would take a good half-day but she was enjoying the crunch of the snow beneath her feet and the sun on her face. It felt intense, real. The air so crisp and clean and the dazzling white of the snow making her shade her eyes. From the Passo it was downhill all the way, and Zaira started to run down the slope of the road, feeling happy and at one with nature.

When she finally got to Poeti she went straight to the house of her uncle Pino, her mother's brother. The house was fairly newly built, quite large for just one man living on his own, yet already somewhat shabby and neglected.

He wasn't expecting her but Zaira would always be a special girl for him, the daughter of his beloved Maria, and he was genuinely happy to see her.

'Zaira, *tesoro*, what a surprise! Come and give your old uncle a hug.'

Zaira dutifully hugged him. He was a widower whose two grown-up sons had emigrated to Wales. He was a lonely old man and craved company. When he had recognised his niece his heart had started beating so fast. She was a lovely young thing, bigger-boned and taller than his sister, but with the same-shaped face – the same beautiful eyes.

'I was just about to make myself something to eat – do join me.'

'Yes please, I am starving.' Zaira always had a big appetite, and now after the long walk from Torretta to Poeti, she was ravenous.

He had a stew of pork, beans and potatoes boiling in the pot. Zaira was so hungry she didn't even notice it, but scoffed it down with huge chunks of bread. Her uncle kept pressing wine on her, which she drank greedily, and soon she became quite dizzy.

'Uncle, do you mind if I have a little rest. I feel really tired after my long walk here, and maybe the wine as well.' She stifled a yawn.

He was rather disappointed – he would much rather have chatted to his niece. He knew she was intelligent and was keen to discuss the political state of Italy with her.

'Yes, by all means, go and lie down in the spare bedroom – but not for too long, mind.'

Zaira slept for over two hours and realised she would have to make a move soon to get back before dark.

'Uncle, here I am back in the land of the living.'

'So what's happening in Torretta?'

'NOTHING – as usual. It's dead,' she sighed

'Any more people left? Here in Poeti five more men have gone to Wales. I have given them the addresses of Andrea and Giuseppe. When will it all stop, I ask myself – this ... this draining of people from here?'

'Well, if there's nothing to keep them here, then I'm afraid the exodus will continue,' suggested Zaira. 'I think one of the Ruggieri family has left recently, for London.'

'All these taxes, all this competition with the landowners in the Po Valley, that's what's killing everything.'

'You'd think that Poeti would be better off. It's a town after all.'

'Yes, but there's nothing here, no factory, no work. Only that huge castle.'

It was true. Poeti was quite big in comparison to Torretta and was famous for its large, imposing castle owned by the Landi nobles. Zaira's uncle said that the castle had become very run-down and attracted very few visitors. The idea of promoting tourism in the area was never discussed, and if it had been, people would not be interested. They didn't think the castle was that attractive but that was because they took it for granted. There was nothing else in the town so men were forced to move away to find work.

Zaira soon said her goodbyes to her uncle. He was so sad to see her leave.

'I must go, otherwise Papa will wonder why I have taken so long. You know what he's like.'

Pino grunted. There was no love lost between the two brothers-in-law. Pino Filippi agreed with the rest of his family that their beloved Maria had been too good for the likes of a Crespi from Torretta. But he loved Zaira, she was so much like his sister, Maria.

On the way back home, passing all the untidy hedges filled with berries, Zaira recalled how as a child she and her brothers used to collect all the sloes, cornels, rose hips and juniper berries – always at Elena's instigation.

Another time, in the heart of winter, Elena wanted to pick some rose hips so she called together the boys and Zaira.

'Dress up warm and wear your longest boots, boys and girl. We're going out to collect *bacche di rosa canina* – rose hips – and juniper berries as well.'

The children were delighted to be going out, as there was lots of snow. They were bored staying indoors. They rushed round finding woollen hats, scarves and mittens, and although their long boots were rather worn, they all wore an extra pair of socks to try and keep their feet as dry as possible.

They took the same road that Zaira had taken today, climbing up out of Torretta onto the higher ground towards the mountains. The village called Tedo was over 1000 metres high and as they headed towards it the snow got deeper and deeper. The top layer was quite hard and icy but once their boots broke the surface the snow was light and powdery like icing sugar. The sun was bright and the snow looked pastel blue. It was such fun to plant their feet in the virgin snow. The boys pranced around, making as many footprints as possible. Zaira hurried to keep up with Elena.

After about two hours' walking they were on the outskirts of Tedo, and amid the soft white blanket they spotted several rose hips and a few juniper bushes. They all rushed towards them and picked as many as they could off the bare thorny branches. Zaira was not so dexterous as her brothers and managed to prick herself several times on the thorns. She had taken her woollen mittens off because she couldn't pick the berries wearing them. Her brothers instead wore old leather gloves, enabling them to pick the berries quite easily. Elena held out two cotton bags – one for rose hips and one for junipers – so the children could empty their hoards into them. 'And don't muddle them up, boys,' she warned. She knew they would just throw them in without caring.

When they had got about five kilos Elena decided it was time to head for home. The sky was darkening and the moon was out. She pointed out the sickle moon to the children. By its side was a shining star.

'What star is that?' asked Zaira.

'It's *Venere*, Venus, the brightest star in the sky.'

All of a sudden Zaira felt a wet thud on her neck. Giovanni had taken careful aim at the tiny patch of exposed flesh on Zaira's neck between her collar and scarf. Zaira turned round and gathered up as much snow as she could. She ran up to Giovanni and aimed at his face. Next thing she knew, Luigi had thrown her to the ground, smothering her with powdery snow. Then Elena joined in and threw three huge snowballs at Luigi. It was definitely boys against girls and they threw as many snowballs as they could at each other before they finally collapsed laughing in the snow. They were covered in slush from head to foot. Their boots were completely soaked and Zaira couldn't wait to get back to the warmth of the *stufa da legna* at home. Luckily it was downhill all the way so the journey home was faster.

The *stufa* was still burning fiercely – fortunately Bartolomeo had kept it going. The children pulled their wet clothes off as fast as they could and hung them on any possible rail they could see.

Elena took the saucepan of boiling water off the stove and made them all some coffee. She boiled some milk and poured it over the coffee, and as a treat she gave them some biscuits she had baked the day before.

She gathered up the bag of juniper berries. She would make a liqueur out of most of them, and the rest could be kept for a tisane.

Now she would concentrate on the rose hips. To make the liqueur Elena boiled up some water and sugar to make syrup, then she added a litre of Grappa – the equivalent of 80% alcohol – some cinnamon and a kilo of the best rose hips they had gathered.

This mixture had to be left for a month and filtered before the delicious liqueur was ready to drink.

'Hmm, some of that liqueur would be nice now,' sighed Zaira. She knew that there was at least one bottle left in the cabinet in the parlour. 'If Papa hasn't drunk it all by now,' she thought to herself.

Zaira had always been rather impetuous, and rose hips reminded her of this. Another time, when out picking rose hip berries with Elena alone, Zaira had mistakenly picked the bitter nightshade berries – belladonna – instead. The rose hips and nightshade were growing entangled together. The nightshade leaves, which are nothing like the rose leaf, are pointed, and usually have two narrow lobes at the base with small violet flowers. When the oval berries appear, they are usually in drooping clusters and deep red, very similar in colour to the rose hip. Zaira had actually put one of the nightshade berries in her mouth, as it was so much softer than the hard rose hip berries she was picking. Immediately she put it on her tongue she realised her mistake. The taste was extremely bitter, not sweet as she was expecting. She bent her head and spat it out as hard as she could. When she caught up with Elena, who was further up the path, she said:

'I think I've done something really stupid. I thought I was eating a rose hip, but it was very bitter. I don't think I swallowed any and I spat it out straight away.'

'Oh dear, it must have been belladonna; they do look quite similar. Keep spitting, from the back of your throat. Make sure you have enough saliva to sluice your mouth out. There's a stream up ahead. You can rinse your mouth out there.'

They reached the stream.

'Be careful not to swallow the water. Gargle and spit it out.'

Zaira did this several times but she could still feel the bitter taste in her mouth. Her tongue and throat felt dry and furry. Elena looked at her pupils.

Yes, they are slightly dilated, but don't worry, I think you'll live. And you know women purposely use belladonna to make their eyes sparkle? And it's made into a beauty oil. That's why it's called what it is.'

Zaira felt such a fool. How could she have mistaken nightshade for rose hip? She wouldn't dare tell her father or her brothers.

'Please don't tell anyone about this, Elena.'

'Oh, you goose, it's no big thing. It's very easy to do. And you would need to swallow it for the poison to work. Luckily for you, you spat it out straight away. And anyway belladonna will make you even more beautiful, you bella donna', said Elena chucking Zaira under her chin.

Zaira recalled something she had read. 'There is a poem in a book you gave me:

Oh Belladonna

Beautiful woman:
Deadly nightshade's
Velvet violet flowers,
Bright red berries,
Sensuous yet fatal,
Not sweet in the mouth,
Bitter-tasting to the tongue.
Acrid nightshade oil,
A medicine for asthma.
Unctuous lotion too
For the bella donna.
Full red-lipped woman,
Sultry, passionate,
Poisonous art you?
Unpleasant remedy
Simultaneously
Healing, destroying.
Shade of black night's
Mysterious allure,
Ambiguous charm,
And cause for alarm.
Oh scarlet woman,
Shade of the night.
Shining purple eyes,
Beautiful parted lips,
Sweet in the mouth,
Poisonous like you.

'I think that's how it goes, but I don't think that's fair at all. It's implying women are poisonous. I know a man wrote it, can't think of his name, but so typical!' said Zaira.

'I think you're right,' said her aunt.

6. **Bartolomeo**

Bartolomeo Crespi had dreams once, dreams of making something of himself, of leaving Torretta and making his fortune, but it was not to be. However, he kept these thoughts to himself and had never spoken of this to anyone else. He was so much part of village life nobody could ever imagine him living anywhere else. To the people of Torretta, he was solid and dependable old Bartolomeo, reliable but not at all outward-going, quite reserved and taciturn. Most people pitied him. His dear wife Maria had died in childbirth and he was left to bring up three small children on his own. He had been quite good-looking once, with sandy-coloured hair and a reddish moustache, and bright grey-blue piercing eyes. Now he was much plumper, yet nonetheless quite proud of his protruding stomach – at least he wasn't starving like some.

At one time Crespi had been a respected name, a name that was synonymous with Torretta. It was said that the first Bartolomeo Crespi had come from the valley slightly further north in the Monte Alta, and sometime in the Middle Ages had purchased several hectares of land from the monastery of St Salvatore. He had constructed a fortified house with a small tower attached. However, it was possible that the tower was already there when he bought the land. Nothing was left of the house, which had been destroyed in a landslide, but there were still a few piles of stones recognisable as a tower. It became known as La Torretta dei Crespi, and that is how the village got its name. The village was quite long and sprawling, and the top part near the church was known as Crespi.

Subsequent generations of the Crespi family had farmed this land, and had added to it by buying up various other pieces from the ruling families of the area: the Visconti, the Sforza, and the Scotti. All the land at this time was sold in the form of perpetual leases, and the Crespi were never considered less than its rightful owners. However, they had never really been successful farmers. The winters could be bitterly cold up in the foothills around the Val Tara, and the earth, unlike the rich fertile land of the Po Valley, was a stony mixture of clay and limestone. The biggest threat to this area, though, were the many rock falls and landslides and little remained of the once quite numerous fortified houses.

For centuries the Crespi reared livestock, grew fruit and vegetables and produced wine, but their biggest assets were the walnut and chestnut trees. Both the nuts and the wood were very valuable. It was the custom in these parts to divide property and land equally between any male children, as the primogeniture system was not practised among the peasant classes. Over time, the land had been multifariously divided and sub-divided, every son of each generation inheriting an equal share, while the daughters shared any monies available. It was a fair system but proved to be complicated, leading to arguments. Every son had to agree to accept his division before a will became valid. If one brother thought another brother was getting a more fertile piece of land than his, he could refuse to sign his acceptance. Big farms were reduced as the land was split up. Different people ended up owning adjacent fields, and if there was a dispute, the land could lie untended for years. It was in the aristocratic landowners' interests to have this system in operation with the peasants squabbling thus. 'Let the stupid peasants continue to argue. They will never be a threat,' said one of the landowners who lived at the top of Tortello.

By the end of the nineteenth century life had become exceptionally difficult in rural areas such as the Val Tara and many farms were abandoned as the peasant farmers left for the industrialised cities or emigrated further afield to France, Belgium, Britain or the Americas.

*

The present Bartolomeo struggled to make a living out of his now quite small farm. And to add to his problems, it wasn't all in one adjoining piece. He had a few adjacent fields in Torretta, with some other plots of land scattered around the village, others near the Monte Alta, and some leading up to Vernazza, with others going down to Lunano. Most of his chestnut woods were way up beyond Torretta after the rocks where the millstones were cut.

Bartolomeo had a huge map given to him by his father, and it was like looking at a jigsaw puzzle – plots of land the size of postage stamps outlined in red, all numbered and belonging to different people. At least he had managed to persuade his brother Franco to sell him his share. It meant that the farm would remain the same size as in his father's time. Their mother, Elvira, had died quite young, and his father had married Elvira's sister, Leonora. Bartolomeo's young half-sisters, progeny of his father's second marriage, were left money only.

When Bartolomeo was a young man he had been reasonably optimistic about his prospects and that he would make a success of the farm. He had met and married the lovely Maria from Poeti and almost immediately they had two fine sons, Giovanni and Vittorio, born almost within a year of each other. Maria had persuaded him to put a stop to the family tradition of naming the eldest son Bartolomeo. He remembered her words exactly.

'It causes so much confusion and I think our first-born son should be named after my father, Giovanni.'

Bartolomeo would do anything for his Maria and readily consented.

In the early years of their very happy marriage, the farm was doing quite well: producing tomatoes, pears, apples, plums and various vegetables, mainly potatoes, which sold well at market. They had a little wine to sell and every year a proportion of the chestnut and walnut trees were cut down and sold as furniture wood. Even the small amount of livestock was breeding well and the cows were producing good quantities of milk. They were virtually self-sufficient, but gradually the big farmers in the lowlands started to make things very difficult for the small farmer like Bartolomeo. They were able to cut prices and Bartolomeo couldn't compete. He found it difficult to sell his produce at market.

'*Grazie a Diu per la legna!* – Thank God for my wood!' His trees kept him going.

Then after a few years Maria became pregnant again, and he forgot his worries about the farm. He felt wonderfully happy that he was to be a father again. But his happiness was not to last – Maria died giving birth to her baby girl, Zaira. The breach birth was complicated, the labour very long and the girl baby surprisingly large, unfortunately for the somewhat delicate Maria. The baby thrived with the help of a wet nurse – their neighbour, Delfina – and Bartolomeo found himself hating and loving his daughter in equal measure. Yet she was a tiny, defenceless baby. He had to care for her, love her, and carry on with his work as usual.

'Poor Bartolomeo, he has a struggling farm *and* three children to worry about,' was the general consensus of opinion in Torretta. Everyone felt sorry for him. Unlike most men in the area, he refused to remarry. Maria had been the only woman for him. He had been so proud when she had consented to marry him. They had met at the horse fair in her home town, Pocti. 'It's good to mix the blood like this. There are far too many cousins getting married in Torretta; it isn't right,' he used to say to his cronies.

Some of the other men of Torretta disagreed with this. 'If the women in your village are pretty, why go elsewhere to marry?'

Bartolomeo was a genuinely kind-hearted man but Maria had been a good catch for him and her family had not been very pleased with the match to a Crespi from a dead-end place like Torretta. Yes, he was safe ... steady ... kind ... hopefully he wouldn't beat her, but he had no ambition. 'A man going nowhere,' said his future father-in-law Giovanni.

'There will never be another woman like my Maria with the green eyes,' Bartolomeo used to say. Zaira looked like her in many ways: the same chestnut hair and almond-shaped eyes, their greyish-green colour a combination of those of both parents, and she was much taller and bigger-built than her mother. He was thankful his daughter reminded him so much of his dear wife, but it tormented him just the same.

Bartolomeo became increasingly depressed and the farm became more and more run down. He could not cope with all the taxes he had to pay and the problems with poor-yielding crops. And the weather was so unpredictable. If it rained in Torretta, it never seem to be an average-size shower, it was always a storm, dramatic lightning filling up the sky and loud peals of thunder shattering the silence. And the wind – it was so violent, blowing seedlings and plants over, damaging roof tiles, sometimes even wrecking the trees ... 'and then the rain turns into hail, just when

I least want it, just when it will do most damage to the grapes,' thought Bartolomeo to himself.

One day Bartolomeo got caught in just such a storm. He was out in one of the far-off fields, separate from the rest of the farm, fixing a fence. Without warning the sky got very dark, and the rain came down, instantly making puddles in the earth. The water felt as heavy as a thick curtain. Bartolomeo had nowhere to shelter and he was drenched to the skin. He had left his hat at home that day and his by now white hair was plastered to his head, with huge drops of water dripping down his face, like tears. He wanted to cry, and he did start to weep. Nobody would be able to tell the difference, his face was wet anyway. '*Porca miseria*! – What a miserable pig's life!'

Fortunately his two sons were growing up fast, and they were filled with natural enthusiasm. Gradually they were taking the farm over. They introduced new crops – maize, wheat and barley – and sold hay at quite a good profit. Bartolomeo was proud of their efforts, but he didn't want to relinquish all control so he continued to supervise the ploughing with the oxen and the managing of the chestnut woods.

He had only one interest outside the farm: he loved collecting mushrooms, especially *porcini* – ceps – and, if he was very lucky, *tartufi* – truffles. He would take Berillo with him for long walks through the woods leading up to Vernazza. Sometimes a couple of men from Torretta would accompany him and they would stop and have a bottle of wine and some cheese and bread in a clearing in the forest. Bartolomeo had the best nose for collecting. One had to be careful with mushrooms; many were very poisonous, such as the *Amanita Phalloides* or the *Boletus Satanus*. It was not that easy to tell the difference between the edible and the dangerous. If Bartolomeo picked something though, then one could always be sure it was safe to eat.

It was he who always found the biggest mushrooms: *porcini* or *ovuli* – Caesar's mushroom – the most *colombini, chiodini* or *galletti* and, on a special day, the most perfect black truffle. Once he had miraculously found a rare white truffle and couldn't help boasting about it when he got back to the village. 'It was *that* big, the usually modest Bartolomeo would say many times, making a circle as big as an orange with his thumb and forefinger. When he returned from one of his forays he would cook the *porcini* and other mushrooms himself. It was the only time he ever felt comfortable in the kitchen. He would make a big *frittata* – omelette – on the stove. First he would sauté the mushrooms in garlic and then throw the egg mixture over them. He never trusted anyone else to do it, never a woman, and especially not Zaira. She was not interested in collecting mushrooms, although she loved spotting them as she strode through the woods on one of her walks. She loved the feel of the soft squashy golden-yellow autumn leaves under her feet, and seeing so many different-coloured mushrooms on or around the path: hues of pink, purple, grey, brown, blue, yellow, white. She knew not to pick any of them because they were usually inedible, and above all she didn't want to disturb them. They looked so beautiful peeking up against the bed of leaves, and bracken and ferns.

*

Bartolomeo had heard a story about a married man who used to cavort in the woods with a young virgin he met surreptitiously while he was out picking mushrooms. He got careless and wasn't always vigilant about which mushrooms he chose. He was too besotted with the girl. His wife had heard about the goings-on but didn't know how to confront him about his behaviour. One day when he returned home, she insisted on cooking him a meal of mushrooms herself. What he didn't know was that she had recognised one of the mushrooms as an *Amanita Phalloides*, the

Death Cap, aptly named because death is always inevitable. She mixed it in with the rest of the mushrooms, not saying a word. The man in question had a stomach ache the following morning but soon recovered. However three days later he died in agony as his liver and kidneys collapsed. Nobody ever suspected his wife because he didn't die immediately. Bartolomeo thought that this was a more common occurrence than people realised and that malicious spouses had poisoned many men.

When Bartolomeo found a truffle he would ask Elena or Zaira to cook a risotto and then he would carefully grate a tiny piece of the truffle over it. 'What luxury and all for free,' he used to think to himself, as he carefully savoured the exotic truffle taste. He would put the rest in a tight-capped jar and use it sparingly over the next few days. Nobody knew the woods as well as he did, and he never came back empty-handed.

*

His youngest half-sister, Elena, had been a great help with Zaira, and had moved in to help out after Maria had died. The aunt and niece became very close and Elena was good with the child. Zaira was a strong-willed yet enchanting child, and Bartolomeo gradually learnt to forgive her for her mother's death. She was very different from her father, quite temperamental in character, stamping her foot when angry, and never frightened to show her feelings. She reminded him of Leonora. Zaira was always rushing around, causing mayhem. Bartolomeo had always been reticent and he found it difficult to show his feelings to his daughter: he never hugged or kissed her. Yet sometimes even he lost his temper with her: *'Fermati un pò'* – stop still a minute.'

Elena had a way to calm her. She told her long, fantastical stories about princes and princesses, knights and crusaders, fairies and witches, and it seemed to do the trick. Zaira would sit there with her thumb in her mouth concentrating on the words, as quiet as a mouse. When Elena came home from school, the little Zaira was always grabbing her aunt's schoolbooks, trying to copy what her aunt did and read them, pretending that she could understand the words.

Elena had a strong character. She had to have – she'd been with the family for many years, and had sacrificed her life for the sake of her poor half-brother and his children. It really wasn't fair on her. She was 25, and still unmarried, when out of the blue she met some young chap from Tortello who took her fancy. Then things changed very dramatically. Elena was going to be married and leave Torretta for good. Zaira could not bear to think about Elena leaving. How could she do this to her?

'Aunt Elena, what will I do when you are gone?'

Zaira was growing up to be a beautiful and striking woman. She was intelligent and learnt things very quickly. She looked very different from the other girls of the village, tall and slender, almost haughty in stature, and Bartolomeo worried about whom she would marry. Delfina and he had already discussed it. He agreed with Delfina that Matteo would have been a good match but Zaira refused to have anything to do with him, especially after that incident at the *fontana*.

'That pimply brute! Never!'

But there was another young man, Alberto. 'He might be a possibility,' thought Bartolomeo. Perhaps he would talk to Alberto's widowed mother about it, after church next Sunday. Alberto was part of the Ruggieri family. The Crespi had always been at loggerheads with them, but maybe now was the time to heal old wounds. The village was shrinking rapidly – soon there would be no one left. It was time to forget the past; they had to stick together. Alberto was the only son. He worked the land he would inherit one day. Zaira could marry him and have a farm of her own, while his own two sons would continue to run his farm.

But his daughter was so truculent, so contrary. He knew she might not agree to his plan.

Bartolomeo sat down at his kitchen table. He was not yet sixty, but he felt older, worn out and weary. All the people looked older than their years in Torretta.

'I'm getting on, I can feel my bones aching. Climbing those hills is getting harder and harder, and sometimes I can hardly catch my breath. *Dio buono, non ne posso più!* – Good God, I can't go on!' he moaned to himself.

'My sons are good boys, they will try to keep the farm going. But what about Zaira? What will she do? Yes, it would be good if she could marry Alberto, or Matteo, but will she ever consent? Boh!'

Zaira had given no sign of being interested in any boy, at least no boy from the village. In his heart of hearts he knew she wouldn't marry either Alberto or Matteo. And it was partly his fault: he had urged her to learn to read and write, had encouraged her to think for herself, and now she was too different. She would want to go further afield to find a husband, go against her father's wishes. 'So much like her dear mother,' he thought.

7. Don Aldo

The priest of Torretta was called Don Aldo. He was short and fat and tottered around everywhere on his brand new bicycle donated to him by the Abbot at the Monastery of St Salvatore. The parishes of Torretta and Vernazza were both under the jurisdiction of the Abbot, so the priest at Vernazza, Don Angelo, was given a brand new bicycle as well. There was just as much rivalry between the priests as there was between the inhabitants of Torretta and Vernazza.

Don Aldo was surprisingly popular with the people of Torretta, mainly because he wasn't Don Angelo. Even so, he cut quite a comic figure on his bicycle, panting up the hilly tracks through the village to the church of Sant'Antonio. It had taken him quite a long time to learn how to ride it. He had toppled off quite a few times and looked very red in the face as he climbed back on, trying to get his breath back. Some people sniggered as he pedalled past, looking very insecure on his saddle, his fat posterior squashed over its sides, 'like a bag of potatoes', one local wit announced. The black robes he wore ballooned out around him, while his chubby little fist tried to clutch at his black hat, pulling it down tight against his head. But if he took one hand off the handlebars, he wobbled all over the place. He was very short-sighted and wore thick pebble glasses, and sometimes he nearly ran people over as he pedalled unsteadily along, shouting at them to get out of the way.

One day he was cycling past an old woman's house and she emptied her chamber pot out of her bedroom window just as Don Aldo passed underneath. The brim of his hat filled up with urine and overflowed onto his cassock. Some of the villagers witnessed the incident, and didn't know whether to laugh at the poor priest or cry. Most of them were laughing uproariously. *'Che buffo! –* What a buffoon!'* It was just typical of the kind of thing that happened to him. Eventually he would purchase a bell to warn people he was coming, and he could be heard all over the village, continually ringing his bicycle bell as loud as he could.

However, when it came to the Sunday sermon, he completely changed character. His voice became deep and resonant and many of Torretta's inhabitants found him quite terrifying, especially the women and children. He was fond of shouting at them about hell and damnation. 'You are all sinners and you will have to stand before God on Judgement Day. If you continue to sin without remorse, you will be damned for eternity into hell fire.' He positively relished the idea. The women sitting in the pews hurriedly muttered prayers to themselves, *'Signore, pietà, Cristo, pietà'* or *'Santa Maria, piena di grazia...'* They couldn't bear to think of hell and all those flames, bodies burning, people wailing.

As in most communities all the women sat in the pews on either side at the front half of the church and the men stood around at the back so that they could make a quick exit when Mass was over.

The men shifted uncomfortably, coughing nervously. They had better go to confession next week, and take Holy Communion; they had to repent, say penance, stop hitting their wives, stop swearing, stop having bad thoughts about the young girls in the village, especially that chestnut-haired one. Yes, they would all definitely start going to confession next week, regularly – but they never did. It was always next week, procrastinating as normal. They left it to the women to worry about God and the church: the women would pray for them. However to assuage their guilt they put extra money in the collection.

Zaira went to church every Sunday and was normally bored stiff. She believed in God and Jesus Christ, and wanted to be a good Catholic, but Don Aldo was so blinkered in his views that his sermons were never about love or charity, only about sins and fear.

Yet his words didn't frighten her. She usually daydreamed during his sermon. She tried to force herself to listen to him.

'Jesus died on the cross to save your sins,' he shouted. 'You sinners, do you ever think to yourself about this enormous sacrifice that our Lord made to save you, to save you from hell and damnation?'

'Well,' Zaira thought to herself, 'if Jesus died to save us, then why can't people commit sins, if they are saved in any case?' She would have liked to ask the priest this question, but knowing him, he would have refused to respond. Although he had received his training in a Jesuit college, his gift for logic was somewhat lacking.

She turned round to glance at the men looking uncomfortable at the back of the church. 'I wonder if that's what they think.'

The priest continued: 'We must repent, we must sin no longer.' Sometimes it didn't make sense to Zaira. Don Aldo was always going on and on about sins as if people were totally evil and committed sins all the time. Well, she certainly didn't. She didn't realise that pride was a sin, or reading unsuitable books behind her father's back was a sin. No, she was thinking more along the lines of men and women sinning together. She was sure that was what Don Aldo was really talking about. He was always talking about the carnal sins, and the temptations of the flesh. 'Ha!' Zaira laughed to herself as she turned round again to look at the men. 'That bunch of ugly-looking things – who on earth would want to commit sins of the flesh with any of that lot? There's not one good-looking man amongst them.'

Well, that was her opinion anyway. The old ones were either shrivelled up or had big fat bellies, and hairs growing out of their ears and nostrils, or they had lost all or most of their teeth, or, even worse, were hunched up or lame.

She didn't think the young ones were much better. They were spotty, and had greasy lank hair and bad teeth. And worst of all, they couldn't string two sentences together when they saw her, especially that Matteo or Alberto. They were completely tongue-tied in her presence. She thought they were scared of her. They knew she could read and write, and they were virtually illiterate. She made them feel highly inadequate. Not one of them was brave enough to get into conversation with her, but they certainly had impure thoughts about her. They definitely knew what the priest was on about.

Don Aldo surveyed the congregation. He felt so superior to them. He too had come from a peasant family, but he had been lucky, his parents had encouraged him to become a priest. They were very proud of their oldest son and the life suited him. He never felt lonely, he enjoyed saying Mass and preaching sermons. He wouldn't have wanted to work the land like his father. He had been privileged to become a cleric. Lots of boys from round here had done the same. Don Aldo hadn't really thought he'd had a genuine vocation, but he enjoyed his single life: he had never been interested in women, not at all. He was well fed and the Abbot was very generous. He lived in a comfortable little cottage just below Torretta, nearer to the monastery, with his housekeeper, or *perpetua* as she was called, and a shy young curate, just out of the seminary.

He used to live at the '*canonica*', attached to Sant'Antonio, but it was in urgent need of repair. The work hadn't even started yet, and he was in no hurry to return there. He liked living near the monastery with the timid young priest.

Don Aldo enjoyed the way the young man blushed when he had to speak to any women in the parish of San Salvatore. He rarely ventured up to Torretta; his duty was to help the *Abate*. Don Aldo could see the young priest was truly committed to God and the Church. The boy knew he had a proper vocation for the priesthood from when he was very young.

Not like that imbecile from Vernazza, Don Angelo. It was common knowledge he was having an affair with his *perpetua*. And all those women who flock to Mass in Vernazza every Sunday, just to eye up that Don Angelo: '*Che vergogna!* – the shame of it!' Lots more people attended mass at Vernazza than they did at Torretta. Don Aldo was seething about this: all that extra money in the collection plates. His favourite topic of conversation was the 'viper' from Vernazza:

'And the way that toad rode his bicycle, really showing off, one-handed sometimes, his swarthy face glowing in the sunshine, eyeing the local girls as he rode past. It was disgusting.'

He enjoyed nothing more than to gossip about Don Angelo with the villagers of Torretta. They grew more and more incensed about his exploits. The nerve of the man, strolling down the main street of Vernazza with that woman, in front of everybody, as if he didn't care. Sometimes he even came down to Torretta, the cheek of him. Don Aldo used to chew the fat quite often with Bartolomeo. They enjoyed drinking a sparkling glass of white wine together, and sometimes they were joined by a couple of other men and played card games such as *Briscola*, a form of

Whist, or *Settebello*. Occasionally Bartolomeo's daughter used to make them coffee. 'Strange girl, very confident, very full of herself, proud and haughty,' Don Aldo thought. 'She'll come to a sticky end, mark my words,' he used to say to others when Bartolomeo wasn't around.

*

Don Angelo was not from a peasant family, but he too had joined the priesthood to escape poverty. He came from an impoverished, minor aristocratic family from Parma. They were related to the Pallavincini clan. He had been the youngest of five brothers, and it was his fate to become the priest. He had fought his father bitterly: 'Me, a priest, it's impossible!'

He had loved women from a very young age and had lost his virginity at the age of ten. How would he manage being a celibate? He believed in God, but not in celibacy.

'It isn't healthy for a young man. Why can't priests marry? It's so absurd. Protestant priests in Northern Europe can marry, Orthodox priests can marry, why can't Catholic priests do the same? It is nearly the twentieth century after all!' But his father wouldn't listen to his protests and with great reluctance, he joined the seminary.

Yet he couldn't renounce his opinions. Priests have had sex with women for centuries. In fact in the early days of the church priests did marry and have families. 'Why were the rules changed?' he asked himself.

'All those corrupt, pompous popes in Rome. They were the worst, having children all over the place, making them cardinals, giving them titles in return, like Pope Paul III and his son Farnese.'

Nothing much had changed really. There were still lots of illegitimate children milling around, *'un fieu del pret* – son of a priest' as they were called, or, more plainly, bastard. Most bastards around here had priests as fathers.

And since he had become parish priest at Vernazza, he worried about his *perpetua*, Irene. 'We have to be more careful – she might get pregnant too.'

He was fed up with being a priest. What he had always wanted was to open a bookshop. He and Irene had already discussed it. He fancied getting as far away as possible from Vernazza.

What a hell-hole it was – most of the women, apart from his Irene, were ugly! The only one he had ever thought beautiful was a girl in Torretta, but she had never even noticed him.

Still, he was content with Irene; she gave him everything he wanted. He was thinking about going to Florence, or maybe to the university town of Perugia. Think of all the beautiful women there! He had heard that there were now quite a few female novelists writing romances for women. He could make a fortune selling these sorts of books to women. They would flock to his shop. He was thinking all this as he cycled effortlessly on the mountain tracks to Riga.

*

Oh dear, Don Aldo had to hurry. He had to meet that loathsome priest, Don Angelo, up at the Shrine of Our Lady of the Afflicted, further up the mountain at the place called Riga. There was not much there, only an '*osteria*' or little inn, run by a very old lady. The place was full of chickens and geese running around.

The shrine had been erected about forty years before during the cholera epidemic. A shepherd afflicted with the disease alleged he had seen the Madonna appear to him, surrounded by light, and holding her hands in prayer. The shepherd had been miraculously cured of the cholera in an instant. As soon as he was able, he ran down to the village of Torretta as fast as he could, (it took about half an hour) to declare to the locals how he had seen the Madonna with his own eyes. The shrine was built about a year later, and sick people visited it in droves. There was talk of many more similar miraculous recoveries. Women left plaits of hair at the site and people left their walking sticks or crutches, flowers and other mementoes.

Then a story started circulating about a little girl in Torretta called Lucia. One day she had a vision as she was sitting on a bench outside the church of Sant'Antonio. Our Lady of the Afflicted came down from Riga and appeared to Lucia. She was holding the baby Jesus in her arms, and at her side was the tall figure of Sant'Antonio, dressed in his usual monk's habit. The Madonna said to Lucia that the people of Torretta must promise to look after the shrine at Riga for eternity, and then she gestured towards Sant'Antonio and said to Lucia: 'Remember, Sant'Antonio church will always stand on this spot, and whatever the difficulties, cherish it always.'

The story of Lucia's vision spread to the Monastery. The Abate decided that a properly enclosed chapel should be built at the shrine of Our Lady, with a new statue of the Madonna dressed in blue and white, holding the baby Jesus in her arms, to be erected on a tall plinth. The place had become neglected and somewhat untidy, so Don Aldo and Don Angelo had been ordered to go up there to survey the land and report back to the Abate about what size and type of chapel would be appropriate.

Don Angelo got to Riga first, not even out of breath, after climbing up the steep hills on his gleaming new bicycle. The views were quite spectacular from here. He could see the plains of the Po valley, and the far-off cities of Piacenza and Parma. How Don Angelo longed to be back in a city.

'Why in heaven's name was I sent to such a remote place?'

He had definitely had enough; he and Irene would certainly be leaving soon. The gossips would have a field day, he thought.

In the meantime, Don Aldo had decided not to take his

bicycle: the hills were too steep. He had reverted to the old mule he used to ride before. The grumpy old animal was reluctant to make the long journey to Riga, and Don Aldo arrived there much later than Don Angelo, huffing and puffing, his chubby cheeks a deep purple. He was furious: that cretin Don Angelo was there already, pacing up and down, looking impatient, making sketches in a notebook.

The two men were barely on speaking terms. Don Angelo despised the rotund, decrepit old priest, and as for Don Aldo, he loathed Don Angelo with a deep passion. He hated his dark, swarthy good looks, his charming way with the women of Vernazza – why, he had even tried sniffing around the young girls in Torretta. But most of all he couldn't bear the idea of that man and his housekeeper fornicating together, committing heinous sins right under people's noses.

'How could he show his face, how could he swagger around as if nothing was going on with that woman? Irene was her name,' he thought. 'More like *'carogna'* – bitch.'

There was not much said. They grunted a few sentences at each other. There wasn't enough space for a large chapel as the site was right on the bend of the road. The chapel would have to be quite small inside, not adequate for a proper congregation, but big enough for the odd pilgrim or traveller to say a quick prayer to Our Lady of Afflictions. Don Angelo continued making notes, and Don Aldo felt foolish because he hadn't brought any pen or paper with him. He would never have thought of it in any case: his handwriting was poor and admittedly he had really struggled with his Latin and theology at the seminary.

They were finished, and muttered brief goodbyes to each other. Don Angelo sped off away down the track, freewheeling down the hills. Don Aldo followed him, still puffing and panting, his mule making heavy work of it all.

The Chapel at Riga was built and to this day, every year on the feast of Corpus Christi, the locals celebrate with an open air mass followed by lashings of food and wine.

8. **Zaira and an ending...**

Zaira was growing more and more restless. She was eighteen now, and both her brothers were married. As was the custom, and since the house was big enough, the wives had come to live in Torretta. Both couples were keen to take over the entire farm from Bartolomeo. Zaira's sisters-in-law did all the housework and helped out on the farm far more enthusiastically and energetically then she ever had. They didn't really need her there now, so there was far less for her to do.

She was getting quite desperate to leave Torretta, her 'prison' as she called it. Only Bartolomeo prevented her. He would never consent. She thought about asking him whether she could go and visit Aunt Elena in Turin. But Elena hadn't been married long. She and her husband were still finding their feet. Poor Elena had sacrificed her childhood to look after Zaira. It wouldn't be fair if she visited them so soon; they were busy building their lives together and she'd be a gooseberry. Elena had invited her to go and stay, but it was all very tenuous – she never ever suggested an actual date. Her husband had been promoted in his engineering job at Fiat, and things were going very well for them. And Elena would start to have children. Zaira didn't fancy the idea of playing nursemaid like Elena had done for her. No, she wanted to go somewhere where there was no family, no ties. Milan was where she really wanted to go and then who knows where after that?

Bartolomeo woke up on the morning of his fifty-ninth birthday. Birthdays weren't usually celebrated. It was traditional to celebrate a name day or saint's day as it was called – *l'onomastico*. His saint's day was St Bartholomew but that wouldn't be for a while yet. He had a strange premonition that he wouldn't live to see that day. He felt tired even though he had just woken up. He was already wrinkled and feeling frail, his face quite red and blotchy and his eyes puffy. He shouldn't be feeling like this. He could hardly get out of bed. He went to the cupboard where he kept his will. Not many people in Torretta made wills, but he had wanted to do things properly. He sat down and read it through very slowly. He couldn't read it all, but he had memorised the words. He had bequeathed his properties and the farmlands in equal portions to all three children, which was unusual. Bartolomeo's original will had left all the property and land to his sons. Daughters normally inherited money only. But he had changed his mind. If Zaira didn't marry, and there was no sign she would marry anyone in Torretta, then she was entitled to her share. She could always sell this third share to her brothers if she wanted. Bartolomeo had decided to treat each of his children equally. He couldn't leave Zaira out. He had a complex relationship with his motherless daughter, possibly brought about by guilt. He felt ashamed of his hatred of her when she was first born, and how he had slapped her when she got back from the *fontana* that day.

Bartolomeo was still reading his will when he felt a strange pain, where exactly he wasn't sure. He tried calling out 'Zaira!' She was in the house somewhere. But no words came out. He started to rasp, he couldn't breathe and then he keeled over and fell onto the cold stone floor.

Zaira was in the seldom-used front parlour, trying to keep out of the way, reading a book. She heard a noise overhead coming from her father's bedroom, which was directly above her. She rushed up the stairs, flung open his door and saw him lying on the floor on his back with his eyes wide open.

'Papa!' she screamed.

She knew something dreadful had happened. She let out a strange whimper, but forced herself to remain calm, trying not to think the inevitable. She rushed over to him and tried to feel a pulse, felt his heart, listened for a breath, but there was nothing. Bartolomeo was dead.

He was both her father and her mother. A sometimes reluctant parent, he had never really been sure how to handle his lively daughter, but their love for each other had been very deep, very strong. He was all she had. Her grief was complicated and overwhelming and she started to sob hysterically.

'Papa, Papa, no, no,' she cried continually.

His friend, Don Aldo, buried Bartolomeo Crespi two days later at the church of Sant'Antonio. His sons Giovanni and Vittorio and two of their cousins had carried the coffin into the church for the funeral, and then out to the cemetery at the back of the church for the burial. It was a tranquil, beautiful spot – Zaira thought her father would be at peace here.

Giovanni and Vittorio were obviously both upset about their father's death, but they were keen to get on with running the farm. There was work to be done and they had lots of ideas about improvements. The only problem was Zaira. Giovanni discussed it with his brother:

'What on earth was Father thinking when he left a third of everything to her? We cannot consent to this.' According to the law, all heirs had to agree to what was stated in a will. Daughters normally only got a share of money, not land.

'Why should she benefit from all our hard work? It's we who have invested so much time and energy on getting the farm ready for the next century. We bought the new machinery, invested in new crops. Our wives are doing more work on the farm then Zaira ever has. She always has her head in some stupid book!'

They had to talk to her about it and soon. On the evening of the funeral they were still sitting in the front parlour where Bartolomeo's body had been laid out the day before. This room was filled with the best furniture, and the best china and cutlery used only for occasions of this nature. The black velvet curtain that had been draped over the wall behind the coffin was still there. The golden tassels hanging from it were shabby and sparse. After the funeral there had been no wake. All the relatives and friends had gone to the house the night before for the laying out, and to say the rosary. Drinks were handed round but everyone was solemn, no badinage, no jokes. Zaira had spent the whole time sitting in a chair, being comforted by Delfina. Elena hadn't been able to get back for the funeral. She was heavily pregnant with her first child.

The family had just completed their first meal without Bartolomeo. The atmosphere had been heavy and unusually silent. Now the wives were busy in the kitchen washing up. Zaira had slipped up to her room. The brothers both called up to their sister to come in to the front room. 'Zaira, we have something to say to you.'

Zaira had been lying on her bed crying – she still couldn't believe her father was dead. She thought the funeral and burial would make it more real, make her accept it more, but it hadn't. She could see him in front of her, a large but slightly bent, ageing white-haired man. She could hear his voice, deep and slightly hoarse, similar to hers, and she could smell him, a mixture of carbolic soap and earth, and maybe a hint of wine. Yet she couldn't touch him, something they rarely did. How she longed to hug him, to tell him that she had wanted to be a good daughter to him, that she knew he had worried about her – her temperament, her difference from other girls, 'Oh, Papa,' she cried out as she came down the stairs. She was still sobbing when she came into the room.

'Zaira, pull yourself together, we have important things to discuss,' said Giovanni, her eldest brother. 'Sit down at the table. You know that Papa left you a third share of everything, well, this was a very strange thing for Papa to do. He always told us that we would have the farm. You would get your share of the money. We think it would be best if you relinquish your share. It will be fairer as we are running the farm, not you. We intend to expand; we want to invest and make some profit for a change. It makes sense to keep it this way, just with us. We propose that we set aside some money for you, if you ever need it, and of course you will always have a home here. But I know Papa was keen for you to marry, *magari* – maybe Alberto.'

Zaira stopped crying. 'Alberto, what a joke!' she screeched. 'I told Papa already. How can I marry someone so ugly? His big ears stick out so much he looks like a donkey!' She forgot her grief for a second at such a comical thought. Zaira could cry a lot and then the next minute something would make her laugh.

'Zaira, stop that,' said Vittorio. 'As Giovanni said, we don't think it's fair that you get a third share of everything. We will make sure that you are looked after, and you will have the money Papa left you, but the farm should be owned by Giovanni and me.'

'Wait a minute,' said Zaira, slowly realising what they were saying. 'If Papa left me a share, then that is what he wanted. Why should I give it up? What do I get in return? I could sell it to you, I suppose,' she pondered.

'Don't worry, we shall make sure everything is settled. But you surely can't expect much money for your share. This land is worthless.' The brothers were both thinking she would have to marry someday (maybe not Alberto) and then they wouldn't have to worry about her. She had some money. That would be enough. Why should they have to pay her for something that she didn't deserve?

Zaira started to think. She was free, 'I can do what I want now – poor father is no longer here to stop me. Giovanni and Vittorio can't prevent me from leaving.'

She had no interest in the farm or the property. She could leave whenever she wanted. She sensed her brothers wanted her out of the way, one less worry for them. It was strange though, she had been planning this for months, but now she could actually do it, it didn't feel right. She would rather have her father back than her freedom. Yet she must do it now, leave Torretta: this was her chance. She would miss it in a funny way, yes, miss the mountains, the rapidly changing skies, the dramatic sunsets, the stars, *le lucciole* – the fireflies, but certainly not the bats and snakes. Maybe she would come back one day, have her own place here. She would be entitled to it.

'Dear father, he was thinking of me.' Zaira knew it was unusual for women to inherit a share of property or land. She was proud of her father: he had been forward thinking after all. Maybe she was more like him than she had realised.

She decided to bide her time and not tell her brothers her decision straight away. 'Keep them guessing,' she thought. A week or so passed and she told them she had come to a decision. 'I agree that you can have my share of the farm, but I want some money for it now. And I would like the old barn and the land around it, maybe make it into a house one day.'

'Yes, yes, of course,' said both brothers simultaneously. They thought she would forget about this soon. If she married, she would have a house to go to in any case.

So it was agreed, although nothing was put in writing, and the brothers got what they wanted. Zaira was troubled for days afterwards. She couldn't help worrying whether she had made the right decision, but this was her chance to get away, to have adventures. She knew her brothers wouldn't stop her.

When she told her brothers her plan to go to Milan, they were very surprised. 'Zaira, going to Milan! What would Papa say?' they virtually said in chorus.

However it suited them to have her out of the way. They agreed to give her a small amount of extra money on top of the money her father had left her. All in all it was not much, but enough for her journey to Milan and to pay for lodgings for a week or so. Then it would be up to her...

Giovanni accompanied her to the train station at Tortello after she had said her goodbyes to some of her relatives and friends in the village. She made a point of saying a fond farewell to Signorina Maestri, her schoolteacher, and of course Delfina, her old wet-nurse. Fortunately Matteo wasn't there.

Zaira and Delfina had a long hug and Zaira told her what she planned to do.

'I will really miss you, Zaira,' she said.

Delfina was terribly disappointed that things hadn't worked out between Zaira and her son. She would never say anything to Zaira about this but she wouldn't give up on the idea just yet. She reminded her that she could always return if things didn't work out.

'You can come back to Torretta any time you want, Zaira,

don't forget that. And make sure those brothers of yours keep their promise to you about having a house here one day. You will learn to swallow that pride of yours eventually. Milan is a big place, but you might not find what you are looking for – even there.'

Zaira hugged Delfina closely; she would miss her too, after all.

At the main-town station which they had reached via a tramline from Lunano, Giovanni waved sheepishly at his sister as the train departed. He knew his father would be furious to see his daughter travelling alone in the train to a big, dangerous city like Milan.

9. **Rodolfo**

Rodolfo Ruggieri's family had originated from Torretta. They were distantly related to the Crespi family and rivalry had always existed between them. The Crespi boasted that they had founded Torretta. It was their family after all who had originally bought the land from the local monastery. This was true but at one time all the people in the village were called Crespi, Rodolfo Ruggieri's family included. To differentiate between the ever-increasing and flourishing clan, people had started to be called by different surnames. The name Ruggieri was given to the sons of Ruggiero, another family was called Rossetti, after a son who had red hair and was nicknamed *'Rossetto'*. Then there were the Franchi, named after Franco, and the Bianchi named after someone who went prematurely white. Consequently, even the same surname had to be distinguished somehow. So there were the Crespi di Capitano (Captain), the Crespi del Latte (Milk), the Crespi della Seta (Silk), and so forth. The names possibly depicted a place or a job, but nobody really knew the origins of these *'sopranomi'* – nicknames. There were even some Ruggieri who were nicknamed *'del papa'* after the Pope, so that led to all kinds of gossip and intrigue: *'Figurati'* – 'Imagine! Sons of popes, no less!'

But the point was this: the Ruggieri had once been Crespi; they had been there as long as Barto' di Capitano. The Crespi hadn't owned Torretta at all, like they boasted. Everybody originating from Torretta could say that. The Ruggieri were equally important.

And then the infamous family dispute occurred. It was a familiar story: an argument over a woman. The similarly named grandfathers of the present day Rodolfo and Bartolomeo had both been in love with a local girl called Candida. Now this girl was capricious, playing the two fellows along, promising to marry both of them, when she had no intention of marrying either. She ended up marrying someone from Tortello and moving away. Rodolfo and Bartolomeo had never been close friends, and instead of any mutual consolation, now they couldn't stand the sight of each other, each reminding the other of their dismal failure with the lovely, yet callous, Candida. Rather than forgetting their differences, they relived the indignity and embarrassment of it all every time they met.

Bartolomeo had inherited a drystone-built property, which stood in a large garden. The Ruggieri had always claimed that the garden fence had been moved and that they actually owned some of the land, and so therefore they could say that they had some rights to the house as well. 'In fact, nearly half of it is ours,' they said. Because of the dispute, Bartolomeo couldn't claim the house as his. He had been thinking of moving into it if he had married Candida, but now nothing was further from his mind and the house was left empty. However Rodolfo was sick of seeing this house. It reminded him of Bartolomeo and it also reminded him of that two-timing trollop Candida. So one night he persuaded a group of friends to come with him to the house, and very stealthily and cleverly they managed to dismantle the key stones from the structure. These they carefully took down to the river and placed on the riverbank between other stones and rocks so that they were completely disguised. By the morning the house was quite unsafe, and was already starting to fall down. It would soon be flattened, especially after a high wind or a storm or, even worse, in one of the notorious landslides.

Bartolomeo had been to the horse fair at Poeti for a few days, and had not seen the house. When he arrived back in Torretta all the villagers were talking about it, 'Ca Capitano', after the nickname given to Bartolomeo's branch of the Crespi family. The 'ca' was falling down. Bartolomeo couldn't believe his eyes. His house was ruined. However, because it reminded him of the unfortunate episode with Candida, he left it alone. He wanted it to collapse even though he was still angry and wanted to find out more. 'Che diavolo è successo' – 'How the devil has it happened?'

'Santo cielo!' He should have guessed! He couldn't help but hear the gossip in the village.

'I knew it. Rodolfo and a few of his friends are the culprits. They have knocked the house down overnight – they must have used witchcraft!'

Bartolomeo's hatred for Rodolfo became even more intense and from that day the two men and their families never spoke, and they constantly argued about any trivial matter. If there were any adjoining fields that they each owned, one or other of them would construct a high fence, then the other would say it was infringing their property and try and tear the fence down. If a Crespi tree fell into a Ruggieri field and damaged some fruit or whatever, they would push it back and try to duplicate the damage. If the Ruggieri family donated an amount of money to the Church of Sant'Antonio, then the Crespi family donated double. If there was a festa or dance in the village at harvest time and the Crespi family offered to donate the wine, then the Ruggieri said:

'We will donate double the amount of wine from any Crespi, and five salamis as well!'

When the late Rodolfo's only son moved away and went to work on the Castellengo estate near Tortello, the Crespi were left to lick their wounds, sulking that they had never managed to get justice. Nobody ever forgot the story of the *Ca' Capitano.*

However they found new things to argue about with the remaining members of the Ruggieri family. One of the sources of the spring water that supplied the village drained through both Crespi and Ruggieri land. Sometimes the spring ran dry and they always blamed it on each other. Water was the most important commodity in the village, even more vital than the land, the houses, the animals. Without water they couldn't survive in this remote village. They were lucky that the water flowed down in waterfalls from the higher mountains. There was also the river, of course, but the pure, fresh, spring water was their primary drinking water supply. The Crespi and the Ruggieri in days gone by had engineered it so that where the water passed through their adjoining land, they were able to partly reroute the water into a tank, so that they could use it to water their fields. The rest of the villagers were not happy with this, but what could they do? The Crespi and Ruggieri always thought they were superior. Then if a Crespi saw a Ruggieri watering his fields he would accuse him of using too much water. If a Ruggieri woman saw a Crespi woman filtering off some water from the tank to wash her clothes, she'd remind her that water was scarce, and that it shouldn't be used for washing trifling amounts of laundry. Not that the women's opinions counted for much. Yet even they were indoctrinated with the rivalry: 'Never trust a Crespi; never marry a Ruggieri.'

They viewed each other as if they were from a different species. It was usual for a man to be suspicious of his neighbour, the people in the next village, the next province and so on. 'Only trust your own, never trust someone who looks different, or acts differently' was their motto.

*

The present-day Rodolfo Ruggieri had heard the story of the *Ca' Capitano* several times from his father. He thought that it was ingenious of his grandfather to know exactly how to destabilise a house, just by pulling out a few stones.

Rodolfo's late father never forgot his relatives in Torretta. He always sent them money, and even found work for them either on the estate or further afield in Milan or even England, but the more he did for his relatives, the more ungrateful they seemed, or the more they expected from him. They were always coming to him, caps in hand, asking for more money for new building works, repairs, or to pay for medical bills. Yet they never expressed any gratitude towards him, and he could never count on them in any family disputes. They treated him as if he were a stranger rather than a blood relation. By the end of his life he was very bitter towards his relatives in Torretta and forbade his son to have any further contact with them.

However Rodolfo had other things on his mind these days. He was making plans for his daughter Livietta's future. He had been to pay a visit to the Contessa Camilla Bertini, now widowed and always dressed in black. She called herself by her maiden name now, as was the custom. She lived high up in Tortello near the castle. Word had got out that, as the dowager of the family, she had decided that it was about time her nephew Leonardo got married. He was in danger of becoming dissolute and bringing ruin to the family. He consorted with many notorious women of the stage, all utterly unsuitable. A local match would be far more advantageous. Besides, the Bertini needed an heir, and Leonardo was the only member of the family who could achieve this. She had given up on the Marchese, his brother Claudio, who was busy squandering his share of the family fortune in New York, of all places.

Rodolfo hurried back to the Azienda, quite hot and bothered, and very grumpy. The Contessa certainly had airs and graces – as if he wasn't good enough. Well, he would show her. Livietta was graceful and docile; she could speak French, and play the piano sublimely; and most of all, she was an obedient, extremely loyal and innocent girl.

'*Perbacco!* What more can a man want from a woman?'

Rodolfo was right about the Contessa's snobbery. She had thought Rodolfo a terribly fawning little man. His black, thick wool suit fitted badly and his fat neck ballooned over his tight white starched collar. He had patchy black balding hair, a pencil-thin moustache, and a pointed goatee beard – 'All incredibly black, out of a bottle most likely, hmm!' she speculated.

However he was rich and it would be wonderful to unite the Bertini and Castellengo estates. She didn't give a fig for Livietta, but it was useful she was an only child as she would inherit everything. The Contessa could never understand why in the peasant communities everything was shared equally between siblings.

'How ridiculous and how stupid!'

As far as she was concerned, Leonardo's marriage to Livietta would be a purely business arrangement. There had been a disastrous marriage some time back between a Bertini and a Perdoni that had ended in a feud. The lands had never been united so now was the time. Even if their wine failed, it was still a prime site. Italy was on the verge of a new age. Industries in Northern Italy were becoming more and more important and land was needed for factories. The road out of Tortello to Castellengo would be good access for such a factory, or even more than one. The Contessa had invested heavily in the steel industry through her late husband's family. It was already producing dividends. And her nephew Leonardo was mad on cars. There was great potential for them to set up a car company and what better place than Castellengo!

'That little man Rodolfo could be sidelined easily enough,' she said to herself.

Back at Castellengo, Rodolfo was anxious to speak to his daughter. He knew that the Contessa would be likely to change her mind and not honour their agreement.

'I must strike now while the iron is hot!'

And he knew that Livietta would take some persuading.

Rodolfo changed out of his tight, uncomfortable suit into a loose shirt and a pair of baggy trousers. How pleased he was to be home, out of that stifling hot apartment in Tortello:

'All those dark old paintings on the walls – all of dead people!'

How he preferred Castellengo – it was so much grander, but more comfortable as well. He had noticed that stringy old battle-axe looking him up and down as if he were her inferior.

'Damned cheek. I'm just as good as her, if not better.'

He bet he had more money in the bank than she did!

10. **Leonardo and Livietta**

'But, Papa, I don't want to get married, I'm happy here with you and Mama. I have everything I want, my music, my books, my pretty dresses, and besides, who will help you with the accounts?'

'Livietta, I am serious. You are nearly twenty-one. It is time for you to get married. Leonardo Bertini is a great catch. Surely you realise that? I have discussed everything with his aunt, the Contessa. It is all decided. You will get married as soon as possible, before the end of October, after your twenty-first birthday.'

'Papa, I don't even know him. How can I marry someone I don't know? You know how shy I am. The very idea makes me tremble. No, Papa, I will not go through with it. I can't. I won't...'

Livietta was wringing her handkerchief, panting heavily, on the verge of tears.

'Livietta, you are becoming hysterical. This is so unlike you. Please stop it this minute. Now calm down and listen. You will live in a fine manor house, you will have many servants and you can call yourself Contessa. Even if Leonardo doesn't use his title, his aunt assures me you can style yourself Contessa Livietta Ruggieri Bertini. Think of it! Don't you know what that would mean to me and your mother? It's everything I have ever dreamed of – me, Rodolfo Ruggieri, from the humble origins of Torretta, and my daughter a Contessa. Bah, daughter, I have never asked anything of you before now, but you must do your duty. You must marry him!'

For the first time in his life, Rodolfo was angry with his daughter, so angry his face was beetroot-red with rage.

Livietta was worried about him. She started to tremble even more and was feeling faint. She held her handkerchief to her cheek then dropped it to the floor, her head quite dizzy when she picked it up.

Father and daughter could not help each other. They both looked to be in need of medical attention during this painful conversation.

Livietta didn't know what to think. What could she say? She loved her father with all her heart; she didn't want to make him so upset. But then again, she didn't want to marry. She wanted to stay where she was, where she was happy, for the rest of her life. She was so torn, she was being pulled in one direction and then the other. She burst into tears.

'Oh, Papa, I don't want to get married, I don't want to get married, I don't want to get married...,' she sobbed, repeating the barely distinguishable words over and over, the effort nearly choking her.

'Livietta, stop behaving like a child. You will get married and that is final.'

Livietta ran out of the room and up to her bedroom. She felt so alone. Where was Mama? She would see her point of view – she wouldn't let her suffer like this.

However Livietta's mother had already had a long discussion

with her husband. She knew Livietta would be reluctant, whoever the man was. Livietta wasn't interested in men. But it had always been their wish that their daughter make an important match; all their efforts at Castellengo would have been pointless otherwise. 'Perhaps if we'd had a son it would be different, but Livietta is our only child. She must get married, and to Leonardo Bertini,' Rina had persuaded herself. 'He's an amazing catch. He is handsome and rich – well, we heard he had squandered some of his fortune, but that's as maybe. He'll settle down once he's married.'

The couple had decided that Rodolfo should speak to Livietta alone. His wife knew she wouldn't be able to bear to listen to the conversation. She knew her daughter. She could faintly hear Livietta crying, and it was breaking her heart.

Later on, Livietta dried her eyes and tried to pull herself together. She went in search of her mother. She had to talk to her. She found her in her bedroom, sitting on the window seat, wringing her hands and looking quite distraught. Livietta knelt down beside her and held her hands in hers.

'Mama, I don't want to leave you and Papa. Why do women have to marry? Things are changing for women now.'

'Women have no need to change, my darling. We are happy as we are. I don't understand why these days some women feel that they are – what do they say? – oppressed. They want to fight for workers' rights, the vote, whatever. I have never felt that. Women should know their place. It's natural for a woman to want a husband and family. When I married your father, I was the same age as you. I always knew that I would get married and have children. Unfortunately the dear Lord only allowed me one, you, my little treasure, but I prayed to him that I would be a good wife and mother, whatever happened to me.

'When I met your father for the first time, I didn't feel love for him, and our marriage was more or less arranged, like yours, my darling. My parents thought that the owner of the Azienda was a good match for me. My father was of noble lineage, but his family had become quite poor over the years. When I saw Castellengo for the first time, it felt like home. And I wanted to do my duty by my husband. He has been very kind – a wonderful father to you as well – and over the years we have grown very fond of each other. I have always been contented. I knew my place in life. He was the breadwinner, the provider; he made it possible for you to have everything you could ever want. My place is to provide a home for him and my family. And that is what I have tried to do all these years.'

'Maybe, Mama, some women now don't want to get married and have a family. I have never even thought about it until now. And my life is so pleasant here, why should I have to leave? I don't want to marry and move to Bertini.'

'Don't worry my love. You will feel differently soon. Leonardo is a wonderful catch, a fine, handsome man. I am sure you will be happy with him, *cara mia.*'

Livietta shivered. She hadn't found Leonardo at all attractive when her mother had pointed him out to her one day at a musical event in Tortello. He was too big, too male. He seemed so arrogant, so confident, so full of himself, as if every woman should fall at his feet.

'Well, I'm not like that,' she thought to herself.

Her mother was thinking too. She thought that Livietta had to learn what life was really like: she knew her daughter would marry; she would do it for them, for her parents' sake.

*

Leonardo had been very amused when his aunt had suggested marriage to Livietta Ruggieri, the Countess treating it like any other business proposition.

Leonardo thought he would be able to wriggle out of any

wedding plans, and then he changed his mind. 'Well, why not? Maybe this is what has been missing for me. It might not be so bad after all, this marriage business ...' He was prepared to give it a shot, and after all he would require an heir one day.

'Aunt, well if you think so, I suppose I should get married sometime. And, of course, Castellengo produces the best wine around. I can have a crate of their best *Riserva* every week!' he said flippantly.

His aunt scolded him, 'Now, Leonardo, you must take this seriously. You don't get married every day. My marriage was also arranged, but I grew to care for my husband, and even though we were not blessed with children,' at this she made a sign of the cross, 'we were very devoted to each other. We had a good marriage, like a true partnership.

'You must arrange everything as soon as possible and set the date. There is not much time; she needs to be snapped up at once. I thought an autumn wedding ... all the trees ... such lovely colours. And of course, it must be before Christmas. I thought about All Saints Day, before All Souls, but then maybe not. It will have to be before the end of October. I think that was what that Ruggieri man and I agreed. And then, what plans I have. I thought that, with your love of cars and my business connections, we could think about setting up our own car factory. The Azienda would be the ideal site.'

'What are you talking about, aunt! I love cars but I don't intend to set up a car factory. Heavens above, what a thought, business doesn't interest me. I want to drive cars, not make them!'

In fact, Leonardo had recently taken part in his first race in the summer, in a circuit around Piacenza, via Busseto and Fidenza and then back to Piacenza.

'And what do you mean? Castellengo castle and all those

beautiful vineyards, you couldn't possibly think of destroying them!'

Leonardo laughed at the absurdity of it all, but his aunt was not so easily dissuaded.

'You don't know how important this could be. You and Claudio have wasted so many of the family assets already. This is a great opportunity. Cars are the future. Of course, I wouldn't touch the castle. We could use it as hospitality for prospective customers. But think of the grounds. We Bertini must get involved. I have been planning this – why else would I want you to marry that girl?'

Leonardo yawned. He would humour his aunt, but after the wedding he would have to persuade her to go to her house in Portofino for a long stay, or visit Claudio in New York. He didn't want her to interfere. She so loved to meddle. And if the marriage turned out to be a failure, he wanted to keep his options open, and his aunt would have to mind her own business.

'Well, aunt, I suppose I had better go and meet the young lady in question,' – Livietta or whoever she is, he thought to himself. 'This is the first step in your scheme, I take it. I have to see the girl first, or should I marry her sight unseen?'

Leonardo changed into one of his smartest suits, made from imported Scottish wool, and the next day, at four o'clock in the afternoon, as previously arranged, he rode over to the Azienda. He had persuaded his aunt that it would be better if he took the plunge on his own.

Leonardo had passed the Azienda several times and had always admired the clean proportions of the castle, much more geometric in style than Bertini with its odd pair of towers. He was entering the place for the first time and was shown into a drawing room by an old female servant. Signor and Signora Ruggieri were sitting on a deep, heavily upholstered velvet sofa, on either side of their daughter, Livietta.

Leonardo was quite disappointed with her appearance. She was a slight, dark little thing. His aunt had said she was a talented beauty. Well, he couldn't agree. 'More like a frightened little animal, actually,' he thought to himself.

Rodolfo jumped up from the sofa where he had felt very uncomfortable and overdressed in his slightly too small suit. Rodolfo had a vain streak, pretending he was slimmer than he really was.

'Conte, I mean Signore, what an extreme pleasure it is to finally meet you.' He was so eager to make a bow, he didn't realise how close he was to his prospective son-in-law and his head bumped into Leonardo's chest. Rodolfo was so embarrassed he staggered back, and fell noisily onto the sofa.

'So sorry,' he muttered.

Leonardo found himself profoundly irritated. 'What an absurd little man,' he thought. 'I can't believe he has made thousands of lire out of this place.' But he overcame his irritation and said in his normal charming way:

'Not at all, no harm done, and may I say the pleasure is all mine.' He bowed with a flourish, showing poor Rodolfo how it should be done.

There was an awkward silence, so Leonardo decided to continue. 'And this is Livietta, how charming!'

Livietta continued to sit on the sofa. She was not sure what she was supposed to do.

'Livietta, get up!' chided Rodolfo.

Livietta got up reluctantly and looked up closely at Leonardo for the first time, this imposing man towering over her. He looked at her as if he was very amused about something. She didn't appreciate that at all. She had hoped for her parents' sake she would learn to like the man she was being forced to marry, but she thought there was something cruel, even sinister, about his smile.

'How do you do, sir,' she said and curtsied.

'Well, at least she got that right,' thought Leonardo. He liked her voice, like a bird's, so musical and light. It reminded him of the nightingale he sometimes heard during the night as he tossed and turned in his bed. 'Maybe it would be better if we were alone together, so I could get to know my "betrothed",' he pondered.

'Livietta, please would you do me the honour of showing me around the Azienda? This place has always fascinated me,' he stated rather imperiously.

Livietta smiled at him for the first time and her face changed. 'It will be a pleasure.' She loved the Azienda and would gladly show anyone around, even this stranger, Leonardo. She could see her parents were pleased. They were grinning at her. It was all so odd. Before this moment she had always been completely segregated from the opposite sex, and she was baffled that her parents were so keen for her to be on her own with a man.

Livietta took him to some of the vineyards first and showed him examples of each type of vine: the dry black Barbera and the sweeter Bonarda, the dry white Ortrugo and the sweeter Monterosso. Then they passed through the wine-presses (in Torretta people pressed the grapes with their feet, but not here) and the vast vaults used for storing the barrels of various types of wines. Next they moved on to the bottling plant: the beautiful glass bottles, the corks, the labelling machines, each with the fine engraving of the Castellengo coat of arms. And finally the cellars where each type of wine was specially shelved, each row meticulously labelled with name, year and a number.

Leonardo was fascinated, he loved the smell of the cellars, a combination of dampness and fermenting grapes. He was getting thirsty – all that beautiful wine to taste and drink. Afterwards in the wine-tasting room Livietta shyly offered him some *Riserva* to taste.

Leonardo licked his lips, '*Caspita*, it's divine!' he thought to himself.

Finally she led him through the courtyard to the chapel and bell tower. She sweetly explained about her bell-ringing duties, telling him to be careful not to touch the rope.

'The chapel is wonderful, so plain, so simple,' said Leonardo quietly, looking around the elegant building. Even Rodolfo Ruggieri had not managed to ruin it. Castellengo was indeed beautiful, even though the Ruggieri choice of furnishings was far too fussy and overbearing.

Livietta had become quite animated, quite charming. 'Well, maybe marriage to her will be tolerable,' he pondered.

He thought about kissing her. 'Maybe not, she is the kind of girl who would have a seizure if I did,' he decided. He had made love to so many girls in his time, and being an expert on the matter he could tell she was an innocent.

Livietta was pleased that Leonardo liked her beloved chapel. She would have dearly loved to get married here, in this very place. However the Contessa had already decided that they were to be married in the big church at the top of Tortello, the Pieve.

Livietta stole a glance at Leonardo as he admired the tall clear windows, the simplicity of their design. She trembled at the idea of what would happen on their wedding night, a big man like him on top of her. Mama had tentatively tried to explain it, but she had put her hand over her ears. Young women were encouraged to remain ignorant about sex. Ignorance was a virtue. Mothers thought that silence was the best protection against vice. Unmarried girls such as Livietta always walked beside their mother when out in the street. She would never have been allowed to walk alongside a young man, even if she had wanted to, which she hadn't.

Unmarried daughters couldn't go out alone until the age of 40. But at the same time it was felt that that there was more danger of freedom if a woman was married. 'Marriage – ugh!' She couldn't bear the idea ... but it was too late now. She had promised her parents she would go through with it. Maybe Leonardo had a more sensitive side after all. She could see that he loved beautiful things. Maybe she would gradually settle down at Bertini.

'But will I ever love him?' He was so huge.

Leonardo was starting to get bored. He'd had enough of scared young women. He strode through the courtyard back to the house, Livietta trailing behind. Rodolfo offered him a further glass of his best Gutturnio Riserva, a very good vintage from 1895. This cheered Leonardo up enormously, and he felt quite warm towards his future father-in-law. He drank the wine slowly and appreciatively. 'Yes, a very good vintage, indeed.'

When he finished the wine, Leonardo decided it was time to make his departure, but then remembered his good manners. His aunt had badgered him to extend an invitation to the Ruggieri family.

'Signor, Signora and Signorina Ruggieri, you are all invited to Bertini tomorrow at nine for supper. I so look forward to your being my guests there,' he said affectedly.

Oh God! He had forgotten. Margherita would have to decide what to cook; he couldn't be bothered to think about it.

The dinner wasn't as bad as Leonardo had anticipated. Rodolfo was on his best behaviour, and his wife talked about their various acquaintances in the area. They discussed Verdi's last opera, 'Falstaff', which they had all seen at La Scala.

'I remember that the baritone was exceptionally good and the orchestration superb,' said Livietta quietly.

They discussed other Verdi operas. Leonardo's favourite opera was 'Rigoletto'. The quartet was so beautiful, the story so tragic. Livietta unhesitatingly agreed, although she said she also liked 'La Traviata' and Puccini's 'Tosca'.

'Yes,' replied Leonardo, '*Le dolci mani* is sublime.'

Rodolfo thought Livietta was playing her role beautifully, and he was relieved that that old hat, the Contessa, was not there.

It was time Leonardo played the host alone, she had said. She had often helped him entertain in the past, but he would have to get used to playing the host at Bertini. Besides she had important business to do in Milan.

Leonardo showed Livietta around some of the house. She didn't think it was as beautiful as her home. It was a large, solid type of house, but somehow its proportions were wrong. Yes, it was full of treasures: miniature sarcophagi, statues of Pharaohs, and jewelled scarabs from Egypt, seventeenth-century silk paintings and wooden sculptures from India, Ming vases and huge ginger containers from China. Best of all were the wonderful paintings: one by Bellini, a few by Parmigianino, and some very contemporary ones that she liked but she didn't recognise the artists. Livietta could have looked at the paintings all evening. And the panorama from the house was superb. Although the house was set in flat countryside, to the south there was a wonderful view of the medieval town of Tortello, with its castellated walls, majestically dominating the rest of the landscape. Tortello couldn't be seen so clearly from Castellengo.

Bertini was interesting, such beautiful *objets d'art*, and its very own library. 'Well, maybe this would make marriage more bearable,' thought poor Livietta, trying to convince herself that it wouldn't be so bad after all. Then she looked at Leonardo and she felt quite queasy.

They looked an unlikely couple as they stood together by the huge marble staircase, surrounded by numerous paintings. She, tiny and nervous-looking; he tall, straight and imposing.

After dinner Livietta played the elegant Bechstein grand piano and sang a couple of lively traditional songs. Leonardo was sitting beside Rodolfo who was beaming proudly at his daughter. Leonardo was surprised. She had a good soprano voice, and her piano-playing was quite accomplished. In repose she looked timid, almost pathetic, but when she talked about something that interested her, or did something she enjoyed, like playing the piano, then yes, she was quite radiant. Her rather beaky nose was too long for her to be considered a beauty, but she was a sweet little thing, mused Leonardo, twirling his moustache as usual.

In mid-October, on a sunny but chilly day, Leonardo and Livietta were married in the *Pieve*, high up in the main piazza of Tortello. The church was a great example of the Romanesque style, with its simple westerly façade, the rounded towers and cupola of the apse, and its cloisters at the side. The main building, dating back to the eighth century, was made of huge oblong chunks of volcanic rock and had been rebuilt in the twelfth century after an earthquake. Inside, it was not so impressive; it had been completely redecorated in the Rococo style, with lots of white plaster swirls and sickly, melodramatic paintings.

Livietta was shrouded from head to toe in a cloud of white lace, and was weighed down by an enormous bouquet of lilies. She felt it was her funeral rather than her wedding. It was very windy as she entered the church on the arm of her father, and she could not stop her teeth from chattering, both from fright and the cold.

The father of the bride stood in the church as straight as he could, and looked quite distinguished in the suit he had had specially made in Milan. He had finally agreed to order a larger size. His hair and beard had received special attention. 'From a bottle!' someone muttered. He and Rina, dressed in dark blue lace, of a similar pattern to her daughter's, both started to weep – this was the proudest day of their lives.

For Leonardo, the ceremony was endless, lots of swaying incense burners, coughing, and thousands of candles. He had always disliked that incense-filled, waxy smell churches invariably had. It made him want to sneeze. There was a full Nuptial Mass and the choir sang the Easter Hymn, *Panis Angelicus*, *Ave Maria* and various other renditions of religious songs, whining on and on … Three overdressed priests hovered around the altar, muttering in Latin. Finally after what seemed like hours, the most senior priest in the middle, a Monsignor, uttered the important words. Leonardo and Livietta muttered the same words, then the priest muttered some more words and that was it: they were finally man and wife. They walked back up the aisle together and it was over. 'Thank God it's ended,' muttered the bridegroom.

Even though the ceremony had been so tedious, Leonardo was rather enjoying himself. He had never been a husband before. What would his actress friends think of him now! He in his morning coat and top hat made for him in Savile Row, London. He had slept with so many beautiful women, but he couldn't remember half of them. Maybe Livietta, his *'merlina'* – 'little blackbird' as he had started to call her, would be different, more pliable, more in tune with his needs; someone who would see the real him, not the cold persona he pretended to be.

Outside the church, the horses and carriages were waiting to take the wedding guests back to Castellengo. There would be a huge wedding feast for all the friends and relatives of the couple, and the workers from both the Bertini household and the Azienda. Everybody was aching to get down to the serious business of eating and drinking. It was a typical autumn day and a wedding was a very welcome celebration before the more sombre one of All Souls. It was indeed a momentous occasion – at last the uniting of the Bertini and Castellengo estates.

Rodolfo was overjoyed. The guests were praising his most

selected and prized wines: 'Exquisite, quite exquisite!' And the food was endless: various sizes and shapes of salamis, Parma ham, *coppa di Piacenza, mortadella, culatello* to start. Then a selection of *ravioli, tortelli,* and *gnocchi,* followed by dozens of guinea fowls, partridges, pigeons, pheasants, then veal, beef, lamb, pork, and, of course, wild boar, with various vegetables and potatoes. Heaps of tiny little fruit or chocolate tarts, served with coffee and the local grappa and finally the multi-tiered cream wedding cake and champagne. Glasses clinked together and voices were raised to toast the couple:

'Tante belle cose.'

Rodolfo had been quite offended when Leonardo had insisted on importing some champagne, and absolutely refused to touch it, but after a few extra glasses of his precious Gutturnio, he forgave his new son-in-law. He decided that he didn't mind in the slightest; champagne was exactly right for a wedding.

Livietta was in a daze. She had never been so much the centre of attention before, had always hated being in the spotlight. Her marriage had happened so quickly. 'I am a wife,' she told herself but she couldn't yet believe it. This was the first day of her utterly new life. She had scarcely eaten or drunk a thing and was walking around haphazardly, not sure what she was doing, where she was heading. Some of the guests tried to engage her in conversation and she just nodded and smiled wanly, unable to say anything sensible. She made a point of going over to Gianetto and his wife who had worked on the estate since she was a baby. They had looked uncomfortable, standing alone, overwhelmed by all the noise and excitement of a wedding day. She was just about to say something to them when Leonardo grabbed her by the arm.

'Come outside, I have something to show you.' He pulled her through the reception rooms to the main door.

Armando was standing next to the new highly polished chrome motor car.

'Come, Livietta, we are going for a ride in my car.' With that he leapt into the driver's seat. 'Come on, get in.'

Livietta had never been in a car before. She gingerly climbed up into the leather seat next to Leonardo. He hadn't even offered to help her get in. She was still in her huge wedding dress, and it was difficult to stuff all that lace inside the vehicle. Leonardo made a few half-hearted attempts, but quite a lot of it was still trailing over the side. He gave up and put on his goggles. He made Livietta do the same.

'Hurry up with that dress, and hold on tight,' he commanded. He was impatient to get off. Armando was fiddling with something at the front of the car, turning a metal lever of some kind, and then with a shudder and a few bangs they were off.

Leonardo was hoping that his new wife would find the experience exhilarating. Things hadn't been going too well with her physically. When he had first tried to kiss her, she turned her head away, and when she did finally allow it, she went stiff and would not kiss him back. He wanted to impress her, stimulate her. He thought the speed of the car would make her feel excited, passionate...

He guided the car expertly down the driveway of the Azienda and headed north up the road away from Tortello. He accelerated as much as the car would permit, and gathered speed, loving the feel of it moving bumpily along the road, and coaxing it to reach its top speed of 35 kilometres an hour. The road was quite newly made, but parts of it were still quite rough and lots of dust was flying around. Livietta was paralysed with fear. She was terribly cold. The wind and the dust were smacking her face, and her hair coming out of her headdress was blowing around so much, she couldn't see a thing through her goggles. Freezing and frightened, she reached out and tried to grab hold of something, but there was nothing secure to hold – only Leonardo and she couldn't bring herself to touch him. They were going faster and faster. She was rigid, her white-knuckled fists clenched, her goggles askance on her face. It was a nightmare. She couldn't wait for the car to stop.

Leonardo was enjoying the feel of the car, but then he looked at Livietta. She was white with fright and he knew he had made a dreadful mistake.

11. Zaira in Milan

When Zaira sat down in the third-class carriage on the hard wooden seat, she couldn't believe what she had done. She was filled with anguish, exhaustion and excitement all at once. All alone on a train, not knowing what was in store for her. She realised that if Bartolomeo hadn't died, she wouldn't have left Torretta. She would have stayed there even though she hated it so much; she would have stayed for her father's sake. She would have been a companion for him. She imagined him looking at her now, shaking his fists at her headstrong behaviour. She smiled to herself and then sighed. She was truly an orphan now – no mother and no father, and her brothers didn't care about her. She thought it was strange how things had turned out. She had got what she wanted, but at what cost?

'What would have happened if my mother hadn't died when I was born. Would I have been very different? Would I be a more tranquil person, more resigned to my fate?'

When Bartolomeo had described her mother, he had always said how gentle and loving she was. She wouldn't have hurt a fly.

'Would she and I have really loved each other?' Zaira didn't know why she was like she was, but she knew she wasn't anything like her mother in character. Even though her father was hard on her in some ways, he had indulged her in others, making sure she had all the things that other children in the village had lacked. Nice clothes for Sundays, sweets, some wooden toys he had made himself, and he had even encouraged her love of books. When Elena had lived with them she had been so free, so used to getting her own way. Maybe a mother would have had a firmer hand, made Zaira realise that she couldn't have everything she wanted in the world, and Zaira wouldn't have been quite so restless. She would have been content in her mother's love.

'I will never know what it would have been like to have a mother,' she sighed.

The train juddered slowly along and luckily her carriage was quite empty. She pretended to sleep. She didn't want to start a conversation with anyone and be asked awkward questions. The train stopped every so often and Zaira half-opened her eyes to see where they were: first the station of Piacenza which looked quite elegant and grand. The train stopped there for a few minutes. Zaira blinked her eyes and a thrill passed through her: here she was heading towards the biggest adventure of her life. The train thundered on, gathering more pace now, then came to an abrupt halt at Lodi and a few other unmemorable places. And now the train had sped up again and was already approaching Milan.

When Zaira arrived in Milan and got off the train, the massive grimy Central Station with its neo-Gothic architecture completely overwhelmed her and her legs wobbled. The huge steam trains filled the endless platforms, their fronts like frightening faces, and smoke and soot everywhere, making the atmosphere dark and mysterious. Some were starting to leave the station, funnels puffing, whistles blowing. There were people everywhere: passengers arriving or departing, a lot of civilians, mostly men, but for the main part soldiers, dressed in different uniforms, including the Bersaglieri with their tall plumed hats. There were also station workers holding flags or signs, porters wheeling huge piles of luggage, trunks and other heavy suitcases nearly toppling off the trolleys.

Some of the trains were going further north, to Switzerland, Germany or France. There were signs at the end of each platform: 'Rome', 'Munich', 'Geneva', even 'Paris'. Zaira's mouth was almost watering. One day she would get on one of these trains and never come back. But first things first: she had to seek her fortune in Milan, find somewhere to stay, get a job.

It took her ages to descend the huge staircase carrying her few possessions in her little valise and find the main exit from the station. She was not sure where to go but after asking directions and a few minutes' hesitation, she slowly made her way on foot to the huge white highly ornate *Duomo* – cathedral – in the main square, where to the side stood a huge wrought-iron and glass-enclosed gallery of shops.

Her walk had taken her longer than she expected, but it was certainly worth it. Everything here looked magnificent compared to the rest of the streets near the station that she had passed. Milan was a heaving, disgusting mess – smoky and foggy, and the factory buildings in the distance burping nasty black smoke out of their chimneys. There were people begging, horses and carriages reeling in all directions, and one or two motor cars stuttering and stalling on the main thoroughfares. 'What chaos!' she thought. She didn't feel very safe either: lots of shady-looking men standing on street corners, waiting, waiting maybe to attack her, to steal the small amount of money she possessed. In Torretta, there was no such thing as crime, but here:

'*Dio buono*! God knows what might happen.'

Zaira was having second thoughts already. She was away from home for the first time ever, a young, orphaned girl. She felt frightened and totally out of her depth. She tried to pull herself together: she couldn't give up yet.

She still had aspirations to be a governess, or even one day to train as a proper teacher. And she had to find lodgings. She would have to stay in a hotel for the first night, and then look for work the following morning. She trudged around many streets and eventually found a small hotel for '*signorine*' and struggled up the stairs with her small amount of luggage to a room on the fifth floor. Even if there had been a hotel lift, she wouldn't have used it; she wouldn't have known what it was. She looked bedraggled: her wavy hair flying about, soot on her pert little nose, and her one and only good dress looking so old-fashioned compared to those of the Milanese women, betraying the fact she was a poor country girl. Zaira thought that she had looked quite smart on her departure from Torretta. She had pressed her best blue-and-white-striped calico dress and had put on all the jewellery that had been her mother's. Yet as she strolled around the galleries near the *Duomo* and saw all the sophisticated Milanese women she realised what a country bumpkin she was and how old-fashioned she looked.

'The first thing I must do tomorrow morning is to buy a new dress!'

As she lay in bed that night she realised she really was alone in Milan. It was the first time she had ever slept in a strange bed. When she first lay down on the soft feather mattress she realised her life had now radically changed.

'There is no going back. I am free now. I am completely alone in the world, in this little bed, in this dirty street in Milan.'

No one to stop her from doing exactly what she wanted. She had done her duty to her father and now she could go anywhere she pleased, and sleep in as many different beds as she wished.

She knew she had made the right decision in leaving Torretta, excited to be starting her new life.

She was so tired she slept soundly that night. It was the first time she hadn't thought about her father, and her hopes were high.

But it was much more difficult then she realised. 'How do you set about being a governess?' she asked herself when she woke up next day. She had been so intent on leaving Torretta, she hadn't really thought about how she would actually get a job. She needed to know people. She required a recommendation, but she knew nobody.

'Milan is too big, too frightening – how will I survive in such an imposing, dreadful place?' she asked herself.

After a week, Zaira was still trying to find work. She had given up on the idea of being a governess. Signorina Maestri had been right: she didn't look the part and the couple of leads she had managed to investigate had proved fruitless. The two people who had interviewed her looked her up and down contemptuously. Her clothes, her accent, her demeanour were all wrong, but she desperately tried to remain optimistic. She knew there were educational or philanthropic institutions, private agencies or newspaper advertisements and shop notices to read. But it was not easy. Even knowing French hadn't helped. Zaira's education was far from complete. She was mainly self-taught from books; she hadn't got the qualifications or the connections to get the kind of job she thought she deserved.

And Milan was so expensive. Everything cost so much more than it cost in Lunano or Tortello. She had only been able to afford a rather plain, high-collared, dark green dress, a straw boater, some black leather ankle boots and a cream and green patterned shawl. The autumnal weather made it necessary for her to wear her shabby black woollen cloak, so although she was pleased with her new clothes, she couldn't really show them off the way she would have liked.

Accommodation was another problem: rooms were very hard to find and the rents were so high. Eventually she found a tiny attic room at the top of a big *palazzo*. The money she had left covered only a further two weeks' rent.

'So much for my inheritance! What will I do when my money runs out?'

She started to dream about her mother. She felt guilty about her: her mother had been perfect, she had been cherished, she had died young, free of sin, but Zaira was all alone in a big city, unprotected, at anyone's mercy. She thought of the heroines in the novels she had read, penniless and down on their luck. Her expectations grew lower and lower.

That morning she had seen a notice in a shop window:

UN PO DI CUCINA
STIRATO SEMPLICE
PULIZIA DELLA CASA
18-35 ANNI
A LITTLE COOKING
SOME IRONING AND
HOUSE CLEANING
18 TO 35 YEARS OF AGE

'Is this what it has come to? Will I end up as a maid for a family, or a chambermaid in a hotel?'

She could have stayed at home in Torretta; got married even and carried on her life as a skivvy to some man there, rather than becoming a servant in Milan.

Zaira found the advertisement quite amusing really.

'Would somebody who was 17 or 36 be rejected? Does the

age limit mean they can't apply? It's only a housemaid's job, *per carità!* – for pity's sake!'

She knew that she could possibly find work in the textile industry, as Milan was the most important city in Italy for this trade. Maybe she could become a dressmaker, but she hated sewing: her clumsy fingers could never make neat stitches and she would never master one of those sewing machines, or whatever they were called.

After nearly two weeks of searching she realised how difficult it would be for her to find a proper job – one which would transport her out of her humble peasant-class background.

She was beginning to revise her options, lower her sights. Then, out of the blue, she suddenly remembered her cousin, Rosa Crespi, who had left Torretta to work in a button factory in Piacenza. Rosa had said there were lots of jobs there, especially for women, but 'What menial work!' Zaira had thought to herself.

Zaira was torn – she wasn't sure what to do. She was running out of ideas. Should she return to Torretta and find herself a husband instead? She had never cared for any boy. She had once fallen in love, for about a minute at least, with a boy she saw fleetingly in Tortello, but she had never seen him again and forgot all about him. She had never, ever seriously thought about men and love. She was intrigued by the idea of romantic love in the novels she read, but she had never imagined herself in love. If she did marry, it would have to be for love, not an arranged marriage. Her father had always been trying to arrange betrothals with boys in Torretta. He and Delfina were convinced she would marry Matteo. She laughed aloud at the thought. Matteo who had pinched her bottom but, when he tried to speak to her, couldn't string two words together without stammering, without blushing. The whole idea of marriage was ludicrous, utterly impossible, but girls like her only had two alternatives: marriage or work.

Her only option was to find work. She was willing enough. She had read in a magazine that 'girls should enjoy work and learn to work well and work according to the needs of the family'. Well she no longer had a family, but she knew she was clever – surely she could learn how to do anything, even if her previously high aspirations could not be met.

Yet Zaira was tired of trying to find a job in Milan. So far all she could find was work as a maid to some awful family. This was not what she had expected.

Finally she took a deep breath and decided to travel to Piacenza to see her cousin, Rosa.

Piacenza was nearer Tortello, and if things didn't work out there she could always go back to Torretta to her brothers. Zaira didn't want to think about this yet, but it was there, always there, in the back of her mind. She remembered what Delfina had said about swallowing her pride.

She packed up things at her lodgings, paid the bill, which left her with barely any money, and walked as quickly as she could back to the enormous central station of Milan. She looked around the many platforms, filled with the smoke from the train funnels, the atmosphere still so dark and dangerous.

She wondered to herself whether she would ever go back there. It had all been such a bitter disappointment to her. She just about had enough money to buy a third-class ticket to Piacenza, and then she would have to find a job. Her situation was becoming desperate.

Zaira fidgeted for the whole journey:

'What will become of me now?'

When she arrived at Piacenza railway station, she climbed down from the train onto the platform, walking slowly and wondering what to do next. Suddenly she found herself accosted by an aristocratic old lady waving her umbrella stick. The woman was dressed in black from head to foot, and her face was half-covered by a lace veil, topped by a tall hat with a black feather in it. It was the Contessa Bertini.

'My dear, can you please help me?' she asked, holding out her hand at arm's length to stop Zaira in her tracks. 'You seem to be the only person around to ask. I have mislaid a piece of luggage, and the porter has already gone off somewhere else.'

Zaira looked round and saw the porter a few platforms away. She climbed down the platform and ran across the tracks to reach him. She told him in a breathless voice about the lady on the other platform:

'That old lady over there says she has lost a bag.'

'Ah, yes the Contessa Bertini.'

The porter told her that he had spotted it already and went to retrieve the valise. He and Zaira both went back to the Contessa and Zaira explained to the Contessa what had happened.

'It was at the far end of the platform. It got muddled up with someone else's luggage, but the porter recognised your family crest, erm, should I say, the Contessa Bertini's family crest?'

The Contessa was extremely grateful to Zaira for her help.

'Thank you so much, my dear. You have been very kind.' She looked Zaira up and down, and although she could tell she was not of noble birth, she also noted her unusual good looks and her pains to speak perfect Italian. After two weeks in Milan, Zaira was attempting to put on the airs of a city girl.

'Where are you going, my dear? Can I offer you a lift in my carriage?'

Zaira was just about to say she was going to find her cousin who worked at the button factory, but with sudden inspiration she changed her mind.

Well, I am looking for work. I did try in Milan but there didn't seem to be any suitable work available, or I mean nothing that was of interest to me, nothing that I wanted to do ... erm ... I just thought it would be easier, that's all ...'

Zaira was breathing heavily, trying not to twist her fingers, trying not to get flustered, not sure what she was trying to say.

The Contessa considered her for a while longer. How old was this girl – eighteen, possibly twenty?

She knew that Livietta, her niece by marriage, was almost entirely useless in the house. This girl could be the ideal solution. She could help Livietta run things, organise the meals.

'But is she too young, too pretty? What will Leonardo think of her?' the Contessa pondered. 'Well, he only seems to be interested in sophisticated actresses or opera singers, women as unlike Livietta as possible. She is still so baby-like and demure. He wouldn't be interested in another innocent, surely! And if he were, would it really matter? Leonardo has always been one for the fairer sex! This girl seems pleasant enough, cheerful and articulate. She will be company for Livietta.'

The Contessa knew that Livietta was dreadfully lonely and homesick, missing her parents and the Azienda, and that she felt at such a loss in Bertini.

The Contessa knew even better that her nephew wasn't faithful to Livietta. She was aware of his exploits in Milan.

'But he is a man, after all. That's life; one has to accept these things,' she said to herself. To Zaira, she asked:

'How old are you, girl?'

'Twenty.' Zaira had never lied before in her life. She thought back to those times in the church when she had mocked the priest's sermons. Well, she was sinning now. When she used to go to confession there had never been anything very bad to confess: she had been disobedient to her father, she had lost her temper. She sometimes wished there had been some juicier sin to own up to, but she had never lied before.

'Nearly twenty,' Zaira corrected herself, but in fact she was still 18. She knew the Contessa was weighing her up, perhaps even going to make her a proposition. The Contessa thought herself a good judge of character and Zaira seemed honest-looking and trustworthy.

'Well, I'm thinking … my nephew's wife does need some help. She is about your age, but you seem so much wiser than she is, more self-possessed, let's say. She needs help in the house, but you being nearly the same age, you could also be her friend, a maid-cum-companion. Yes, that's it, she desperately needs some companionship.'

Zaira's mind was racing. 'Work in an aristocratic family's house, companionship for a young wife. *Caspita!* – Gracious! This is much better than being a servant in some dreadful place in Milan.'

She took a deep breath. It wasn't what she had planned, her dreams of a teaching diploma, or being a governess, rising above her peasant girl origins, but she couldn't be so choosy now, after all.

'Oh, Contessa, I am indeed looking for work, I am sure I could be just the person you are looking for. I enjoy housework very much. I used to run my father's house *and* farm in Torretta, further up in the mountains.' She was lying again: she had deplored the odious tasks of the cooking, the washing and cleaning, the sewing, the animals. Her mind was racing ahead. Surely there would be several servants in a house like this. She even thought she might know which house it was. She had heard talk of the Bertini family. Weren't they connected to the Visconti somehow? They had a manor house at the place also called Bertini on one of the roads from Tortello to Piacenza. It was built in the plain, about two hundred metres from the road, with big gates and magnificent pillars at the roadside and a long drive leading to the huge house with two oddly shaped towers and surrounded by castellated walls.

The Contessa was impressed with the way Zaira held her head up proudly, her beautiful hair and almond-shaped eyes. She was a very charming girl, unusual even, not shy and retiring like poor Livietta.

'So what is your name?'

'Zaira.'

'Ah, Zaira.' She liked that. It was the name of that rather unusual opera by Vincenzo Bellini based ona story by Voltaire.

'I am very pleased to meet you. Well, come with me now. I'm going to Bertini – on my way to my house in Tortello.'

The Contessa and Zaira approached the carriage, the same coat of arms embossed on the doors as the one on all the luggage pieces: three lions – *leoni* surrounding a shield, '*Nihil time* – 'Nothing to fear' written on it in Latin.

Zaira was about to climb in by herself but remembered to allow the driver to help her. She had never been inside such a carriage before. The interior was button-upholstered in deep crimson velvet. There was an ornate silver cylinder on the floor on one side of the carriage and the old lady rested her booted feet on it. Zaira didn't realise what it was, but it was filled with hot water to keep the Contessa's feet warm. The horses and carriage sped off, taking the road from Piacenza to Tortello. It was quite a long, boring drive. The landscape was flat and uninspiring but the foothills of the Apennines could be seen in the distance.

Zaira tried not to think about Torretta. After her sojourn in dirty Milan she had missed the clean mountain air, the pure spring water, the lush green hills, the brilliant stars at night, the tranquillity.

12. Zaira at Bertini

Just before the medieval town of Tortello, the carriage slowed down and turned into a long driveway. Zaira had been right: this was the house she remembered. It looked even grander as they approached it. Zaira had seen it a few times from the road in her father's horse and cart but the house hadn't been very distinct because it was partially hidden by tall poplar trees. Now she could see it was a sixteenth-century manor house, made of small reddish bricks, with rows of tall shuttered windows. The extensions at the back and the surrounding high walls were in yellow ochre stucco. The two odd-looking towers made the rather simply designed house look even more imposing. One of the towers had been added at a later date and was taller and rounded, unlike its shorter and squarer companion, a contemporary of the original house. The two dissimilar towers gave the house a slightly disjointed, irregular look, as if they were struggling to be compatible, like two old people locked in a loveless marriage. Zaira started to think of that other tower, *'la Torre dei Crespi'* in Torretta. There was nothing left of it now, just a few piles of stones. How different from these two imposing, discordant structures!

'Come, my dear, we have arrived at Bertini.'

Zaira had been lost in her thoughts: 'Well this is it, the start of my new life, not in Milan or Piacenza as I had planned, but in Bertini. How long will it last?'

The Contessa rang the bell impatiently and an old man opened the door. Zaira could see that the house itself had been modernised. There was a huge central staircase, its marble steps curving round to the first floor and beyond.

'Dio mio!' Zaira couldn't help exclaiming to herself. Electricity had been installed. Zaira had never entered a house with its own generator and electric lighting before, but she had heard her brothers saying they had seen electricity being installed in a new house in Piacenza one day. The hotel and lodgings where she had stayed in Milan had only gaslights and candles.

She was itching to go to the switches to turn the electric lights on and off.

Zaira looked round and told herself she had made the right decision.

'I think I will be happy here.'

At that moment Leonardo strode down the huge staircase in his riding boots, swinging a riding crop, ready for hunting. He stopped when he saw the girl with chestnut hair and large grey-green eyes – she looked vaguely familiar.

Zaira looked up at Leonardo on the marble staircase, and felt as if she had received a blow. She swallowed and took a step back. Maybe she had made a mistake after all. Who was this man? She knew instantly she felt a physical attraction to him, but it was also a feeling of dread that a man had aroused her for the first time in her life.

He had dark brown, longish, wavy hair brushed back from his forehead, and a rakish moustache curled up at the ends. His penetrating, deep-brown eyes were set above a long, very straight nose and broad sensual lips. He was tall and quite slender, although his shoulders were broad and his thigh muscles were straining against his tight riding breeches. His voluminous white shirt was open at the neck showing his smooth skin. He was unlike any man she had ever seen before. When he looked at her he stared, holding her gaze. She felt as if he were trying to see inside her. He made her extremely uncomfortable and very agitated. She swallowed nervously.

The Contessa beckoned to her nephew. 'Allow me to introduce Zaira,' she said, and before Leonardo could say anything, the Contessa added:

'This, my dear, is my nephew, Leonardo. He likes to be called Signor, rather than Conte, heaven knows why.' The Contessa snorted with obvious disapproval.

'*Buongiorno, Signor*, I am very pleased to meet you,' Zaira forced herself to say. Leonardo was relieved: her accent was local, even though she was trying to hide it. For a minute he had thought she was one of his acquaintances from Milan. How could he have been so mistaken? She was obviously from the country, albeit dressed in city clothes, and admittedly very beautiful. And what on earth was she doing here? He turned to his aunt and was about to confront her when she interrupted...

'Leonardo, I met Zaira today at Piacenza station, such a helpful girl...'

He looked at the girl again. So she was coming to live at the house, as a servant/companion to Livietta! It would be amusing to see how the two hit it off.

'This girl seems quite confident, unlike poor little Livietta,' thought Leonardo. 'Still, it might well do her good, and maybe we can all be entertained.' He started to smile to himself and looked at Zaira intently.

Zaira tried to avoid his gaze. He seemed to be smirking at her. She was embarrassed: 'Is he insulting me by looking at me like this? How can I possibly be attracted to a man like him?' He was like an 'evil villain' from one of her novels.

The Contessa went out to find Livietta, and Leonardo and Zaira were left alone together for the first time.

'So, my lovely Zaira, what did you do to impress my aunt? She doesn't usually gather up waifs and strays off the street.'

Zaira started to blush. Then she swallowed, pulled her shoulders back, put her chin up, and recounted how she had helped the Contessa retrieve her luggage at Piacenza Railway Station.

'I have been to Milan to look for a job, but it was quite useless, nothing there of interest to me, not quite what I had expected. I confess I thought that it would be so much easier.'

Leonardo found the girl surprisingly refreshing. She was amazingly fearless and unusually confident for a girl of her age and background.

'And how old are you, Zaira?'

Zaira found she couldn't lie again. 'Eighteen,' she stammered. She felt young and innocent in front of him, not twenty and wiser than she was.

'Ah, old enough,' Leonardo thought to himself.

'Well, Zaira, welcome to Bertini. I am sure your coming here will prove to be a pleasure for us all.'

The Contessa had returned with the Signora of the house. Zaira was rather surprised when she laid eyes on Livietta for the first time. She was such a slip of a thing, very reserved and so young and coy, her eyes lowered all the time.

Zaira was aware of Leonardo peering at her again, and she felt tongue-tied. Livietta's shyness also prevented her from speaking.

Finally Zaira plucked up her courage and found herself speaking:

'It is a great pleasure to meet you.' But inside she felt strangely mute. She wasn't really thinking what she was saying. She had actually been looking forward to meeting Livietta, a girl of her own age living in a beautiful house. Zaira wanted to be friends with her, but her mind was full of Leonardo:

'Why is he having such an effect on me?'

She was irritated with herself.

At this point, Leonardo decided it was time to leave. The two young women needed to get acquainted with each other. He would have plenty of time to get to know the new girl later. He made a slight bow in Zaira's direction.

'Delighted to meet you, I'm sure, signorina. Goodbye Aunt. Goodbye Livietta,' he said coolly to his wife. 'I must get out to the horses – they will be getting impatient.'

He strode out of the main door whistling to his dogs and shouting to the grooms.

'*Sprigatevi! I cavalli ci aspettano!*' – 'Hurry up! The horses are waiting!' And with that he disappeared from the great house. The hall seemed empty without his presence.

Zaira couldn't stop herself from breathing heavily, yet she was relieved this impelling man was out of her sight. She couldn't even think about Livietta, who looked so dull and boring in comparison to her husband. He was obviously a man who got what he wanted – quite a rogue even – but there was something else about him, something that was quite intriguing...

...Livietta was speaking to her.

'Sorry I didn't hear what you said, hmm, Signora Contessa.' Zaira wasn't sure what to call her.

Livietta had spoken to Zaira for the first time. 'I said should we go around the house, then? And please call me Livietta,' she said in her sweet, very quiet voice. Although Zaira was distracted, she could see that Livietta was a natural, gentle girl, possibly not at all at home in this big house. There didn't seem to be much affection between husband and wife – they had almost ignored each other.

In return, Livietta was now staring at Zaira. The newcomer intrigued her, and she was not entirely stupid. She could see that Zaira was completely bowled over by her husband and that Leonardo seemed quite smitten as well.

But Livietta was not jealous and asked herself often: 'How can one be jealous of a man one can't love?' A man she found intimidating, domineering, cruel and demanding.

She sighed. She had become somewhat resigned to her life at Bertini, but being married was even worse than she had expected. The sexual side absolutely horrified her. Although her mother had tried to explain, Livietta had had no knowledge of anatomy, especially of a male, and she had always been kept away from male nude statues. And now it would be unthinkable to discuss her sexual problems with her mother.

The Contessa, whom Livietta found just as formidable as her husband, also decided to leave at this point.

'Well, I must be off to Tortello now, Livietta.' Nodding to Zaira, 'I hope *you* settle in,' she said in a commanding voice, and with that the old woman in black, who had so dramatically changed Zaira's life, left the house waving her umbrella stick in the air yet again.

'Thank you so much, Contessa.' Zaira remembered to curtsy. The old servant suddenly appeared from nowhere and let the Contessa out.

Livietta showed Zaira over the entire house. They visited the huge kitchens on the ground floor where all the elderly-looking servants eyed her suspiciously. There was a summer kitchen with tall windows, which was attached to a conservatory leading to the garden, and also a winter kitchen with much smaller windows, and between them a huge larder room where the cheeses were strained and the hams and salamis were cured. From there they walked to the laundry room with the big, rattling boiler and the nearby courtyard where rows and rows of brilliantly white-lace-edged *'biancheria'* – bed linen and towels – were blowing in the wind.

Then they went downstairs to the *'cantina'* – cellar – below the house. It was stacked full of countless bottles of wine and liqueurs. Zaira thought it would take hundreds of years to drink them all.

Livietta then ushered Zaira back upstairs to the vast dining room filled with a long oak table and at least twenty oak chairs with long, plain, upright backs and beige-silk-cushioned seats. Then to the two drawing rooms sparsely furnished with plain hand-carved furniture and to the ballroom with its grand piano. Each room had ornately carved white ceilings, striped wallpaper – either in powder blue or crimson, huge marble fireplaces, all engraved with the Bertini family crest, and tall windows draped in pale gold-coloured velvet curtains held back by silk tasselled cords and with pelmets of the same fabric. They finally came to the library, the walls of which were completely covered from floor to ceiling with rows and rows of shelves of books. There were books on every subject imaginable: some very old with faded leather covers and torn bindings; others new and glossy, with shiny gold lettering on their immaculate spines.

'So many glorious books! I do hope I get a chance to look at some of them,' thought Zaira, her mouth watering as she gazed at what looked like millions of hardbound gilt leather volumes stacked very neatly and arranged either thematically or alphabetically on the shelves of the tall walls. Livietta and Zaira were both staring in wonder at this impressive sight and then they turned and shyly smiled at each other.

'I love books!' they both said simultaneously. They looked at each other and then laughed.

Then they climbed up to the first and second floors on the magnificent marble staircase. Zaira couldn't believe how many bedrooms there were as she wandered through the corridors: dozens of them. And the bathrooms ... they all had proper fitted baths, water closets and washbasins and those other oval-shaped porcelain containers, like washbasins but much nearer the floor. Zaira wasn't sure what they were.

'What is that?' she asked Livietta, pointing to the bidet.

'It's called a *bidet* – it's for washing yourself, erm, that is, not your face or hands...' Livietta didn't know how to go on.

Zaira laughed. 'I think I can guess what you mean.'

She thought back to Torretta – there you had to urinate or defecate in the barn, just like the animals.

On very hot days Zaira used to go to a little hidden stream, surrounded by gigantic boulders, where nobody could see her. Sometimes she would climb further up to the waterfall, undress, and bathe in the pool of clear spring water. She wasn't ashamed of her naked body, smooth and shiny with youth.

'Why am I thinking of this now?'

She tried to shake these thoughts from her head and pay attention to Livietta but she couldn't – after they had left the library the same awkwardness, the same coolness between them, had returned. She didn't think they would ever become friends.

Instead, she couldn't stop thinking about Leonardo. She couldn't understand why she was having these thoughts. She had never, ever really thought of a man in this way before. She and Elena and some of the other girls in the village had discussed the subject of babies and sex, but Zaira had never really been interested. She knew she was expected to marry, and have children, but she could never fully imagine what it would be like.

The idea of sex with a man had never entered her head. It was what animals did; she had always found it disgusting.

*

What had interested her was how to escape that kind of life, that bondage to husband and family, to the ties of a place like Torretta. When a woman married she and anything she owned became her husband's property. Legally, women had very few rights. If a woman became a widow, she had to wait ten months before she could remarry, so that there would be no uncertainty about the paternity of any child born thereafter. And if a woman committed adultery, she could be imprisoned for two years.

*

'Adultery,' shuddered Zaira. She was having adulterous thoughts about Leonardo, a man she had only just met.

'What would Don Aldo say to that?' In spite of herself she smiled at the idea of the priest. He would absolutely love it. He thought all his parishioners were adulterers, sinners; he was convinced everyone was up to no good all the time.

Livietta thought Zaira was a strange girl: obviously intelligent, but completely self-absorbed, daydreaming all the time.

'I think she's treating me with disdain, as if I don't really exist,' thought the young Signora to herself.

Livietta's next task was to introduce Zaira to all the servants. There must have been at least a dozen of them. They all looked aged and wrinkled, including Guerrino, the old man who had answered the door. Zaira knew instantly that she and Guerrino would become friends, but some of the women were downright rude. She could almost read their thoughts:

'What the hell is this young girl doing here?'

'She'll be bossy and interfering.'

'She'll have airs and graces, ideas above her station, and pretend she's better than we are.'

Most of them had been with the family since the time of Leonardo's grandparents.

Zaira didn't know exactly what her domestic duties would be. She and Livietta would have to get to know each other, which was the main reason why she was here after all. There had been talk of Livietta and herself deciding on the menus for each meal together.

When Livietta had finished showing Zaira the house, she timidly instructed Guerrino to take Zaira to her room. Zaira was delighted with the lovely big room that contained a four-poster bed, draped in muslin curtains. The Contessa had instructed Livietta which bedroom to give Zaira before she left. It was at the top of the house, and set apart from the servant's quarters. It was a proper guest room with a balcony and a view of the hills, her hills. Zaira, for all her misgivings and confusion about Leonardo, realised she would have been much worse off being a chambermaid in Milan, or working in the button factory in Piacenza. Now she, an obscure peasant girl from Torretta, was living in some luxury in the Bertini family home. She started grinning to herself.

'And how am I supposed to help Livietta in the house? I know nothing of these things. Choosing menus, me?'

She laughed out loud – all she knew about was bread and polenta!

That was not strictly true, and she was a quick learner. She would be able to help Livietta. She would force herself to learn how a house like this had to be run. She flopped on the bed and immediately went to sleep. She was woken up by Guerrino's knock on the door.

'It is time for dinner, signorina.'

Zaira felt embarrassed. She had been asleep for nearly three hours. She didn't realise how tired she had been, wandering around Milan on foot, spending restless nights in that shabby, dirty, cramped attic room. She deserved a rest after surviving there, she told herself as she got ready to go downstairs.

13. Zaira's awakening...

Guerrino showed Zaira to a dining area in the winter kitchen where the servants were already seated and eating at a great long table. Zaira had never seen such a spread of food and this was just for the servants: firstly antipasto of *prosciutto crudo*, salami, pickles, and lots of hot, fresh bread, then *pastasciutta*, and finally rabbit. The ham and salami had been cured on the estate along with the pickles, *sotto aceti*, or *agrodolci*. Cauliflower, broccoli, carrots, peppers, small onions and beans had been blanched in white wine, vinegar and water; and for the *agrodolci*, also some sugar. The pasta was tagliatelle with *sugo dei porcini* – a fresh mushroom sauce of the best variety, always served without Parmesan cheese. The local red wine was served around the table in round white bowls, and as it was drunk any sediment remained at the bottom of the bowl.

'And Signor killed the rabbits himself,' Guerrino told her proudly.

Zaira was suddenly ravenously hungry and ate as much as

she could; she had never tasted anything so good. She had hardly eaten anything in Milan – bread and cheese mostly, and a little fruit.

The other servants were very curious about her and asked her lots of questions. She decided it was easier to tell the truth, more or less: she had left her village of Torretta looking for work, and had met the Contessa at Piacenza Station. She hammed it up a bit.

'The Contessa was so friendly to me; she said I would be the ideal companion for Livietta. It was fate that we met like that!'

She deliberately left out the word 'servant' from her speech. She wanted them to think she was a cut above the rest of them.

The servants around the table laughed, some sniggering to themselves:

'This girl will soon learn not to be so cocky!' one whispered to her neighbour at the table. Then they forgot about her and continued their usual round of gossip.

'Hey you know old Brutto who runs *la pasticceria* – the pastry shop in Tortello?' someone asked.

'You do know him; his wife is called Fortunata, hee hee.'

'Well Fortunata was less than fortunate when she discovered Brutto had a mistress. You'd never guess how. She saw him packing up some dainty little pastries onto lace doilies. She saw him place them in a gold box and then he tied them up with pink ribbon, his big clumsy fingers having great trouble tying up the delicate ends into a bow. Usually it was Fortunata who did the packing up of pastries so she wondered what he was playing at. Soon after, when he had a spare moment, he left the shop. She was curious and as she couldn't work out whom this order was for, she shut up the shop and followed him through the streets of Tortello. He climbed up and up the winding alleyways and finally stopped at the house of Signora Landi, that widow – you know who I mean.'

'Yeah, that one who doesn't behave like a widow: she stopped wearing black after only one month, and she wears rouge and lipstick! No shame, that one, and she has the cheek to say she was the best dressmaker in Milan before she got married, and her husband wrecked her life.'

'*Che scandolo!*' Margherita muttered, crossing herself.

'Anyway, Fortunata saw Brutto kiss that trollop's hand. Well, she was so angry, she didn't know what to do: whether to beat him with her rolling pin or what. She decided to watch and wait. It turns out that Brutto often visited the widow. He used to stand outside her house and if she lit a candle at the window that was his signal to enter.

'Fortunata had a plan. She made up her own box of little pastries. But instead of pastries she put bits of charcoal into the doilies and when Brutto prepared another box of pastries, she substituted her box without his knowing. Brutto picked up the wrong box and made his way to the widow's. But he soon came back with his tail between his legs. The old widow kicked him out, and Fortunata hasn't had any trouble with him since!'

'And, don't you know, that trollop has found herself another lover already!' said another servant.

Everyone laughed, even Zaira.

Margherita the cook got up from the table and started to make the fresh pasta for Leonardo's dinner. Zaira was fascinated and watched intently. It was one of the few things Zaira had enjoyed doing at home, but her pasta was always doughy and heavy. She wanted to see how Margherita did it.

She watched as Margherita threw a quantity of white flour onto the scrubbed pine pasta table. Into the heap of flour she broke six eggs and added a little salt and finally a few drops of water, a little at a time. Then she started kneading the flour with her fingers, swaying her hips and moving her weight from side to side, the rhythm of the kneading a ritual dance. Zaira had always loved it when the women of the village did this. It was a homage, a prayer almost, to the making of good food.

The secret was to roll the dough out several times, not just once as Zaira lazily used to do, until it was paper-thin. Then the cook filled the pasta with a simple stuffing made from a mixture of breadcrumbs, *Parmigiano* – Parmesan cheese, garlic, egg and a small amount of a tomato and onion sauce, called '*soffritto*'. She carefully placed a spoonful of stuffing on the pasta in neat rows, equal in distance to each other. Next she laid another sheet of pasta carefully over the bottom one so that they fitted together exactly, and pressed the pasta down gently between the rows of stuffing. Then she took a little serrated wheel and cut out the filled pasta in squares so that each square had the stuffing at its centre.

Even though Zaira had eaten a huge meal, she could feel her saliva rising, almost tasting the delicate soft pasta melting between her lips.

'It's wonderful to be alive,' she thought, even though things weren't quite how she had planned.

After the servants had finished eating, they all started getting ready for the dinner of their master and mistress.

'Those two will be sitting there looking glum as usual,' said one.

Zaira wasn't sure what she was supposed to do now. While some of the servants waited on Leonardo and Livietta at table, she half-heartedly cleared away some plates, but Guerrino told her to stop.

'Miss Zaira, please go to bed now. We can discuss what your duties will be tomorrow morning.' The other servants, especially the women, started sniggering at her again – why she didn't know, nor did she care.

The people in Torretta were exactly the same, always

gossiping and whispering. Zaira had always been a good topic for conversation:

'A motherless girl allowed to run wild.'

'Why isn't she betrothed?'

'Why can't Bartolomeo be more disciplined. Why did he let her go to school for so long, at her age. Why...?'

Zaira realised that people gossiped everywhere, not just in Torretta. It was what kept the world moving. But she had never been that interested in talking about other people. Her mind was racing. She would be happy to retire to her bedroom early and think about what had happened to her that day, and maybe to dream about the man of the house.

She ran up the stairs, not having seen or spoken to Livietta or Leonardo since their first meeting. Just as she was climbing to the second floor where her bedroom was, she felt somebody grasp her arm from behind. It was Leonardo. She swung round quickly, angrily, and stamped her foot. Then in spite of herself her body relaxed.

He laughed. 'Don't worry, Zaira. I won't hurt you. Come here.' He tried to gather her into an embrace, and managed to brush her lips very lightly and kiss her long graceful neck as she struggled to escape.

'What is he doing? The insolence of the man – and what about Livietta? They have got through their dinner very quickly.'

All these thoughts rushed through her head as she tried to remain calm, but inside she was seething. Leonardo could see how annoyed she was. He laughed again.

She was one step ahead of him on the wide staircase.

'Signor, please don't laugh. I know that I am a poor country girl, and it is common knowledge that people like you take advantage of girls like me. I was invited into your home by the Contessa, your aunt. I was given the impression that I would be safe here, that I would have a respectable position, and – your wife, your wife, Signor, what about your wife?'

After her little speech, she arched her back and stood up as straight as she could, her chin in the air, still facing him.

Leonardo looked at her in amused puzzlement:

'Well, you have spirit. I'll say that for you!' He coughed.

'*Do* please excuse me, Zaira,' he said in a laconic, lordly manner. 'I was just having a little fun. We've never had a young, beautiful serving-girl here before.'

'I am not a serving-girl,' Zaira was thinking, but she said nothing.

Leonardo continued: 'I promise I will do nothing to offend you, nothing against your will, I assure you.'

With that he held her hand to his lips, looked up into her eyes, pretending to be contrite. Then he raised one eyebrow questioningly and smiled again. He bowed, and went back down the stairs.

Zaira ran to her room. She was in turmoil. Even though she had spoken calmly with the utmost purpose and precision, she was shaking. She might easily have succumbed instead. She wondered what would have happened if she had. It was just a bit of fun for the illustrious Sir, but what about her? What would she have felt? She already knew that she had power over men from the way they had looked at her in Torretta and Lunano. But she had never been kissed, had never felt this sexual attraction until now.

She climbed into the comfy four-poster bed, and started leafing through a book, but for once in her life she couldn't read. She couldn't stop thinking about Leonardo and the contradictory feelings he had aroused in her.

Still wide awake, she started playing with the electric cord hanging down by her bed, but finally she fell into a restless sleep. She woke up in the middle of the night, and heard noises outside.

She could see under the bottom of her door that the electric light was still on in the corridor. Zaira was accustomed to the dead quiet and the utter darkness of the countryside. The light would keep her awake. She twisted herself out of bed, and went to the door. No, she couldn't go out there. maybe Leonardo would be there again. But she finally plucked up the courage and turned off the electric light at the switch she found just outside her door. In the dark she could see the shadows of many men and woman drifting away from her along the long corridor. What was this? They seemed to be wearing strange clothes. The men were wearing short tunics and thick stockings on their legs! The women wore long, full dresses and tall ruffs around their necks. She must be dreaming. She switched the light on again and everything was as it should be, but then, when she switched the light off again very quickly, she could see the silhouettes of the men and women again. She let out a gasp and hurried back into her bedroom. She was going mad. No, she must be dreaming. But she'd better lock her door. Maybe Leonardo would try to come back. But Leonardo hadn't been among those strangely dressed men and women. Who were they? She had never seen anything like them.

She spent the rest of the night tossing and turning, sometimes thinking about Leonardo, sometimes about those strange apparitions. Perhaps she had been dreaming about some characters from a novel she had read.

'No, they were ghosts. That's what they were – ghosts. The house is haunted. I've got ghosts to worry about as well as Leonardo!'

Very early the next morning Zaira rose from bed, exhausted, not at all refreshed and trying not to think about that man Leonardo. She realised he was a worse threat than any silly ghost might be.

'How can I live in the same house as him now?'

No, that was stupid of her. She had to forget what had happened – it obviously hadn't meant anything to him; he was just amusing himself. What did men like that think, that they had the *'droits de seigneur'* to have their way with any girl?

'Well, not with me, he won't.'

She had to concentrate on Livietta and what her duties would be.

She had a quick coffee for breakfast and then Guerrino showed her into Livietta's private sitting room. Livietta had tried to put some of her own things in the room – the crocheted antimacassars she had made herself, which hung over every chair, and the heavy lace curtains at the windows, her own velvet footstool and her sewing box cum table she had brought with her from Castellengo. Yet it was not enough. The room was too vast, too full of empire-style furniture and portraits of long-forgotten Bertini ancestors. For someone as unassuming as Livietta, it was difficult to impose her personality on such a room.

Zaira decided that she and Livietta must be friends. She needed at least one ally at Bertini. And it didn't prove too difficult after all. She discovered that Livietta was also interested in reading novels and that as far as food was concerned 'the simpler the better', a philosophy with which Zaira agreed wholeheartedly.

The estate grew its own fruit and vegetables, reared much livestock and produced some of its own wine and vinegar.

'Maybe it will be quite easy to work out menus after all,' she told Livietta.

'All we have to do is concentrate on what is available on the estate, and make meals from that. It's what we did in Torretta, so we can be even more self-sufficient here.'

They made their own butter, but Leonardo preferred his food to be cooked in olive oil, so all the olive oil was imported from the Contessa's estates in Liguria.

'If Leonardo wants anything more fancy, then he can get it in Milan.' Zaira and Livietta agreed about this.

Zaira had already discovered from the servants' gossip that after only a month of marriage, Leonardo had already started spending more and more time in Milan with his actress acquaintances. She tried not to let it worry her, but she experienced a feeling she had never known before – jealousy.

14. Zaira and Livietta

As Christmas approached, Zaira and Livietta tried to build up a relationship. They were both still shy of each other, but they had common interests and both liked to discuss the current problems of Italy. They also liked talking about their families. Zaira mainly spoke with derision about her brothers, although every so often, when she was completely alone, she had a little cry about her father. She did miss him: his funny old ways, his obvious pride in her. He was never overly affectionate but he had loved her in his own way, even though she knew she had constantly reminded him of his dead wife.

She could see that Livietta was truly homesick and missed her parents. She visited them regularly but they didn't come to Bertini very often. Leonardo had made it very clear that he considered his father-in-law inferior.

Gradually, the more they talked about each other's families, they realised that Rodolfo's father had actually come from Torretta. They both knew about the family feud and the *Ca' Capitano* – they had heard the story umpteen times. They started to laugh uproariously about it all.

'These peasants and their feuds,' Zaira said in an affected, condescending tone. She started to describe some of the more recent feuds occurring in Torretta. They mainly concerned the water source. 'Our families have always rowed about water, and the other villagers are no different,' she said.

'There are three springs feeding water into Torretta,' Zaira explained. 'One spring is used as a common source of water for all the inhabitants and the water comes out at the *fontana*, the focal point of the village. This is where people gossip and generally congregate. Where the women fill their pots with water to take home to heat up on their wood-burning stoves, or where some naughty men and women even start to intrigue,' whispered Zaira, rolling her eyes.

'There is a further spring that drains through the land of both the Crespi and the Ruggieri,' she continued. 'As I said, this is also a subject of dispute between them. In fact, they have to share it, as it dates back to the time when the families were much more closely related and lived on the same land.

'The third spring is further up the village and it comes out right on the boundary between two pieces of land owned by different people. These two, Pietro and Federico, were in constant argument about who owned the spring. Pietro used it as drinking water for his family and for his array of animals: some pigs, four cows and two oxen, I think.

'Federico was incensed by this: "How dare you use my water to give to your filthy animals?" He was further convinced that all their excrement fed back into the water. Finally Federico said he could prove that the spring was on his side of the boundary. He had gone to the town hall at Lunano to get the correct maps, but unfortunately the maps had been lost, and had to be redrawn. In the meantime he forbade Pietro to take the water. Pietro ignored him and that night he started to put up a wooden fence on the other side of the spring. Now this was clearly Federico's land, and when Federico saw it, he quickly pulled it down. He then put it on the other side of the spring, which again was clearly Pietro's side. They continued to argue, every day or so one person pulling down the fence and replacing it on the other side of the spring.'

Zaira said: 'Typical of the people in Torretta! They are always bickering, always arguing about who owns what. They are obsessed with land and property because they have nothing better to think about.'

'Yes, I am constantly amazed at people's selfishness, their pettiness, their mean-spiritedness...' replied Livietta.

'Why can't they just share the water?' asked Zaira rhetorically. 'Why can't they think of the common good for a change? Why is there always this constant feuding?'

'And then there were the factions. Some people sided with Federico, others with Pietro, and then there were those who had their feet in both camps. You couldn't win, whatever you did. People always have something bad to say about their neighbours. Nobody ever says anything good – oh no, that would be too easy.

'Everyone talks about this man and that woman being seen together in the fields. Men having non-existent affairs with their sisters-in-law, mothers sleeping with their sons, daughters sleeping with their fathers, boys having sex with goats, women being raped by the devil – *'il forletto'* or the incubus as it's called – or one-eyed monsters roaming the woods.'

Zaira's tales got more far-fetched by the minute. Livietta laughed incessantly, and so did Zaira. Their sides were splitting, their tummies hurting. Zaira continued between laughs:

'They're all so bored in Torretta, the feuding keeps them going. It's so isolated up there; most of them only leave once a week to go to the market in Lunano. They have nothing to occupy their minds. It doesn't take much to offend them. Only their anger and so-called honour keep them going.'

'Yes,' agreed Livietta, 'how would they spend their time if there was nothing to feud about? There wouldn't be anything else for them to do.' She giggled.

'And what makes me laugh even more is that they are supposed to be Christians, to believe in Jesus, the son of God, to turn the other cheek, to love thy neighbour as thyself, help others less fortunate than yourselves, to be charitable and all that. No, they can't do that. The only thing they ever do is give money to the priest, Don Aldo, who makes the church look ever more ridiculous with even more painted statues and rows of candles. I bet they'll be putting in electric lighting next. This is being Christian; this is how they ease their consciences...'

Zaira stopped her outburst in midstream. Leonardo was standing at the door looking at her. They had been avoiding each other. Zaira blushed and Livietta continued with her sewing. She had been trying to teach Zaira to sew, but her student was so impatient. Livietta smiled to herself, thinking of Zaira, and totally ignored Leonardo.

'Livietta,' he said sternly. 'I am going to Piacenza and won't be back until ten this evening. Can you make sure that some supper is left out for me?' With that he left the room abruptly.

Livietta and Zaira both burst out laughing again. He had sounded so touchy, looking at both of them as if he were envious of their companionship.

Zaira had settled in quite well at the house. Her duties were not particularly onerous. As she had hoped, she was in fact more of a companion to Livietta than a domestic help. They planned the menus together. They shopped in Tortello and occasionally travelled to Piacenza. But Zaira never went to Milan; the memories of her failure there were too painful for her. She wanted to forget the past and preferred to think of her present life at Bertini, with Livietta. The two young women had grown fond of each other, like sisters. At lunchtime they ate together in a small dining room, but in the evenings, when Leonardo was there, Zaira continued to eat in the winter kitchen with the servants. She was happy to do this; she would have hated to eat with him. She just wanted to avoid him.

Zaira tried to stop herself from thinking what might have been. She had to accept her lot in life, as Signorina Maestri, her teacher, had always told her.

15. **Zaira and Leonardo**

It was now January 1900 and Zaira had been at Bertini for well over a month. She and Livietta had spent a lot of time getting ready for the Christmas Eve supper. The Contessa and Livietta's parents had both been invited and unsurprisingly the evening had been quite strained. Livietta had pleaded with Zaira to attend the family dinner, but Zaira declined. She had felt uneasy about dining in the same room as Leonardo. She preferred to stay with the servants. Some were even quite friendly to her now, and chatted away to her in dialect, usually giggling and uttering some cheeky proverb or other, such as:

Puleinta e latt
Ingrassa il culatt.
Polenta and milk
Fatten the buttocks.

New Year's Eve had been a very quiet time for her, but she didn't mind. It was all a fuss about nothing. She was excited about the new century, but as far as she was concerned New Year's Eve was a day like any other day. They had never celebrated in Torretta. Livietta was staying with her parents and Leonardo was off celebrating with some of his male friends in Milan.

Somehow Zaira had managed to keep out of his way – most of the time. Occasionally when she and Livietta lunched together, he joined them. Every so often she caught him staring at her. Yet he hadn't really spoken more than a few sentences to her at all since that first night. When they saw each other they exchanged pleasantries very briefly. Zaira tried to be polite to Leonardo in front of Livietta, but avoided being alone in a room with him. He always had a slightly preoccupied air, and luckily didn't seem to take much notice of her.

He went hunting early in the morning and usually was away from the house all day. He and his aunt had business affairs in Milan, and sometimes he went to Turin and Genoa, the other two main industrial centres. There was servant gossip about him opening a factory to make cars. They had heard him and his aunt talking about it a lot.

There were four car factories around the north of Italy. In the last year four of Leonardo's acquaintances had designed their very own car which had since been driven in the World Drivers' Championships. Giuseppe Merosi, the car's designer, wanted Leonardo to join them and set up a car factory in Piacenza (in fact, later Merosi was to join the Alfa factory). Leonardo was having discussions about this at the moment: he thought Piacenza was a much better place than Castellengo. In any case, Rodolfo would never agree to their taking over his estate for a car factory, and Livietta would be even more ill-disposed towards him than she already was. Leonardo had decided that he would do what he could to placate Livietta; she was a harmless little thing really. He didn't want to annoy her more than was necessary. It was Zaira who puzzled him, 'the little firebrand'. He wished he could get to know her more intimately.

Zaira tried not to think about Leonardo, but at night she dreamt about him – his powerful yet graceful body, his long slender hands touching her. Sometimes those dreams would turn into nightmares. She would be falling through the air about to crash on the ground, and her teeth would crumble inside her mouth, and she would wake up thinking she was toothless. She felt tormented.

She wanted to forget about him but she couldn't.

'Where did he go to in Milan?'

She knew the servants' gossip; that he had many mistresses there. She often saw him setting out in his motor car, controlling it skilfully as he drove off out of Bertini. She would love to have a ride in that car, she thought enviously.

She was good at physical things, which was unusual for a girl like her. Most girls stayed inside the house, but she had always been allowed to roam around the countryside. Her two brothers had taught her to climb the huge rocks, swim in rivers, jump from great heights. She had even managed to ride the priest's bicycle one day when he was inside with her father, and had left it outside their house. She sneaked out of the back of the house while they were busy trying out some newly bottled wine in the kitchen. She tucked in her skirts as best she could, and gingerly climbed on the bicycle, trying to balance on it without sitting on the saddle. She finally managed to sit down on it and started pedalling up the hill until she mastered the art of keeping the handlebars and wheels straight. She had felt so good, so free.

But driving a car, what would that be like, the wind blowing in your hair, being able to go anywhere you wanted? She would love to find out.

'I don't suppose Leonardo would ever teach me to drive.'

One bright morning she went out on to her bedroom balcony that overlooked the stables to feel the winter sun on her face. Leonardo was standing below her with his favourite mare, Lola, a chestnut with a light golden mane. Leonardo was caressing her so gently, so lovingly. Zaira knew he adored his horses. She thought of an old saying:

Cavai e donn seinsa difett
Guardia in dla stall e in lett.
Horses and women without defects
To be inspected closely in the stable and in bed.

He reached up to the mare's ear and spoke to her, stroking her long mane. Zaira imagined him stroking a woman in this way. At that moment Leonardo happened to look up at her balcony as if he knew she was watching him. As he continued to stroke the mare he stared intently at Zaira. It was if he were touching her rather than the horse.

She felt herself flush from tip to toe, and hastily withdrew inside her bedroom. In her mind, she could still see his penetrating stare, and his strong body. What would he look like naked? She had seen her brothers naked when they were boys, but not a man like Leonardo. She forced herself to block these thoughts out. She was being silly, she told herself.

She was happy as she was. She liked her life at Bertini – it was just right. Livietta and she were now such good friends. They both agreed that men complicated life too much. Zaira had guessed that Livietta hated the physical side of her marriage. Sharing a bed with Leonardo offended her idea of feminine 'pudore' – modesty. Zaira was right. For Livietta, sex was a violent and brutal act. She had thought that the first night of her honeymoon at Lake Garda, and she had not changed her mind: she found the physical act of love with Leonardo absolutely disgusting. Although she had not told Zaira this directly, she had intimated it very strongly.

'I really don't understand the point of it all,' she had said once about the 'private life' she led with Leonardo.

The following morning Zaira had some time to herself. Livietta was out visiting her parents at Castellengo and Zaira decided to explore the library. She had been meaning to do this for some time. There were so many books she didn't know where to start. She could see some books in French high up on one of the shelves: Racine, Jean Jacques Rousseau, Voltaire, the names sounded so beautiful. She climbed the stepladder and reached up to get a red leather-bound edition, embossed in gold lettering. It was Emile Zola's *Nana*. She started to read...

Leonardo entered the library. He hadn't gone hunting that day; he felt restless, bored, uneasy. It was a new century; he wanted something new to happen, something that was missing from his life. He saw Zaira across the room at the top of the library steps.

'She is an unusual girl,' he thought, 'beautiful and intelligent. She loves reading, she has opinions of her own' – he had heard her talking many times to Livietta. He felt shut out of their conversations; they excluded him in his own house! He hated the intimacy she shared with his wife.

'Poor Livietta, I ignore her totally. Why did I ever marry her? To please my aunt?'

Not to please himself, that was certain. They had never attained any affection for each other; she was still frightened of him and yielded to him like a scared animal. Sex with her was no pleasure. At first he was intrigued by her reserve; he wanted to break it down. Now he had run out of patience. He had been willing to be take things slowly – he liked the idea of the hunt after all – but she hadn't changed, hadn't accepted him, felt no passion for him. She was only happy when she was with her family, or with Zaira.

Now, Zaira was completely different. He knew she had passion; she was fiery, hot-tempered. She tried to ignore him and he had gone along with that. 'But why shouldn't I have her?' he often asked himself.

Sometimes he could see she was trying to sneak a look at him, with her eyelids slightly closed. He knew he had affected her in some way: she tried hard to contain her feelings for him but failed miserably! She always blushed when she saw him, and stammered when she spoke to him.

He desired her physically, but would the chase of the hunt be satisfying enough? What then?

He had mixed feelings about her. He didn't want to hurt her. As she had said, she was under his protection in this house. Yet when he heard the two women together, the way they laughed, the way they laughed at him – yes, he was convinced they were laughing at him, too absorbed by their female companionship to need him – it aroused him even more...

'Zaira,' he called. She turned round to him, startled, and nearly lost her balance on the steps. Leonardo rushed over to help her, but she righted herself. She had no need of help from him. 'There is no need, Signore, thank you all the same.'

'Zaira,' he whispered.

'Why is he whispering?' Zaira asked herself. 'Doesn't he want the servants to hear?'

She guessed his mood was strange – he looked so intense.

'Zaira,' he said again. 'please talk to me, tell me what you are thinking about, tell me what goes on in that lovely head of yours.' He snatched the book from her: 'Emile Zola, eh? A girl like you reads Zola?'

'Is he making fun of me?' she asked herself. 'Yes, Signor, I enjoy reading in French. I hope I am not causing you any offence?' she said with a slight irritation in her voice.

He scrutinised her up and down, admiring her form up on the ladder. Leonardo had always got his own way with women. But Zaira was different; he could not quite decide how to handle her.

'Call me Leonardo, and no, I am not offended by your reading my books. It gives me pleasure that my library gives you so much pleasure. I certainly do not agree with that old expression, how does it go?

Dio t'in libra d'un visein
E da donna c'sa latein!
God save you from neighbours
And women who know Latin!

Zaira repeated it, correcting him on some words. They both laughed.

Zaira blushed and became self-conscious. She was reluctant to look at him again.

'What has come over him? Is he going to play one of his games again?'

She tried to take the book back, but he grabbed her hand instead. They stared at each other intently. It seemed like hours.

'No, stop,' she said, sighing deeply and trying to wrest her hand away from his.

'But what would happen if I told him not to stop?' she asked herself in turmoil.

Leonardo read her thoughts. 'Do you remember what I said to you the first day you arrived: that I would do nothing against your will. I meant it. I know I hurt your feelings then. I misjudged you. You deserved better.

'If I kiss you now, I will do it because you want me to. I won't force myself on you – no *'droits de seigneur'* here. But please let me kiss you. I see you in my house, so near but yet so far from me. You and Livietta shut me out, don't you? Can't you let me in? I know you think about me.'

He helped her down from the library steps. He put his arms around her and tried to kiss her, and Zaira was not at all sure if he was being sincere. 'He always gets what he wants,' she thought to herself. She hesitated, but she wanted to be kissed, she wanted to kiss him...

And so they kissed and kissed. Leonardo groaned. 'Oh Zaira, you are lovely. I adore you,' he said using the intimate *'tu'* instead of *'voi'*.

Zaira didn't know whether to believe his words. 'I'm just another girl for him; he's just saying this. Or does he mean it?'

He caressed her shoulders, her back. It felt so good. She returned his kisses as if it were the most natural thing in the world. She didn't feel awkward or shy. She wanted to kiss him, to feel his body against hers...

Finally, she moved away. She loved feeling his arms around her, but it was wrong. She was so confused. She didn't know what she wanted.

'No, I can't, he's married to Livietta,' she said to herself reluctantly.

Bartolomeo had instilled in her a sense of duty, a sense of honour. Up till now she had lived by a moral code. Getting involved with a married man was unthinkable, but she had never been tempted before now. She was horrified by the thought of adultery, and here she was kissing a married man and enjoying it. She knew Leonardo and Livietta did not love each other, were not even fond of each other – but no, she couldn't; it was still a mortal sin. She felt his skin on hers, his panting, his passion. She wanted him to continue.

'No, stop,' she finally said. 'Leonardo, please stop, please, please.'

Instinctively she also had used the intimate form *'tu'* rather than the polite *'voi'*. Leonardo and Livietta had never stopped calling each other *'voi'* even when in bed together.

Leonardo stopped reluctantly. He was absorbed in her full wide lips, her soft, smooth skin, her scent, like roses. She was so vibrant, so healthy. Her face was flushed, her breasts were heaving; she was panting as much as he was.

'Is it the first time for her? Such innocence, and *magari* – maybe I could really love her like I never loved anyone else.'

She was just so, oh, so exquisite. He didn't know exactly, it didn't really matter ... 'Zaira, Zaira, Zaira,' he whispered.

'Leonardo, we shouldn't be doing this. What about Livietta?'

'We are loving each other, my sweet, something there is so little of in this house. You know Livietta doesn't love me, and I don't love her. Please love me, Zaira, please.' He was begging her.

Zaira cleared her throat, and in her slightly hoarse voice said very shyly: 'I do love you, Leonardo. There I've said it. I've never, ever said it before to a man, never felt anything like this before, never, ever kissed a man, but yes, I think I love you. I know I can't stop thinking about you.'

Zaira had heard two voices inside her: one told her not to admit this, but the other, the passionate side of her nature, spoke more loudly. There had been no mother to tell her about feminine *'pudore'* – modesty. Zaira did not think it was a question of submitting or not submitting to a man. She had always known that men were allowed a different morality to women, but didn't understand why.

Zaira did not feel so very different from a man: she had no *pudore* – modesty, she wanted to experience these things, to explore the sexual side of her nature.

Leonardo was overjoyed. This girl who had fought against him for so long was finally his for the taking. But he stopped himself. 'What am I thinking?'

What had she said to him before, about taking advantage of her?

'I promise I don't want to take advantage of you.'

Before, he had wanted to teach her a lesson, but now he wanted to make love to her on equal terms, not as a master with a servant.

'Zaira, I promised never to offend you. Tell me what you want to do. I want to be with you. I know this is a difficult situation, but you know how things are with Livietta. My family wanted me to get married, so I did. I never really thought about it. I knew I could continue my life as before, but it wasn't enough. I realise that now.'

'I don't know what to do about this situation, as you call it, Leonardo. Maybe I should leave, and we should forget about each other.'

'No, no, you cannot leave now. Let me come to you tonight. At least we should talk more about this, please, Zaira. Let me come to your bedroom. I know you keep it locked, *tesoro mio*,' he laughed.

'I will knock on your door at midnight. Please say yes.'

She wanted to resist. It was liked being tempted by the devil, and all the things Don Aldo used to warn about. Yet she wanted him to come to her room; she wanted to find out more about this love, if indeed it really was love. She was curious about how her body had reacted when he kissed her – she'd had feelings she had never known about, feelings in her groin, her breasts. She wanted more...

'Yes, come to my room tonight, but not for long. The servants will know, I'm sure.' The servants always knew everything.

'*Maledetti!* – Damn them!'

*

As agreed, Leonardo knocked on her door at midnight. Zaira knew that this knock was her death knell. There was no turning back now. She was scared, but very curious; she had to find out what this love would be like. She didn't entirely trust Leonardo, she couldn't tell what he was really thinking, but she knew that she wanted him. She had tried to fight it, tried to resist temptation, yet the inevitability of it struck her – she had always wanted him, since she first saw him coming down those marble steps, swinging that stupid riding crop...

She unlocked the door and closed it behind him. Leonardo immediately folded her in his arms. She was wearing a long white lace nightgown she and Livietta had bought together. Since arriving at Bertini, Zaira had acquired a whole new wardrobe of clothes; her appearance had changed beyond recognition. Her unruly hair was always tidy, her smart, fashionable dresses always well pressed – she even wore corsets, but now her long wavy hair was loose over her shoulders and flowing down her back. She was wearing white like a bride on her wedding night, thought Leonardo.

*

'Everything has changed now.' Zaira realised as they lay in each other's arms.

'There is no going back.'

She had wanted adventure, and this was an adventure in itself. She had known the moment she saw Leonardo that she wanted him. She could no longer pretend otherwise. Yet now she would have to act as if nothing had happened between them, especially in front of Livietta.

16. Zaira, Leonardo and Livietta

By day Zaira and Livietta spent their time as usual: planning menus, shopping, and discussing daily tasks and future projects with Guerrino and some of the other servants. Sometimes there were evening entertainments for some of Leonardo's small circle of friends. Livietta played the piano for them, while Zaira looked on, trying to behave as normally as possible. She was not particularly musical. The cacophony that was the female choir of Sant'Antonio church and their agonising harmonies had done little to draw out any musical appreciation in her. The women had sounded like wailing cats. Other than that, there had been some quite good accordion music at some of the dances, and there was even an orchestra in Lunano, set up by the first mutual insurance society, but Zaira had not been that interested. She had been too busy telling boys she didn't want to dance with them.

She and Leonardo sometimes exchanged wistful looks but they learnt to be good actors, always behaving properly towards each other. Nobody would ever have guessed, but the servants had already started to gossip before it had happened, so there was no reason for them to stop now.

'There's definitely something going on there,' they muttered amongst themselves. Only Guerrino refused to say anything against Zaira.

Zaira was in a trance most of the time. Sometimes she wondered how she got through the days. She longed for the nights when Leonardo knocked on her door at midnight. She had told him about the first night when she had dreamed of people in strange clothes.

'Well,' he teased her, 'people dressed like that when this house was first built. Perhaps they are ghosts and you are the only one who can see them, *tesoro*. They only appear to special, beautiful young girls like you.'

He tapped her on her nose, and she hit him playfully on the arm. He grabbed at her, pretending to be angry, she grabbed him back; then he started tickling her remorselessly, so she tickled him back and they laughed like children. He had envied the laughter she had shared with Livietta, and now he had it for himself.

He was ticklish on his stomach, behind his ears, and at the back of his neck. When she tickled him he became helpless and went into paroxysms of laughter. So different from his usually cool, sophisticated demeanour, she thought.

They tried to be as quiet as possible but sometimes Zaira was sure the servants could hear their lovemaking or giggling together. She no longer cared though.

'To hell with them,' she thought. She had changed so much, using coarse language, and enjoying sex so much she thought she would die if she never felt Leonardo inside her again.

He always called her 'Rosetta' when they were alone together. He told her that red pubic hair was quite unusual and that he loved nestling his face in it. She liked to encircle his thighs with her hands, knowing it was impossible to reach round them. Yet he could encircle hers quite easily.

Every time Zaira made love, it was always new and different – she never knew how or when her body would respond. Her concept of time changed. Sometimes the days flew past; at other times, such as when they were making love, time slowed right down. Life was exciting now, so different from the deadly, boring routine that had been Torretta.

Leonardo couldn't get enough of her. Obviously he could never marry a girl like Zaira, he told himself, but she was more a wife to him than pale little Livietta. He had tried to make his wife pregnant. Goodness knows, he had tried – that's what it was supposed to be about, this marriage business – but she couldn't even succeed in that. She had suffered two very early miscarriages already, one on her honeymoon and the next barely more than two months later.

Zaira knew something of this. Livietta, although shy of talking about her 'private time', as she called it, with Leonardo, had intimated that more than anything else Leonardo wanted a baby.

'That is what marriage is for, surely, to produce an heir, for God's sake,' he had said more than once to his wife.

According to the servants, Livietta had been confined to bed for a week, just before Zaira's arrival, but Livietta had never mentioned it. It had all been too much for her, two miscarriages so quickly. She subsequently had been very concerned that maybe she couldn't have a baby, and if she couldn't, her life at Bertini would be even more miserable. She could imagine loving a baby in a way that she could never love a man.

Would Leonardo get even angrier and moodier than he was already?

She felt cowed by him, the 'big master' as she called him.

Before Zaira had arrived she had felt so lonely and oppressed by him. Darling Zaira had changed all that. Although she was still unhappy at being married to Leonardo, at least she had Zaira as a confidante. She was a real friend.

'Quiet now, "big master" is coming,' she used to say when she and Zaira were giggling about something together.

Zaira hadn't thought much about Leonardo and Livietta in bed together at the time. She hadn't been interested in hearing the details of their intimacies.

How things had changed. Now that Leonardo was coming to her bed almost every night she couldn't bear to think of him and Livietta together.

'I must really love him then!' she thought. 'I'm jealous of Livietta!'

Zaira never once thought about getting pregnant herself. She was too absorbed by the physical act of love and her body's reaction and Leonardo's reaction to her. She was so wrapped up in herself and her lover that she never really thought about the consequences of getting pregnant. Peasant girls never discussed those kinds of things. She had no idea how to prevent herself from having a baby, although she had heard village gossip about a woman who was tired out after having her eighth child, and the strain it had had on her heart. This woman was so desperate not to have any more children she took a concoction of herbs made up by the *'strega'* – the local 'witch' woman or herbalist, who knew all sorts of remedies and even curses to put on people. These herbs stopped women getting pregnant. Zaira had never taken all this hocus pocus about herbs and witches seriously.

She was totally in love with Leonardo. He was wonderful, unique, her ideal man – she was absolutely besotted with him. She couldn't help saying to herself all the time:

'I love him, I love him, I love him...'

Every time he was sweet to her, told her that she was very special or paid her a compliment about her looks, her body, her intelligence, she loved him even more. She devoured every word he said. She decided he was the only reason for her existence.

Her guilt about his being married was diminishing rapidly. She knew he loved her and had never loved Livietta. She and Livietta were still close friends but Zaira felt the strain, caught in the middle of it all. If Livietta had guessed what was going on between her husband and her maid/companion, she never mentioned it. But Zaira found it more and more difficult to joke about Leonardo with Livietta, so gradually they stopped discussing him and kept to safer topics.

Zaira was desperate to tell someone about her love for him, but there was absolutely no one she could confide in. She had to keep her secret love to herself.

Sometimes they made love nearly the whole night, and both were very sleepy in the mornings. At first Leonardo used to withdraw before ejaculation, but the more their affair continued, the more he wanted to be deep inside her; he didn't want to interrupt their passion. It was even possible he did want to make her pregnant, especially if it wasn't possible with Livietta, but he rejected these thoughts.

Then one morning, even innocent Zaira, who knew nothing about pregnancy, realised that there was something going on in her body. Zaira had been living with the Bertini family for nearly five months, and she hadn't bled for over three months. Her periods had started late, when she was 16, and her cycle was not very regular but even she knew she should have been bleeding by now. In fact, she couldn't remember seeing any blood since the night she lost her virginity. She tried to forget about it, but her breasts were constantly aching and she was feeling sick at various times of the day. Sometimes she wasn't even interested in having sex and just went through the motions of making love with Leonardo. She felt tired and listless, and sometimes she burst out crying for no apparent reason. She knew from the servant's gossip that these were symptoms, and after all she hadn't had a period for ages. Even she in her ignorance knew this was the most important sign. What could she do? She couldn't discuss it with Livietta, and Livietta had recently started staying in her bedroom for most of the morning. Zaira had no other friends with whom to discuss her predicament. She could not get her thoughts in order. She racked her brain for an answer. What could she do? All she knew was that her life would never be the same.

There was no alternative; she would have to leave. How could she have been so stupid? It was Leonardo's fault. He could have stopped her getting pregnant.

'No, it's my fault – why did I fall in love with him?'

She knew him quite well by now. He would try and think up some way of keeping her there. But what about Livietta? What about the servants? Everyone in Tortello would find out, even her brothers far away in Torretta. She would have to think up a plan. She started writing a letter.

The next day she packed up all her things and decided to leave the house that very night.

She was expecting Leonardo, but just lately they didn't have sex every night. Sometimes all she wanted was to lie in his arms. Her sudden tiredness and her emotional outbursts exasperated him. He knew even less about pregnancy than she did. In the past he had left it to his actress friends to worry about contraception; he didn't have to use withdrawal with them. They even knew how to keep venereal disease at bay. And as for Livietta, well she always was delicate, pregnant or not. She had complained of feeling ill recently and he hadn't been to her bedroom for weeks.

Zaira didn't know that when Leonardo first started sleeping

with her, he stopped sleeping with his other women friends in Milan. He just didn't feel the need. He occasionally still went to the theatre or opera to meet some of his male companions, but he never stayed out with any female friends. The men were all puzzled by his behaviour.

'What has happened to Leonardo? He's changed,' they'd say. 'He could never keep his prick inside his trousers. Maybe that wife of his has put her foot down at last.'

Many men of the upper classes were unfaithful, with whomever they wished. There was a story of a Polish count that once went to dine at a house in Milan and left at the end of the evening with the maid who opened the door. Leonardo had been like that once, but not now.

*

Zaira decided it was best to leave without seeing Leonardo. It would break her heart, but she had to do this alone. She wrote a quick note for Livietta, saying:

Darling Livietta, all of a sudden I have decided that I am homesick. I know you will understand what that feels like. I do love it here, and will never forget you but I am going back to Torretta. I didn't want you to try and persuade me to stay, so I am leaving without notice. I am so sorry for everything, and I know you will not be able to forgive me for my behaviour, but I feel I cannot possibly stay any longer. In fact, I am sure you will be better off without me.
Your devoted companion,
Zaira

Zaira realised this was a very unconvincing and lame letter. Just recently she and Livietta hadn't spent much time together, but Zaira hoped she would understand. Leonardo was the problem. She could not bear to think about him.

'Can I really leave him without saying goodbye? My love, my

darling one...' Her heart was broken but she didn't know what else to do. She couldn't stay: the situation was impossible. There was no alternative but to leave.

She knew Leonardo was at a business meeting – he had already mentioned it to her – and wouldn't be returning until ten in the evening. This was his normal routine: he got home late, ate a small supper and climbed up the stairs to her room.

'He can't come to my room!'

She didn't want him to see that her bags were packed. She wanted to leave Bertini as soon as possible before she changed her mind, and she didn't want to run the risk of him coming to her bedroom. She decided to go down to the main door at ten to confront him and to tell him not to disturb her that night as she was feeling ill and tired.

It was nearly ten, and Zaira stood at the door waiting for Leonardo to return. Her thoughts were racing:

'I never thought this would happen to me. All the things I dreamed about, and now this. All those plans I had... Everything ruined...'

She was pacing up and down, growing more and more agitated. At last the big door opened and Leonardo appeared in front of her. He looked tired and vaguely irritated. 'What are you doing down here?' he asked.

All Zaira's rehearsed speeches were forgotten. 'Leonardo, I have a question for you: if things were different, would you marry me?'

Leonardo looked even more irritated. He had spent a tiresome day working on the boring details for setting up the car factory.

'What?' he said. 'What?' he repeated and laughed in his familiar way. 'What are you talking about, marry you? How could I possibly marry you? I'm married already,' he said bitterly, 'and even if I wasn't, how could I marry a silly peasant girl like you?'

His words struck Zaira like a slap across her face. That day when she saw him for the first time she had felt physically struck by her emotions, paralysed almost by the effect he had had on her. She remembered that she had fallen into a trance-like state after that first meeting. Now she had been struck again but back to reality this time. She held her fists out, as if to hit him, but instead she shook her head and laughed bitterly:

'I've been such a fool!'

She turned round and ran up the stairs, desperately trying not to cry – not in front of him at least.

'How utterly stupid of me. How could I think I could love a man like him, so cruel, so ruthless, so heartless. He treats Livietta so badly, like she doesn't exist. Why should I have expected him to treat me any better? A silly peasant girl indeed! I am just as good as he is – him and his ridiculous house with the two towers. He doesn't know about the Crespi Tower. My family was important once,' she thought angrily, trying to convince herself this was true. She was never sure whether she believed the old Crespi stories about their former prosperity and wealth. She was getting angrier and angrier, stamping her foot.

With that, she flung off the ring he had presented to her. She wore it on a black velvet ribbon tied round her neck and hidden in her bosom. He had given it to her secretly on the night of Epiphany in her bedroom. It was a 'poison' ring.

'*Porta mi anell* – wear my ring,' he had said to her as a joke.

Zaira had corrected his pronunciation. 'The accent is on the third syllable: *porta mi anell*.' They kissed as he tied the ring on a ribbon round her neck.

'You can put a lock of my hair inside it maybe, or, if you prefer, some perfume,' he said nuzzling her neck, 'to make you smell nice.'

'Of course,' she retorted, 'your "bella donna" will wear your poison ring for you. But how about putting some belladonna inside it instead? It's a poison ring after all.'

She had never got round to putting anything inside it, but she had been touched when he gave it to her. It was a family heirloom – possibly used to poison one of Leonardo's ancestors.

'I believe one of my ancestors' wives tried to poison her husband who was much older than her. The story goes she put some belladonna into this chamber' – he showed Zaira how to unhinge the topaz stone set in a gold case – 'and then, when he wasn't looking, poured some into a glass of milk she gave him. One of the servants, possibly suspicious of this wicked woman, saw what she had done and knocked the glass over, and he never drank it. Since that near fatality was avoided, the ring has been thought to be lucky.'

'Oh, I see, lucky is it? Well, maybe I really should keep some poison in it, just in case you misbehave,' Zaira said wagging her finger at her lover, 'or shall I cut off some of your hair?' she asked mischievously, laughing her throaty laugh. They had joked about so many things together. How long ago that all seemed now.

She quickly lifted up her luggage, dragged on her cloak and bonnet, and ran down the stairs and out of the house. She didn't care whether Leonardo saw her or not. In fact he didn't. He had gone to the dining room to have some supper. He was starving and couldn't bear the idea of confronting yet another emotional woman at the moment. Mimi, one of his former lovers, had been playing up, causing a scene and trying to get him to sleep with her again. He had thought about it just for old times' sake, but *'Porca miseria!'* he was tired of all that now. In fact, the idea was rather distasteful to him. Those other women: they were so false and insincere in comparison to Zaira, and even she could be tiresome. She had changed recently, he thought to himself. 'Women!' he sighed.

He went off to his study and started reading a page from a book by an obscure philosopher:

'Perhaps the daily experience of life is uninteresting. In the search to deny our fears and frailty, we continue to immerse ourselves in new interests or look for new things to do ....'

Leonardo thought life could be distasteful. Sometimes he just wanted to be left alone by everyone.

17. Zaira in Piacenza

Zaira's plan was to go to Piacenza, to her cousin who worked in the button factory. She had already written her a letter, not saying much except that she would be arriving in Piacenza in a couple of days.

Zaira had spoken to Guerrino about her intentions, and the old servant informed her that she could get a lift to Piacenza at seven o'clock in the morning from the carter. Until then Zaira was going to hide in one of the empty stables. When Zaira left the house that night she was still furious and agitated, pacing around the stable, unable to rest. It was very cold and she didn't think she would get any sleep, but she tried lying down and curling herself up, and soon her eyes closed. She awoke at dawn, with the cocks crowing and all the birds chattering away. She went outside to meet the carter. She knew him by sight and when she greeted him and told him she wanted a lift, he nodded lazily and off they went.

The journey was tedious, uncomfortable, and very bumpy. Zaira felt every stone, every hole in the unmade-up road. She was thrown from side to side and had to hold on tight to her hat. Even her internal organs were jumping around. Her thoughts were in turmoil. Maybe the baby would be harmed.

'It would be for the better if it died right now,' she thought. 'I don't want this baby, certainly not like this. I am all alone in the world.' She wanted to cry out loud but she pursed her lips to control herself.

'How the devil did I end up like this, in this terrible situation? Maybe I should just die now, fling myself off this cart into the road, and kill myself and my baby. No one would care. I have nobody, nothing to live for. Or maybe I should wait until I get to Piacenza. I could go down to the River Po, fill my pockets with heavy stones and drown myself,' she tormented herself.

But she knew she couldn't do it. It wasn't just because of the baby, but because she wanted to live, she wanted to survive. And maybe there was something else as well: she just didn't have the courage to end it all.

'I must be strong now. I must end all this stupidity. I should have left Bertini ages ago. How did I think I could live in a house and share a man with his wife, become his lover?' she agonised with herself.

'Livietta was so kind to me. I knew it was wrong to sleep with him, but I continued all the same. I thought it was because I loved him so much. I did love him. I loved him mind, soul and body, but he has been so cruel to me. And I am so weak, so wicked. I deserve my fate. And now I have to pull myself together.'

She tried to clear her mind but her agonised thoughts continued:

'Why did I fall in love with Leonardo, the first real man I saw? Those silly boys in Torretta don't count. I didn't even know what love was before I saw him. I didn't need a man. I wanted to feel independent, have my own life. But after Milan I was so despondent. My dreams were shattered, I was disillusioned, my confidence was gone. And then I saw Leonardo and everything changed. Just that first image of him changed my life. Why do women need to love like this? I didn't want to love him. He was so arrogant, conceited, so sure of his power over me and I responded, in spite of myself. Are we women really that dependent on men? Will this ever change? Is it in our natures to love like this? And the more they disappoint us, the more we seem to love them. We try to understand their imperfections, we learn to be patient and trusting, like puppy dogs, and when they make us happy, we love them even more because we know what it is to be sad. But it's they who make us sad.'

She couldn't quite explain to herself her feelings for Leonardo. She couldn't understand what exactly had happened, but it was definitely a 'falling' in love.

'I did fall; I felt it so strongly it was physical. Just one look at his handsome face, his strong body, his hair – his maleness *and that mole on his neck.*'

She couldn't bear to think of all her favourite parts of him.

'I fell like a worshipper at his feet. I would have died for him. I still would. I can't just stop loving him, even though I hate him. I hate him. I hate him.'

Zaira remembered Leonardo once saying that love and hate were very close, in his joking, sardonic way.

Zaira continued to torture herself.

'His words have hurt me so terribly but I still love him. I still care about him. But I will never forgive him. I have to forget about him now.'

She tried to tell herself it was more about her proud nature.

'It's my pride that is wounded more than anything else, that's what it is. How dare he hurt me this much. Oh I wish I were dead. What will I do now?'

She tried to get her thoughts in order.

'I have got to try and get on with my life, baby or no baby. Try and get work. My cousin Rosa will help me.'

Zaira arrived in Piacenza around eight in the morning. It seemed a strange place to her untutored eye. The streets were wide and empty. It had been a Roman town – originally called *Piacentinium*. As she passed by the Piazza Cavalli with the two majestic bronze statues of the Duke Farnese and his son on horseback, she could just about see the *Duomo* in another square straight ahead of her. The place had been thought 'pleasing' or 'pleasant', from the word *'piacere'*, and as she slowly walked to her cousin's hotel, clutching Guerrino's directions in her hand, she was thinking that she felt exactly the opposite, very unpleasant. This time she really would have to endure the soul-destroying work at the button factory. She needed to earn her living somehow. She had some money saved from her wages from Bertini but not enough for her to have the baby: to pay for a midwife or, moreover, a doctor...

She soon spotted the small hotel where her cousin was living. It was shabby with paint peeling off the walls. Zaira struggled to get her luggage into the cage-like lift, remembering to close the iron gates behind her. After her time in Milan Zaira was now quite familiar with lifts. It slowly juddered upwards, taking an age to reach the fourth floor where her cousin's room was situated.

Rosa greeted her warmly, kissing her on both cheeks, twice. She had managed to change her shift at the factory that day.

'How are you, dearest cousin Zaira?' Rosa said in dialect. 'I wasn't sure you were really coming. I remember once before you said you were coming and you never turned up. That must have been over five months ago.'

Zaira burst into tears. 'Oh how I wish I had come then, and this would never have happened,' she said, looking down at her stomach.

Rosa had seen enough of the world to guess what Zaira was saying – that she was pregnant.

'Come on, *cara*, you look tired. You have to rest for a few days. You can stay here with me in my room.' Rosa lived quite close to the button factory. She had thought her factory work would be a temporary move, so she had never found herself somewhere permanent to live. The cheap, sparsely furnished room was dank and dreary. It reminded Zaira of that awful room she had herself had in Milan.

Rosa was lonely, and actually rather pleased that her cousin had turned up. After Rosa returned from work that evening, they could sit down and discuss what would be best for Zaira. They would talk things through, most importantly about Zaira working at the button factory. In fact, Rosa promised to make enquiries that very day. Zaira spent the day rearranging her luggage and reading a book on human biology she had borrowed from the Bertini library.

'I should have read this months ago!' she thought to herself.

That night Rosa came home from the factory looking exhausted. Zaira, without thinking of herself or her condition, ran down to the bar next to the hotel to get her cousin a cup of weak tea, with a slice of lemon in it. Rosa drank it appreciatively. She described what the factory was like. There were rows and rows of women sitting at long tables, each operating a machine consisting of a driver-belt which stamped out the buttons from tin, bone or whatever, while the male bosses sauntered around, monitoring their work and making sure they produced their quota. The work was hard and the hours were long and the women were paid much less than the men. They had all come from the farms, driven into the regime of supervised and controlled wage labour.

'It's so unfair,' said Rosa, 'and some female workers have even started talking about setting up a women's union! Zaira, there is work at the factory if you want it, but take your time, rest here for a few days, and if you want, you can start next Monday. We can have a day out on Sunday, just the two of us.'

The next evening, Zaira explained to Rosa what had happened to her since she left Milan. Rosa tried to console her.

'Oh Zaira, you're not the only girl this has ever happened to. Remember Filomena from Torretta, or that little Mariuccia from Vernazza? Poor thing ended up in the institution.'

'Disgraces' such as these happened in every family. Zaira remembered her father telling her about her first cousin on her mother's side. Maria's sister had married someone from Busseto and they had a daughter, who was sent to Giuseppe Verdi's house, the Villa Agata, as a servant. Maria's sister had airs and graces but because it was Verdi, the great composer, she didn't mind the fact that her beloved daughter was only a servant there. However the girl got pregnant, claiming Verdi was the father, and she was packed off to France and never heard of again.

'Well, I thought I was different. I had my life all mapped out. I was going to Milan, Geneva or Paris. And then what happens? I become a servant/companion to a sweet, defenceless little woman, and what do I do? Me, so generous, so charitable, I have an affair with her damned husband, and what's more I'm carrying his child, and she, poor thing, she's suffered many miscarriages.

'I've never thought much about God, about sinning, but now I'm damned for eternity. Why did I give up my virginity so easily? Why, oh why was I so stupid? Why did I fall into the same old trap like any other pathetic girl?

'I even thought he might marry me eventually. They could have got an annulment – Livietta would have happily gone back to her parents. Yes, secretly I had it all worked out. I convinced myself Leonardo really loved me and would do anything to keep me.'

Rosa didn't quite understand what Zaira meant. She was

saying so many things, so fast. Rosa couldn't keep up. Zaira had always been clever, and now she looked like a real lady as well. Her hair was tied up in a neat chignon, and her clothes were truly glamorous. She was wearing a straight, dark brown lambswool skirt, and a cream high-necked lace blouse, with a row of shiny pearl buttons down the front. On her silk shawl, which was a lovely sage green and embroidered with white and red roses, she wore a beautiful cameo brooch.

And she spoke like a real lady as well; she was ranting and raving in perfect Italian!

Rosa had had only had two years of schooling and spoke only dialect. Zaira spoke Italian too fast, too fluently.

'Look, Zaira, the first thing is to decide what we are going to do about the baby. You know there is an orphanage here. You can have the baby quietly; not many people need to know. When you do start work, you can wear loose overalls, and nobody will guess as long as you keep yourself to yourself. You know they mustn't know you're pregnant, or they won't employ you. I can tell the girls you've just arrived from the country, and *guarda* – look, it will be better if you don't speak Italian. You will have to remember to speak in dialect like the rest of us.'

Zaira looked very glum.

'*Cara*, don't worry, quite a few factory girls I know have had babies. There is a midwife that you can hire. She will even come here to the hotel. Then you can give the baby up to the nuns at the orphanage. Some nuns are quite good these days. Girls who have had babies can even go to school and learn how to read and write, and then they are found jobs and everything, or you can go back to the factory. You can make up some story; say you need a few days off work.'

Zaira hadn't thought about that. What was she going to do

about the baby? 'Would I really give it away? Oh, dear, what shall I do?'

She wouldn't torment herself any longer. She would not even think about it.

She couldn't imagine herself with a baby. She knew nothing about them. Maybe Rosa was right – the best thing would be to leave the baby with the nuns. She, however, certainly had no need for any nun to teach her to read and write.

Maybe this would be the beginning for her, not the end. She could leave for Switzerland. She could honestly say she had work experience now. Yes, once she gave the baby up, she could start all over again.

It was Thursday, still early morning. Rosa was on the late shift but she and Zaira were both wide awake and already out of the bed they were sharing. Zaira was finally feeling calmer; she no longer felt as if she was a fictional melodramatic heroine. She could not possibly behave like one of the tragic characters in the books she used to read.

There was a knock at the door. Rosa opened it and Leonardo was outside.

Before Zaira knew what was happening, Leonardo rushed over to her, and flung his arms around her. 'Oh Zaira, my Zaira, why did you leave like that? Why? I have been going out of my mind ... and Livietta too.'

Zaira had made herself quite stiff in Leonardo's arms, but he didn't seem to notice. He continued to repeat her name, murmuring it into her hair, as if she was a long-lost dead relative resurrected from the grave. It was barely three days since she'd left Bertini.

'How in the world did he discover my whereabouts?' she wondered.

'It must have been Guerrino!'

He was the only person she had confided in. She hadn't told him about the baby, only that she had decided to leave and was going to stay with her cousin in Piacenza, and that was why she had wanted a lift there. And then maybe the carter had remembered that Zaira had mentioned her cousin's name and address when he dropped her off near the city centre. Oh, it was so easy. Why hadn't she been more cunning, more secretive?

Rosa was muttering: *'Santa Maria Vergine!'* She didn't know was happening.

Zaira saw Rosa looking bewildered. She released herself from Leonardo and hesitantly introduced him to her cousin. Leonardo was the epitome of charm and kissed Rosa's hand.

Zaira started laughing at him. 'Always such good manners, even in a place like this!' Then he laughed too. They appeared to be having a reconciliation. Indeed, Zaira was ecstatically happy to see him. She had missed him, even if it had only been a few days. He hugged her again and again, then Zaira pulled away from him.

'What am I thinking of?' She wanted him to leave. Her mood changed very suddenly. She tensed her body and said in a very serious voice:

'Leonardo, why have you come here? It is all over between us. I was so stupid to think I loved you and that you loved me.'

'But I *do*,' protested Leonardo. 'How can you say I don't?'

'You said I was a silly little peasant girl. Rosa, tell him about my family, the Crespi Tower...'

'Dio mio,' Leonardo interrupted. 'I was tired and irritable that night. I didn't know you were going to run away, so dramatically ...' – he waved his arms – 'so furtively! When I found your room empty, and this on the bed' – he held out the poison ring on its velvet ribbon – 'I knew you had left in secret.' He made a tiptoeing gesture, then laughed ironically. 'Except that half of Tortello most probably knew where you were by the afternoon,

with everyone gossiping about Zaira up at the Bertini house. Why, it even occurred to me that you must be pregnant to do such a thing.' Leonardo laughed again.

'I am *pregnant*,' screamed Zaira, tearing at her hair. 'That's why I ran away. How could I possibly stay? Isn't it true that unmarried mothers can be locked up in institutions? I knew it would be useless to expect any help from you. You laughed in my face when I mentioned marriage.'

Leonardo was stunned into silence. He didn't say anything for a few minutes, his thoughts all over the place.

'Of course I will help you. Please, *tesoro*, do not worry. I will always look after you. I *do* love you – you don't know how much.'

Rosa was still standing in the corner, mesmerised by these two people. Her cousin Zaira with a *Conte*, arguing like equals. Then she realised she was intruding. They had forgotten she was there, but she mumbled something about going to the market and left them alone. She was going to the factory later that morning for the second shift.

'Zaira, listen to me. I have a friend, an old professor of mine, in Piacenza. He has lovely apartments right in the heart of the city. He will do anything for me. You can stay there with him. You cannot possibly stay in a place like this.' He turned and looked around the hotel room, wrinkling up his nose at the not-too-salubrious surroundings.

'You can have the baby and then return to Tortello after a few months or so, saying' – he spoke in a great rush of words – 'I don't know, you went to Piacenza to get secretly married, it was love at first sight. Or it was someone you knew a long time ago – I know, a soldier whom you didn't see very often – but he died, very suddenly, in firing practice or whatever.' He stopped for breath and spoke more slowly. 'Look, I promise to support you and your child.'

'Our child,' she reminded him.

'Yes, of course, and I will come and visit you as often as I can.'

Zaira was unhappy with this solution and told him of her alternative plan.

'I can give the baby up to the nuns at the orphanage here. Then I would be free to travel abroad, to go where I want.'

'No, Zaira, you cannot do this,' said Leonardo coldly. 'You said *our* child, remember. No child of mine, legitimate or illegitimate, will ever be abandoned by me. I am Leonardo Bertini, you must do what I say. I could ruin you, you silly girl; you could end up in the gutter. You will be branded a prostitute or, as you said, possibly confined to the insane asylum. I would have complete control of the child. You would have nothing, nothing I tell you. Besides, your place is with me. I love you, I need you. I realise that now.

'I know I have had many affairs but all that stopped when you and I first slept together. I want you with me, now and at all times, for ever. Zaira, can't you see that? I can't marry you, but we are indeed like husband and wife nevertheless – we cannot be separated.' He almost spat the words out. He was being ruthlessly honest with her and himself. He realised he wanted her more than ever and he wanted her to have his baby. Perhaps this is what he had planned all along.

He had been brought up by his parents to hide his feelings, to keep control, never to cry, never to fear, *'nihil time'*, as written on the family crest. He had tried to keep a stiff upper lip, as the English would say. Then Zaira had walked into his life, full of fire, full of passion. She didn't care about the *'bella figura'* – the outward image Italians were concerned with. She had changed him; he didn't want to hide his true feelings any longer. It really didn't matter about her background.

'I didn't mean that about you being a silly peasant girl. You are *my* Zaira, that's what's important to me.'

'Oh, I don't know what to do or what to think,' she said desperately.

All Zaira's dreams of freedom and adventure were fading fast. She was pregnant, worse off than most of the girls she had left behind in Torretta. She had never thought that it would happen to her, she who was so clever, so immune to the charms of men.

She felt trapped. She knew Leonardo could be cruel and unfeeling. He could ruin her if he wanted. As he said, he was 'a Bertini' and she was a 'silly little peasant girl'. How often she had heard those words in her head over the past days. Yet there was nothing else to be done. What else could she do? So she agreed, with resignation.

'Yes, all right, let us do it your way. You men have all the power, don't you? I am a woman, I am nothing, I have no choice.'

She had sexual power over her lover, but he as a man still had legal power over her, she thought to herself. So-called society consisted of men who had an inherent dominance over women.

She knew people would still talk – they always did – but she hoped that with Leonardo's protection she would be able to carry this off.

He tried a more soothing tone: 'Zaira, darling, it's not true. You are everything to me. I know I don't always show it, but you make me feel alive. You've changed me, you make me question myself, you make me question everything. I will never hurt you, never let others hurt you.' He grasped her to him. 'You know this is for the best, and then we can be together, always.'

Zaira didn't know what to think. She would never be sure if he was telling her the truth or not. She was exhausted. This pregnancy had changed her – her will to fight him was waning. She had lost control and he had taken charge.

She left Rosa a note of farewell and thanks. Zaira felt guilty about poor lonely Rosa, who had quite liked the idea of having

Zaira to stay with her. Yet Rosa had been expecting something like this: her cousin constantly changed her mind, was always full of surprises. When she returned to the room and found her cousin gone, she wept quietly to herself.

'Who would have thought it, Zaira and that gentleman? I still can't believe it – but I will miss her so much!'

[*Not long after, Rosa, perhaps emboldened by her cousin, set her cap at one of the foremen at the factory. She flirted mercilessly with him. It worked. They married, moved to Cremona and had seven children. She and Zaira never saw each other ever again.*]

18. The Professor

Leonardo accompanied Zaira to his old friend, a retired professor called Giorgio Zerbini who lived in the heart of the city centre, in the street known as Corso Vittorio Emanuele II. It was long and straight, virtually empty of traffic except for the odd horse and cart, and a few covered coupés or landaus, soon to be replaced by electric trams. The grand three-storey buildings had floor-length windows and shutters and ornate stone balconies. The shops surrounding the *palazzo* where the professor lived had heavy striped awnings, some with curtains of the same material covering their windows so it was impossible to see what goods were on offer. The *palazzo* entrance had elaborately decorated double doors and worked wrought iron in the arched windows over the doorway. Through the doors was a courtyard filled with trees, shrubs and a square patch of grass. Across the courtyard was an aviary and an archway and then another door leading to the apartments. The professor's apartment was on the first floor, so they ascended the first flight of the wide marble stairway to reach it, rather than taking the rather claustrophobic lift.

'I don't think we'll both fit in there,' said Leonardo, 'and it's only on the next floor.' He carried her luggage up the flight of stairs.

Zaira was relieved: she hated lifts – they reminded her of her failure.

The professor opened the door for them. He was a distinguished-looking bachelor with immaculately groomed, brushed-back, long wavy silver hair and dazzling white, even teeth.

He was a well-known expert on current affairs in Italy. Leonardo had studied literature and politics at the Catholic University in Milan and the professor had taught him for a couple of years. After his parents died, Leonardo had never finished his degree, much to his professor's regret. Leonardo apologised for their unannounced visit and briefly explained Zaira's predicament and that she needed a place to stay for a few months. The professor did not seem at all disconcerted, and in fact he was delighted with his lovely guest:

'You can stay as long as you want! I would be very happy to have you here as my guest. As you can see, I'm an old bachelor living alone in a huge apartment. There is plenty of room for two people.' He had a manservant who came in every day to cook and do a little cleaning, but the professor enjoyed his own company.

He had always had a soft spot for the charming Leonardo. Leonardo knew this and had exploited the old man's affection in the past when the professor had managed to get him out of a few tight spots at the university. And Leonardo trusted him implicitly: he guessed that he would be very discreet. The professor knew that his former student, the silly boy, had lots of women, but he was completely uninterested in the lurid details about why Zaira, who was obviously one of them, was here.

'Don't worry, dear, I won't ask you any embarrassing questions.'

Zaira's mood completely changed when she met Giorgio Zerbini. She could not help thinking that it would be wonderful to live with a real professor. She would be quite happy to stay there and read books or talk about politics to her heart's content. She felt relaxed and happy in his company. And she did need somewhere safe to stay. It was so much more appealing than poor Rosa's shabby little room.

Leonardo soon saw that the two had hit it off, so he made his farewells.

'Dear Professor, I can't thank you enough. I am sure Zaira will be very happy here.'

He took Zaira to one side, held her chin up and promised he would return as soon as he could. Zaira sighed, and refused to kiss him as he left. He laughed and then bowed to them both.

The professor had never had a relationship with a woman, albeit with one or two men he had to confess. But he had decided a long time ago that the whole business was too distasteful for a fastidious man such as himself. However he had considerable charm, and knew exactly how to treat a woman. Poor Zaira looked embarrassed after Leonardo's quick departure, so he insisted on showing her around the apartment. He fussed over her and made sure she had enough bed linen and towels, and anything else she might need.

He could see that Zaira was an unusual girl, born before her time possibly, and they got along famously. He liked having someone to look after – it was a rare treat for him. He wanted her to be as comfortable and cosseted as possible.

During the months she was there, she ate all the healthiest foods, including lots of fresh fruit and vegetables, and she drank litres of milk. And to cheer her up when he thought she looked a little down, he spoilt her with little delicacies he either ordered by post or sought out in the shops in Piacenza: *amaretti* from

Saronno, *torroncini* – nougat from Cremona, Swiss chocolate, Austrian or Polish biscuits and *marrons glacés* from France.

*

They spent many evenings discussing the political unrest in Italy. The professor spoke to Zaira in his melodic voice, never condescendingly but slowly and precisely:

'The year 1900 has been a watershed in the development of both the Italian economy and the liberal state. But Italy is still divided into the "haves" and "have nots".'

They talked about the tragic occurrence of pellagra in the Po Valley. The disease had been caused by the peasants' starchy diet (rice, bread, pasta, polenta and beans), yet luckily people in Torretta had not been affected. This in turn had led to political uprisings in Cremona and Parma. Big farms with employed labourers were prospering, while small landowning peasants were not. Rice and cheap cereal were imported through the railway routes, and the price of wheat had fallen.

Zaira had heard from her cousin Rosa that her brothers were struggling to manage. They needed more money, and were thinking about supplementing their incomes by seeking work in Milan or Piacenza. She mentioned them to the professor. 'My brothers have a farm to run, but they may have to go and work in the munitions factory here in Piacenza.' She was hoping it wouldn't come to that though.

'It is important that rural workers keep a home and smallholding in the country as a guarantee against hard times and unemployment,' he replied. 'Land means a cheap house, vegetables, chickens, rabbits, firewood and so on, which make them better off than urban workers. Men enter the factory because they don't own enough land. It is important for your brothers to maintain the land as a valuable asset, so they won't be totally dependent on jobs in industry.'

Zaira agreed. 'Although life in Torretta is poor, it is nothing to the squalor and poverty I saw in Milan.'

The professor stated that the peasant was ceasing to be apathetic and aspired to change because of the political transformation in Italy. 'The Po Valley peasants have been the first to organise, many of them migrants from the mountains. Workers have changed mutual benefit societies into trade unions and have established direct contact with industrial workers in Milan.'

Zaira told the professor about the Lunano orchestra, founded in 1880 by men from the local mutual benefit society. The professor, much to Zaira's surprise, had heard of Lunano. Apparently some religious non-conformists from Tortello had settled there. Around this time in its turbulent history the Visconti ruled Tortello, and there had been a war with the Scotti who had tried to take it over, so more people moved to Lunano to escape the bloodshed. In fact, the Visconti had owned many lands in the surrounding area, including large parts of Torretta, and even land eventually bought by Zaira's ancestors.

'The mass emigration from Italy was one of the factors leading to the idea of colonies. As well as trying to compete on the world stage, Italy needs more people to work in the new industries,' continued the professor. 'That was why Italy wanted to get control of Abyssinia, to build up the workforce.'

Zaira thought that this was ludicrous:

'Italy should try and build up a stable economy first,' ventured Zaira.

They discussed the colonial ambitions that had led to the terrible defeat at Adua in 1896 with over 5000 lives lost and the terrible financial burden this had caused, 'The human and financial losses were unforgivable,' said the professor. 'It is almost as if Italy has an inferiority complex. It's folly to compete with the other powers in terms of colonies after what happened at Adua. Rather, we should be trying to build on what we have here in our own country.'

They discussed the 1898 riots in Parma when the telegraph wires were cut and the new electric lights were smashed. The workforce was no longer apathetic.

Zaira told the professor she was fascinated by the new inventions. 'I got so excited when I could telephone my aunt in Torino from Bertini, and the electric lighting we have now is so much more convenient than lighting candles or gas lamps!'

One day she was looking at an engraving in the corridor of his flat and the professor remarked: 'Oh, that's the Liver of Piacenza! It's an Etruscan bronze found in 1877 near Gossolengo. It's a bronze replica of a sheep's liver inscribed with the names of Etruscan deities. The names of the gods imitate the organisation of the sky according to the Etruscans. It is believed that it served as a tool for priests when they practised divination and analysed the organs of sacrificial victims. They say this is an ancient star-finder and calendar, my dear, and certainly an important part of Etruscan religious rituals. It's been dated to the 2nd to 3rd centuries BC. One day you must go and see the original in the Palazzo Farnese, here in Piacenza.'

*

And so, for some time, life continued for Zaira in this way. Some days the hours sped by, especially if Leonardo visited, but on others they dragged, as if time had slowed right down, and all Zaira wanted to do was go to bed. She was getting very big now, and the professor had insisted she see a doctor. When the doctor questioned her about dates, he thought the pregnancy had progressed further then she had realised, but he pronounced her very healthy and strong. Everything was proceeding normally.

Zaira looked forward to Leonardo's visits. He came every week or so, when he too joined in their political discussions. He was proud of Zaira: she could hold her own in an argument. He was also delighted that she shared his fascination with the new inventions.

He knew she loved his motor car. In fact, he had taken her for a drive in it once or twice around the roads near Bertini, when Livietta was out visiting her parents. Zaira loved the speed and always urged him to go faster, faster – unlike Livietta, who after that first time in his car refused to get in it ever again.

Leonardo and the professor discussed poetry and art. Leonardo was a great admirer of Gabriele D'Annunzio, the poet and novelist, whom he had met in Milan together with the magnificent actress Elena Duse, who had inspired *Il Sogno d'un Mattino di Primavera*. D'Annunzio's sensual, decadent writings appealed to Leonardo, and he too had loved speed and cars. Leonardo had especially enjoyed *Il Piacere*, the novel about the enjoyment of the senses. Roses, for instance – the sight of them, the touch of them, the smell, the taste …

'*Un gran fascio di rose rosee, bianche, gialle, vermiglie, brune. Alcune larghe e chiare… freschissime e tutte imperlate, avevano no so che di vitreo tra foglia e foglia, altre avevano petali densi e una dovizia di colore … una strana voglia di morderle e di'ingoiarle, altre erano di carne, veramente di carne, voluttuosode come le più voluttuose form d'un corpo di donna, con qualche sottile venatura.*'

Zaira and the professor preferred to discuss the new female novelists. The professor introduced her to *La Donna* by Sibilla Aleramo. Would she leave her child as the heroine in the autobiographical novel had left her children? Zaira did not know. She did not know what she would think when her child was born.

*

One night Leonardo turned up unexpectedly, very late.

'Zaira, you are coming back to Bertini with me, now.'

He gave her no explanation but tried to hurry her out of

the professor's apartments, not giving her much time to pack her things.

Zaira tried to thank the professor for all his help as she was being ushered out by Leonardo.

'Giorgio, I – I can't thank you enough for what you've done for me.'

The professor, who was bewildered by Leonardo's somewhat rude behaviour, managed to say a fond farewell to Zaira.

'Goodbye Zaira, my dear, good luck to you. Please write to me when you can and tell me your news.' And he quickly kissed her hand.

19. **Births**

Leonardo was driving his car like a lunatic, swerving around corners, and jamming on the brakes. He couldn't get the under-powered engine to go as fast as he would like. On the journey, he quickly told Zaira that Livietta was in labour, the doctor had said both she and her child were in danger and Livietta was asking for Zaira.

Zaira was completely shocked by this news.

'What! In labour you say, why didn't you tell me she was pregnant before?'

'I was so surprised, so stunned by your own news – your own pregnancy, I just didn't know how to tell you. I most probably wouldn't have told you in any case. I thought she would miscarry like she did before, and yet the longer her pregnancy continued, the more I didn't trust myself to mention it to anyone, let alone you. You had your own worries, so please forgive me, *tesoro*, if you think that I have kept you in the dark all this time.'

Zaira didn't know what to think.

'What about Livietta's mother, why isn't she with her at a time like this? I don't understand, why is she calling for me?'

Leonardo explained that although it had been arranged for

Rina to stay with her daughter during her confinement, two weeks ago his mother-in-law had been taken ill with pleurisy, and had been forced to stay at home.

They arrived at Bertini and immediately they both rushed up to Livietta's bedroom. Zaira had reverted to that trance-like state she experienced when she first arrived there. She felt hurt and betrayed by Leonardo yet she knew she had to put on a brave face and comfort Livietta.

'After all, it's my duty,' she thought to herself. She had been Livietta's friend as well as servant.

They entered the sour smelling room. Zaira could see blood stained sheets and towels, and then she saw the midwife, who was already wrapping up the stillborn baby boy. Zaira thought back to her own mother, who died giving birth to her. She sincerely hoped that this would not be Livietta's fate as well.

Leonardo was beside himself. 'Please, no, the baby, can't you save the baby?'

They had arrived too late. He had guessed this might happen, he thought that if Zaira were there, she would somehow be a lucky talisman.

'Oh why, oh why couldn't Livietta have died instead? He thought bitterly to himself, wringing his hands, pacing up and down the room, but he finally controlled himself and begged Zaira to go and comfort Livietta.

'You know she has been asking for you.'

Zaira hesitated.

'Zaira dear, please do as I ask, for Livietta's sake, not mine.'

Zaira had always been surprised by Leonardo, but never so much as now. She had never anticipated his moods, had never understood his motives.

'Does he really want to belittle me in this way?'

He had obviously been making love to Livietta at the same time he had been coming to her bed.

She didn't think he was at all contrite about this. He had told her there had been no other women, but he obviously hadn't included his wife in this statement.

'Poor little Livietta, she wanted to see me and he has made it happen for her, the way he makes everything happen, the way he makes everyone do what he wants,' she thought bitterly to herself.

'But I can't, Leonardo, she will see that I am pregnant,' but she was wrong: her big black cloak hid her condition very well and she could see that Livietta was too weak to notice. She took a deep breath and went over to Livietta's bed. She looked so white, so ill she was hardly breathing. Zaira couldn't help pitying her. She took her hand and said her name, very quietly.

'Livietta, please, dear Livietta, everything will be all right. Try and get some rest now,' she said these words as calmly as she could.

Livietta didn't make any response but Zaira felt her hand being squeezed ever so lightly. Zaira stroked her cheek and Livietta let out a sigh and went to sleep. Zaira tiptoed out of the room, where Leonardo was waiting for her.

Leonardo led Zaira up to her old room. He didn't say much, he was still too distraught.

'Zaira I need you, my love. I know you are strong. We must be together, I will work it out somehow.'

Zaira did not say much – it was impossible to find the words. She was desperate to ask him what his feelings were for Livietta.

'Why did you bring me back here?' she asked coolly.

'I thought Livietta was dying, she murmured your name. I felt so sorry for her. I don't love her but how I pitied her. She was so weak, so delicate, all that blood. When the doctor called me, I knew the baby could die, half still inside her, half outside. It was so terrible, I couldn't manage on my own. I needed you too; I thought you could make a difference, that you would be like a lucky charm for me.'

With that, he left the room. He hadn't touched her once. Zaira was utterly bereft of any feeling, she felt numb and exhausted. She flopped down on the bed fully clothed, not even bothering to remove her cloak, and surprisingly she slept a long, uninterrupted sleep.

The next morning Livietta was a little stronger but crying constantly. 'My baby, my baby.' Zaira was sitting by her bedside holding her hand, neither of them saying anything.

Livietta eventually said:

'I missed you so much. I felt so alone without you. Please stay with me here now, darling. I am so pleased Leonardo persuaded you to come back here, after all your troubles.'

Zaira wasn't sure what Leonardo had told her.

'But please don't leave again, Zaira, I can't carry on like this. Leonardo wanted a son so badly. I am tired of it all, those 'private times'... I can't try again. The miscarriages, and now a dead baby, I can't bear it,' she said in a very faint voice.

Zaira didn't know what to say. 'Shush, try and get some more sleep now. I will be here when you wake up.'

Livietta eyelids closed. She looked so weak and vulnerable. Zaira shook her head. She was back in the house with the man she loved and his wife whom she had betrayed, and they both needed her, it seemed.

The following day without any warning at all, when Zaira was again watching over the sleeping Livietta, her waters broke and the contractions started soon after. She thought that it was too early. She had not gone to the full term of nine months.

She tried to think about dates and count back. 'Surely I didn't get pregnant straight away?'

She managed to leave Livietta's room and tried to find Leonardo, but she was in agony and couldn't move. Guerrino found her writhing on the stairs.

Since returning to Bertini, she had managed to keep out of the servants' way, only Guerrino had spoken to her. Guerrino, always very quiet and unusually discreet, guessed what was happening and ran to one of the younger servant girls and told her to call the midwife again.

'The Signora needs her once more,' was all he said.

Zaira was suffering so much the pain was unbearable. She managed somehow to get up to her bedroom and lay down on the bed, panting and sweating and screaming out: 'Where is everyone?'

She felt so alone, she didn't care whether the servants heard her or not. The midwife arrived after a couple of hours. She was very experienced and knew that this was going to be quite a long birth. She managed to calm Zaira and wiped her brow, telling her to: 'breathe in and out deeply.'

Leonardo who had gone to find Zaira in her room when the midwife arrived, was there the whole time, but he sat in a darkened corner, at a safe, respectable distance. This was unusual; men were normally kept well out of the way for a birth, they hated all the fuss and commotion. Leonardo hadn't stayed with Livietta, but now he felt different – he wanted to be present for this birth. There was so much at stake. He knew Zaira would be very brave and strong.

'Thank God she is so healthy,' thought Leonardo, his fists tightly clenched and rubbing tensely against his thighs.

The pains were getting worse, 'like fire,' Zaira thought. She was totally covered in sweat, and begging:

'Please let this pain stop,' her hands gripping at imaginary supports in the air, her hoarse screaming and choking like a death rattle. She wasn't feeling at all brave or strong after all.

The midwife urged her to push: 'gently, gently, Signora.'

When the baby finally came out of her body, her flesh felt as if it was being whipped and she screamed very loudly:

'I am going to die! I am being devoured! This can't be real, it must be a dream!' Then she looked down at the tightly shut eyes of the baby.

'What a relief', she managed to sigh as the midwife cut the umbilical cord and wrapped up the baby.

Then it started again: another bout of contractions, the sweating, the pushing.

'What the hell is happening now?' She asked the midwife. The pain was bad, but she was more accustomed to it now.

The midwife examined Zaira and realised quite quickly what it was:

'Ah I see. Stay calm, Signora, stay calm.' She could see another baby was coming out.

'Calm, you say? How can I remain calm, what is it now? I thought it was all over!' screamed Zaira. Luckily the pain didn't last long this time. She had given birth to a healthy baby girl and then after about another five minutes, a tiny little baby boy popped out.

Zaira had twins!

The midwife cut the second cord, and quickly wrapped up the babies in more towels and blankets. They had to be kept warm, then after she had rubbed them all over, she placed them both at Zaira's breasts, their little mouths desperately trying to suckle.

Zaira finally relaxed, amazed that these two tiny little beings had come out of her body. When she gave her breasts to those two little mouths, and they both made such a soft gurgling sound, she didn't know whether to laugh or cry. She kissed them both on their tiny foreheads, and then for a long time, gently felt the down of their heads. The midwife continued to show her how to breastfeed the babies. When she was satisfied that Zaira was doing it correctly, she made her departure and promised to come back the next day.

After she left, Leonardo got up from his chair and stood close to the bed to look at Zaira and the babies. He saw that her cheeks were rosy and her eyes were radiant...

'Just like a real mother,' he thought to himself and aloud he said:

'I feel immensely proud of you, my darling Zaira, you were so brave.' He patted her on the arm, and then patted his two babies on the heads.

Yet it would take Zaira a long time to forget the labour pains, the slow progress towards the climax, the hours of suffering and then the final contraction and then the relief. And then, what a shock it was for her, more contractions and another baby.

Zaira breathed deeply and said:

'Why is it only women who have to go through this kind of pain?' she asked. Leonardo started sobbing quietly to himself. He tried not to let Zaira see him and quietly went back to his chair.

'So much has occurred in such a short space of time.' He muttered.

Zaira was so exhausted she could not really take it in:

'Were there really two babies? Am I really feeding them both?'

She seemed to be managing it quite well, taking it in her stride as usual.

*

Zaira gave birth to her premature twins in the early morning of 29 July 1900. The day King Umberto was assassinated in Monza by a worker from Brescia, a revenge killing for the 80 unarmed workers killed in Milan two years before which had led to all the rioting that followed. Leonardo himself was quite sad, the poor king was weak and vacillating, but Leonardo admired his wife, Queen Margherita. She was a scheming, bigoted old thing, but she too was fond of cars.

The king's son, Vittorio Emanuele III took over the throne, and the new liberal government of Giolitti soon came to power. Leonardo was supposed to go Piacenza as soon as he could. There was talk of further rioting in Milan, which could lead to trouble in Piacenza as well. But he didn't go, there were too many things happening in his own life just now.

Two weeks later, Leonardo went to visit his aunt, the Contessa. She had been trying to keep a low profile all this time, so that her nephew could settle down to married life. But she too had noticed how Leonardo and Zaira looked at each other. She had wanted to confront Leonardo about this, but decided to hold her tongue. She knew he thought her an old, interfering busybody.

They briefly discussed the recent events in Italy. The Contessa was going to the king's funeral.

Then, after a brief pause, Leonardo told her everything: about his and Livietta's loveless marriage, his increasing fondness for Zaira, and then the stillborn baby. How utterly upset he was about the loss of his son, and then he told her about the birth of the twins, 'So wonderful, so exciting!'

They discussed how he could resume his life without too much upheaval. He told her his proposal. He also suggested, very delicately:

'Perhaps, dear Aunt, you could keep even further out of the way for a while, until the new arrangements are in place.'

He hinted that she could go to her house in Portofino for an extended stay, or furthermore, visit that old reprobate, Claudio, in New York, whom she still hadn't visited.

The Contessa listened quietly, it wasn't quite what she had expected, but Leonardo seemed determined, and even though Zaira came from peasant stock, there was something about her even the Contessa admired.

Now Leonardo had to talk to Zaira about the future and he quickly returned to Bertini and tried to find her.

She was feeling sufficiently recovered after the traumatic birth of her twins, and was sitting on a secluded veranda at the back of the house, with the tiny little babies on her lap. Old Guerrino was in attendance. She had managed to avoid both Livietta and the servants all this time.

Leonardo told her that Livietta thought that she was ill, ill with grief about her 'dead husband'.

'Ha, what husband!' Zaira thought bitterly and she laughed her throaty laugh to herself.

This veranda was the only part of the house where Zaira could not see the two odd towers. She had got two young twin towers – of trouble – herself now.

'Would they get on or will they be as incompatible as those old towers, that funny old pair, over the house?' She wondered.

Leonardo had been searching for Zaira everywhere, as he had been impatient to speak to her. When he eventually discovered her on the veranda, he felt overcome by the natural way she had with the babies. She looked so beautiful. He gave an inescapable sigh, but he straightened himself and controlled his feelings – the way a Bertini ought to do. The babies were tiny and being premature twins, looked even younger than they were. Leonardo had never had to deal with babies in his entire life, but the boy and girl were absolutely fascinating to him, and he wanted to kiss them both, but not now, later... Leonardo dismissed Guerrino, abruptly.

He wanted to tell Zaira his plan – or rather his proposition –

as soon as possible, get it over with, in fact. He started to explain it in a cold and formal manner, as if they were strangers:

'Zaira, you are feeling better now and I have to talk to you. As poor Livietta and I have lost our very precious baby son, I propose that this boy here should be raised as our own child. He will bear the Bertini name.'

'What?' asked Zaira incredulously, but Leonardo refused to be interrupted. He preferred to keep to his prepared speech.

'The girl, well you can bring up the girl yourself. I don't want to deprive you of both your children. They can grow up together, like brother and sister, in this house. You can play the part of the bereaved widow and young mother. I will cherish the girl as much as the boy.

'I think this is a fair and reasonable solution, don't you?'

Zaira was silent, hearing only the ruthlessness in his voice. He didn't give a fig for the babies, neither girl nor boy, but he was desperate to have an heir.

'Leonardo, I would prefer not to discuss this now,' she said eventually.

He reminded her yet again that she could be thrown into an institution if some hostile person in the church or local authorities ever discovered the truth.

'Would you prefer that alternative? You know you will always have a home at Bertini and I will look always look after you,' his tone softened and he tried to hold her, but she remained stiff. She wanted to push him away but it was difficult with two babies on her lap.

'This is all nonsense, all the servants must know the truth, they surely can't believe my so-called husband is dead already. I have done a lot since I was last here, haven't I? Not only lost a husband but given birth as well,' she said angrily.

'Zaira, nothing has changed, we will all live together in the same house. I can take care of the servants, don't worry about that.'

She realised that he wanted them to carry on as before as if nothing had happened:

'Yet what else can I do?' She asked herself desperately. 'Where would I go with my tiny baby girl?'

And she had two babies. She could not be separated from either of them. 'I know that now. And Fabio would be a Bertini, me not only a mother but the mother of a Bertini.'

Zaira never thought she would feel like this, but these two tiny delicate little beings had to be protected. How could she have possibly thought she could have left them at an orphanage? Zaira had never thought of herself as a possible mother, could never remember having maternal feelings towards any child, but now, these babies were hers, they needed her.

'Ha, everyone seems to need me at Bertini,' she mused sardonically.

So again she reluctantly agreed to his plan.

'Well, yes, I suppose you are right, as usual.' She always agreed with him these days.

A delighted Leonardo kissed her on the cheek, picked up the boy and left Zaira with the baby girl she had named Alba – a new dawn for a new century.

Zaira looked at her little girl: 'Nobody's going to take you away from me, Alba.'

*

Italy, after a period of chaos and upheaval, was beginning to enjoy a period of stability in the new century. The so-called liberal government wanted to make social reforms a priority, even allowing working women some rights: the right to form women's leagues, to be educated, to hold conferences about their democratic right to vote. Zaira would miss all this, but Alba wouldn't, she would eventually reap the benefits of this new age – the twentieth century.

*

Leonardo carried the boy, Fabio – Zaira's choice again, no symbolism this time, she just liked the name, into Livietta's bedroom. Livietta was awake, reading a book, and she visibly shrank away from him, feeling the tears welling up in her eyes.

Leonardo did not even pretend to be affectionate to Livietta, but she was his wife, a Bertini after all. Since the early days of her last pregnancy he had never visited her bedroom and never would again. He thrust a crying Fabio into a crying Livietta's arms. Coldly, he explained his plan to his wife.

'We will bring up the baby boy Fabio as our own. Zaira will continue to live here. She will no longer be classed as one of the servants, but as a bereaved widow, part of the family. She and her baby daughter Alba will have their own apartments on the other side of the house. I am already arranging it. The builders are coming in tomorrow to make the alterations.'

Livietta did not really digest what he was saying, but the little baby was so tiny, so sweet and dainty, she loved him already. She actually thought Leonardo's plan was quite reasonable – in spite of everything she couldn't hate Zaira, whatever she had done and now she and Zaira could be together, as before, both looking after their babies.

On his return, Leonardo had immediately made it known to his wife that Zaira's husband had tragically died while training with his regiment based in Piacenza and that was why he had brought her back to Bertini.

'They met each other before she had argued with her family and left Torretta. Then they finally married in secret in Piacenza when she left Bertini. Alas, the marriage was very short-lived.'

'It was strange,' thought Livietta, 'I can't remember Zaira mentioning any of this.'

Leonardo continued: 'As she had nowhere else to go, she had returned to Bertini to have her prematurely born baby (or babies as it turned out). The baby girl will be a companion to our beloved son, Fabio.'

He was quite convincing and it seemed feasible to Livietta even though she was surprised that Zaira hadn't confided in her.

'That was why she always looked so vague and dreamy,' she said to herself.

Leonardo even called the servants together and announced the same words. He made it sound like a newspaper bulletin. Even if some of the females in the staff speculated about the dates not quite adding up, most of the servants found Leonardo's announcement quite believable.

'Why would he bother to say this?'

'Why would he care about what happened to a girl such as Zaira?' The household continued to gossip, some trying to convince themselves that Leonardo's statement was true, yet there would always be talk about Zaira being the mother of both the babies.

One of the old laundry women swore:

'On my daughter's life, I saw that midwife with the dead child in her arms!'

Whilst others swore they had seen no such thing. 'Well, I never saw any dead child. Why would you lie about something like that?'

Guerrino said nothing.

The same old laundry woman said she always knew Leonardo and Zaira had been carrying on, 'And what was to stop them from continuing to do so?' she asked.

'I always said it: that Zaira has landed on her feet. She's a crafty girl, I always knew she had ideas above her station,' said another.

Livietta gradually also guessed the truth, but she could not bring herself to do anything about it. She saw the way Leonardo and Zaira spoke together, the way he even put his arm around her sometimes, and also how he seemed to dote on little Alba.

She herself was besotted with Fabio and although she was very disappointed by Zaira – 'Why, she used to make fun of Leonardo!' – it was all too unpleasant for her even to think about it. Yet she continued to be genuinely pleased that Zaira had returned to Bertini. And of course, she had Fabio now to worry about, she wanted to be a good mother to him, and another good thing was that Leonardo wouldn't bother to come near her again: no more miscarriages, no more childbirth, and little Fabio would always have the little girl, Alba, to play with.

'Things could be much worse,' she thought to herself. She and Leonardo developed a much better relationship and often discussed their love of music. When Verdi died in early 1901, Arturo Toscanini conducted the orchestras and choirs at his state funeral in Milan. Leonardo, who didn't want to miss this last farewell, had made the journey to Milan to attend. Afterwards he told Livietta, who hadn't wanted to leave Fabio, that it was the largest public assembly in the history of Italy.

20. **Letters...**

The new arrangements at Bertini appeared to work well for everyone. The children were both christened at the *Pieve* at the top of Tortello in September. Alba was baptised in the names of Alba Maria Marta. Her surname was given as Crespi. Zaira had to lie about her marriage certificate saying it had got mislaid when her husband died, but in fact as his ancestors had originated from Torretta he was also called Crespi. It was easy for documents to get lost in the archives at Piacenza. Men who were already married would often commit bigamy because they knew no one would ever check the records.

Fabio Claudio Leonardo was christened with his intended first name, without any family objections. Leonardo was happy: he had the son and heir he had always wanted. Zaira could name him Fabio if she wanted. He told Livietta that it had been his own choice. His aunt the Contessa would die a contented woman, knowing that the family name would continue. She had never had children of her own, and Leonardo's brother Claudio, who was still living in America, could never have been relied upon to get married and have children.

*

Claudio had been very busy getting involved with the film industry in Hollywood, and also indulging the passion he shared with his brother for cars. The Ford Motor Car Company was making great strides and Claudio had offered to test drive their new models. *[He would start racing, and come back to Italy a celebrity, and become involved in the Futurism movement. Their philosophy was a combination of a passion for speed, fast cars and planes, and an ardent support for guns and weapons, symbols of the colonialist ambitions prevalent in Italy at the time. These were the concepts that the male of the species had traditionally always supported.]*

Leonardo too had been interested in these things but was less so now. He had mellowed – his personal experiences had changed his outlook on life.

*

The brothers were, however, still very close, and always corresponded. This was one of the letters Claudio sent Leonardo, whom he called Tino, an old family nickname. *Tino* meant a vat or tub used for winemaking.

Dear Tino

I feel sorry for you, little brother, living in such a backward, immature country as Italy. How different it is to America. Compared to what is happening here in the New World, Italy is still in the Middle Ages. As you know, I am involved in making a movie, as they call cinematic films here. I am one of the producers. It's so fascinating, but very hard work. I am up at five every morning! Me, can you imagine it? The director is king and has everyone rushing round. Everything has to be just right, as he's so meticulous. Even the two leading ladies – absolutely gorgeous but very temperamental – are deferential to the director, but he knows just how to handle them. One of the actors has a really squeaky voice – thank God there is no sound! When you see the rushes from each day's screening, you realise what an artist the director is.

Well, enough of me, I was delighted to get your recent news in your last letter. Good old Tino, you finally have a baby son! By the way, why did you choose the name Fabio? I can't recall anyone in the family of that name. To think one day he will inherit all the Bertini titles. My American friends love calling me 'Il Marchese', yet they can't pronounce it, and say the 'ch' as in 'cheese'!

The Americans are a delightful race but they have no idea about foreign languages whatsoever. They are of the opinion that every being in the whole world must speak American!

So, there's no need for me to worry any more about getting married and having children. And it's all thanks to you. I can't really imagine Amy, my present 'flame', as my wife, or returning to Italy and being an Italian Marchesa! She's great in bed, or good in the sack, as they say here, but I don't think I will ever marry her – life's too short!

You, Tino, have saved me the bother. I must admit I would never have thought it. You used to be so wild. You never gave a damn about anyone. And you were spoilt so shamelessly by our poor parents when they were alive. You were given everything you ever wanted and you always got your own way.

But now, quite unbelievably, you have finally settled down with your wife and son. You seem so different these days, I can tell from your letters: so serious, talking about the government, the social reforms, what's occurring in industry. You never used to be interested in such things. Still, I'm glad you still love driving your latest car. Incidentally, what speed can it do?

In your last letter you mentioned how our parents' deaths affected us so much. I suppose we really did go off the rails for a bit, didn't we? I agree with you that it was mainly out of grief and rage.

We were angry with them for dying. It sounds as if now that you have Fabio, you realise how important family is.

Now I'm getting serious! Your letters must be having a strange effect on me.

There is one thing that intrigues me. What is this I hear (from Lorenzo Lippi) about another woman living at Bertini, a young beautiful mother, and her daughter? A relative of Livietta, was that it? This all sounds very mysterious, Tino dear. Maybe you haven't changed so much after all!

You mentioned Zaira, and now Alba, in your most recent letter, but you never explained who they are. Still up to your old tricks after all, are you? Well I await your next letter with great anticipation.

Your ever-loving brother,

Claudio

*

Dear Claudio,

You rascal! All this curiosity about Zaira! There is not much to say. She is a distant relative of Livietta, she is recently widowed, and she and her daughter, Alba, who is the same age as Fabio, have come to live with us. All I can tell you, brother dear, is that the arrangement suits us all very well. Zaira is an attractive and interesting woman, she and Livietta are great friends and Fabio and Alba are inseparable.

Our dear aunt the Contessa is thinking of paying you a visit soon, so maybe she will give you more details. I'll tell you the whole story one day – whenever they manage to get one of those flying machines off the ground!

*

Leonardo tore up this letter and started again. He wanted to tell his brother the complete truth but wasn't sure what Claudio would think. He was so flippant, would he understand?

Dear Claudio

You want the truth about Zaira. Well, here it is. To be blunt I wanted her the first moment I saw her. And somehow she made me fall in love with her. I wasn't sure how long it would last but now I do really love her, more than I ever thought possible. She came here as a companion/maid to Livietta, employed by Aunt Camilla of all people, and that's how it started. She is so different from any other woman I know – like a breath of fresh air.

It is true that she and Livietta are very distantly related; their fathers both originate from Torretta, a desolate place high up in the Apennines. There's no road, no running water, no anything. Zaira actually wants me to go there one day. Well, we will see.

Now, about Fabio and Alba – not to beat about the bush, both Livietta and Zaira got pregnant around the same time. So, brother dear, you will say that I haven't changed that much! Alas, Livietta gave birth to our stillborn son and when darling Zaira was clever enough to give birth to twins, a boy and a girl, it seemed sensible for Livietta and I to bring up the boy as our own. This ensured the continuity of the family name, making Aunt happy, and relieving you of the responsibility you didn't want, as you have told me a thousand times. I let it be known that Zaira was an unfortunate widow with a newly born daughter who was returning to live with us again. Thus I could protect her and our daughter at the same time. So, now you know the truth: Zaira and I are the parents of both the children. Zaira chose the name Fabio, because she liked it!

If we could talk face to face, this would be so much easier to explain, but I think you have the picture now. You must have guessed that my marriage to Livietta has been quite miserable. She cannot bring herself to love me as a woman should love a man. I really did try but stopped having relations when she got pregnant. Livietta is actually much happier now she has Fabio to look after. She is relieved that we don't sleep together any longer. I think she would prefer to have her eyes plucked out rather than engage in some of the things I tried to show her!

Nevertheless Livietta is a sweet person. I respect the way she is coping with this rather delicate situation, and for that reason she will always be dear to me. She and Zaira continue to be good friends, so all in all, things are going remarkably well.

It is Zaira who sometimes seems doubtful. She obviously wants Fabio to know she is his real mother, and thinks we could have arranged things differently, but I really don't think there was any alternative.

When we are alone together, she makes me deliriously happy. Hopefully you will understand why I am prepared to live this great deception. Maybe one day you will get to meet Zaira and the children, and then you will see.

And, brother dear, it's true what you say about Mama and Papa. I think of them often, and how sad it is that they will never see their grandchildren. I have such fond memories of them, and I do remember they spoilt you even more than they spoilt me; you were the older son after all!

We were very privileged to have such wonderful parents, Claudio, so I hope you never forget them over there in Hollywood. I must close now but with my next letter I promise to send you photographs of Fabio and Alba. She's as beautiful as her mother.

With much affection,

Leonardo

*

Livietta was content. Her adored parents doted on Fabio and relations with their son-in-law were much less tense now that their beloved daughter had finally produced an heir. Leonardo and she had settled into a friendly, yet still formal, relationship. They still never used the familiar *tu* together. Choosing when to use *tu* can certainly define a relationship. And theirs could never be described as intimate. Yet even though they were formal with each other, Livietta was no longer frightened of Leonardo because he had stopped his physical demands. She was happy for Zaira to take care of that department. In bed or when they were alone together, Zaira and Leonardo always called each other *tu*, but nobody knew this. Livietta could not understand what Zaira saw in men and in that whole business. In fact, she felt much more emotionally attached to Zaira than she had ever been to Leonardo.

Yet Leonardo still sometimes called her 'Little Blackbird' or 'Nightingale' and enjoyed her piano recitals. Music was the only thing that they had ever really had in common. Zaira was utterly unmusical but Leonardo had finally persuaded her to accompany them to La Scala. Leonardo, Livietta and Zaira sometimes shared a box, and even in sophisticated Milan they were whispered about: 'Look there's Leonardo Bertini and his two women!'

Zaira really enjoyed the opera, the entire visual spectacle and drama of it, and even she was moved and enthralled by Verdi's passionate music.

After seeing 'La Traviata' which was Zaira's favourite, she was longing to discuss it with Leonardo at a late supper in their hotel that night. They were alone as Livietta had not accompanied them.

'I can identify with Violetta, a woman completely misunderstood and imprisoned by the conventions of her time. She had to give up Alfredo to satisfy his family.

'Leonardo, what would have happened if your parents had been alive. What would they have thought of me, the peasant girl from the country?'

'Oh, Zaira, what a question! How can I answer something so hypothetical. If my parents were alive, I would have lived a completely different life, maybe even in a completely different world. In fact, I most probably wouldn't have met you. But all I can say, my sweet, is that neither of them had a snobbish bone in their body, and they were nothing like my dear aunt, the Contessa. It is only the bourgeoisie that worry about what other people think. A true aristocrat doesn't give a damn about rules and convention. And so they would have adored you – the merry widow from humble peasant origins!'

'Ha, merry widow, indeed! I hope they would have loved me for my intelligence, my natural abilities...'

'Now don't exaggerate. Let's go up to bed, my *lucciola!*'

*

Fabio was very much like Livietta in temperament. She loved him more and more every day. At first, Zaira had continued to feed her son after his birth. Livietta did have some milk after the stillbirth of her son but it was not enough for the hungry little Fabio. Even Zaira's milk hadn't been deemed sufficient by the midwife and doctor, so it had been decided that a wet nurse be brought in, much to the displeasure of Zaira, who wanted to be as close to her son as possible. After some months, however, Livietta managed to get Fabio to drink the milk from the donkey she had specially procured for the purpose. He was a very delicate little boy and suffered many illnesses, and wasn't as robust as Alba, but the children adored each other, and when they began walking, he followed after his sister everywhere.

Alba was the dominant one, always bossing him about. She was just like her mother, forthright, confident and fearless. Fabio was more like Livietta, retiring and shy. In fact, sometimes she convinced herself he really was her son. He even looked like her: he had similar black hair and brown eyes, even her longish nose. She conveniently forgot that he resembled Leonardo as well.

For a short while Leonardo had kept up the pretence with Livietta that Fabio was Zaira's child by her dead husband. However, as Livietta regained her strength, she and Leonardo were able to converse quite sensibly and frankly. As she had guessed, Leonardo admitted that he was the father of both children:

'Look, you will always be my official wife, but Zaira is like a wife to me as well.'

Leonardo was relieved how well Livietta took these revelations. It made him respect her more and she really was less reserved and shy with him now that she had Fabio to fuss over.

'I am happy with things the way they are, I assure you.'

Leonardo understood that the new arrangement suited her much better than before, regardless of his adultery.

Zaira never knew that Leonardo and Livietta had these conversations. She and Livietta still laughed and joked together, but they never discussed Leonardo. There was an implicit agreement between them, and Zaira was sometimes quite nervous about her new status. In fact, as Livietta became more confident, and relaxed in front of Leonardo, Zaira was less sure about herself. She tried not to offend Leonardo and became quite reverential towards him. In private, though, she still made her silly jokes and played games:

She threw herself on top of Leonardo. 'You are a *leone* but so am I!' She was born under the sign of Leo.

But there was something missing. Zaira felt she had no control over her own destiny, no true freedom. She felt somewhat bogged down now by her life at Bertini. She was playing the part of contented mother/lover, but she was envious of Fabio's loving relationship with Livietta. She couldn't be a true mother to him.

Finally she admitted to herself, 'I am the least contented of the three!'

Zaira felt a little guilty because, even though her life was now definitely at Bertini, she wanted to make some kind of contribution in other situations and make a mark. After all, she had so wanted to find a job. Now she was employed in the usual role of mother and wife (or almost), but was it fulfilling enough?

She loved her children and Leonardo more than she could say but she felt she could do more. She had started to write – in fact Leonardo encouraged it. And so she wrote a little something every day, usually in the form of a poem, or once even a short story for possible publication in a magazine. But she didn't feel she had written anything good enough so far.

She tentatively asked Leonardo if maybe there wasn't some kind of work she could do, perhaps help him with the car factory.

'My darling Zaira, I have enough problems with the factory without letting you loose there. Your place is here looking after Alba.'

'But Leonardo, you have always said that you believe in rights for women, the vote; that women should be employed on equal terms with men; yet you don't think I should get a job. I have lots of ideas about your factory.'

'Zaira, *tesoro*, I am sure that you would do a very good job running the factory – you know so much about cars,' Leonardo said sarcastically. 'But I'm afraid that the workers would certainly not take orders from a woman. Women are different, they are home-makers and child-bearers above all else.'

'That's rubbish, Leonardo. What about all the women working long hours for poor pay in all those terrible factories in Milano, Piacenza, Parma or anywhere else? They have to work because their husbands don't earn enough or they have no other family to support them and they would be destitute otherwise. Try telling them their place is in the home!'

'Look, I know there are exceptions but the problem about work and gender is well known by men and denied by women.

'The actual reality is that this will always be a lost battle. It's like men trying to have children or like a woman trying to be the champion in a men's running race.'

'Oh, that's ridiculous! That's not what I am saying at all. I am saying women are entitled to work, just like men. I'm not talking about physical things: having children or competing in male sports. Women are capable of doing most things; their intellectual capabilities are the same as men's. A woman could be a doctor, a teacher, a lawyer, anything like that.'

'Men have greater aptitude for some things, whilst women are better at others, but they are always more emotional. It's a question of nature, chemistry, hormones, brain construction and anatomy. It would be more intelligent to perfect one's skills and attitudes than to try to become something that is not part of your biological make-up. If a woman wants to become very skilled in a field where man historically dominates, she has first to give up her natural femininity and become a male.'

'That is just not true. Women could do most jobs; it's nothing to do with losing femininity. And you are indeed generalising too much. We are not all equally feminine. Look at Livietta and me. I am quite tall and strong, and she is small and delicate. But that doesn't mean to say her brain doesn't work as well as mine – or yours for that matter.'

'I never said that a woman shouldn't become a teacher, a doctor or a lawyer and so on. I simply assert that for a certain kind of work and in general in sports...'

'But I am not talking about sports – how many more times!'

'Well, in either case, women will never be equal to men. Of course, there are exceptions, but this is generally not the rule. I am not judging, only ascertaining certain facts. And, *mia cara,* the fact that you always get angry when I make such remarks is evidence there's something right in what I say!'

Leonardo had this uncanny knack of making Zaira feel

inferior. He sounded so logical when he argued. But she would never agree with him. Women, if they put their mind to it, could equal men in any intellectual activity.

'I am talking about women's mental abilities, not physical abilities. I really don't think anatomy affects our mental processes, and I don't believe our brains are different from men's. But if in fact they are, then they are better!'

Leonardo couldn't help but admire Zaira for her opinions, even though he disagreed with them. For someone without a formal education she had a remarkable knowledge and could hold her own in an argument. She had obviously learnt a lot from those novels she read.

Zaira was thinking of *Romola*, a novel she had read recently by the English writer George Eliot (a woman imitating a man, was she?). There is a Latin quote about there being no such thing as picking out the best woman as it's a question of comparative badness. Romola, the heroine, hasn't entirely been lifted out of *'that lower category to which Nature assigned thee...'*

In the so-called natural order of the world, women will always be made to feel their inferiority by men.

Zaira admitted to herself that although, as a woman, she aspired to be equal to a man in the area of work, she was different from a man emotionally. Women didn't have that male arrogance or confidence to act on their own initiative or take decisions.

She would always feel emotionally weak. She craved Leonardo's affection, his caresses, his love.

'Look, I admit I am emotionally weaker than you, and I can't argue as well as you can.'

Leonardo recognised these weaknesses; he could see that women cry and suffer over men, and he thought that this was typical of their sex.

'So how could a woman hold down a job like a man when you are so emotionally vulnerable?'

Zaira replied that if women were given equal opportunity in the workplace then they would gain confidence, take initiatives and be decisive. They were weak because they had been kept at home, relying on their husbands for both financial and emotional support.

'Emotional strength and confidence are gained through experience. The more women work outside the home, the stronger and more confident they would become.'

In fact, Zaira had no ambition to be a doctor or a lawyer. All she had ever wanted was to be a teacher. She remembered the little school in Torretta and how she had enjoyed teaching the younger children.

'Leonardo, I don't want to argue with you about these things. I think there is some truth in what both of us have said but I still think women should have aspirations and not be told they cannot do things. And I have been thinking, wouldn't it be lovely to have a little school here on the estate? I could help all the children with their reading and writing. Indeed, this would be the first step towards equality for all. I really think that if girls could have the same education as boys, there would be no limit to what they could do.'

'Well, we will have to discuss this another time. I have a dreaded appointment with the bank this afternoon, about the factory, again! Goodbye, my lovely *professoressa*!'

Zaira was frustrated because she thought Leonardo didn't take her ideas seriously enough. But she disliked arguing with him. Sometimes he got quite angry and unreasonable, even shouting at her. And it was supposed to be women who were emotional! She thought that possibly men were so accustomed to having a superior role in general, both in society and at home, that they were actually threatened by the idea of women being their equals, taking their jobs.

'You men have always been on top – at work and in the bedroom,' she giggled, 'and now you're frightened we'll take over and leave you powerless! You wait until you get home. I will show you who has the power round here!'

Zaira was aware that she could use her sexual power over Leonardo, and maybe her arguments were made weaker because of that. Men had the impression that women use, and abuse, sexual power to get what they want.

'There will always be this conflict between men and women,' Zaira predicted.

Zaira thought that it was all very well living in a wonderful house like Bertini and looking after Alba, but she really would like to do something more worthwhile. Women's brains were just as good as men's. She didn't believe that women were that different.

In their many repetitive arguments Zaira continually tried to get her point of view across. She thought Leonardo was so stubborn.

'The only difference, as far as I can see,' she often said to Leonardo, 'is that you are stronger than I am, you impregnate women, and women get pregnant.'

'But it's so much more than that. Your brains are different – you think differently, you act differently, you change moods; it's all to do with the moon and menstruation.'

'Well, I think men are just as moody. Anyway, we always repeat the same arguments. I am happy to disagree with you on the subject of men and women. I see their similarities and you see their differences. We will never see eye to eye on this.' So saying, she pretended to shoot an invisible arrow at his eye.

'Did you know that I'm a very fine archer?'

He pretended he had been shot in the eye: 'Yes, I knew, my goddess Diana!'

Zaira did wish to start up a small school. She had it all planned. The room, the children. She thought it was silly to have two kitchens. The summer one could be made into a bright, airy classroom, with three rows of desks and shelves of books on the walls.

Above all, she wanted to instil the idea into both boys and girls that they could do anything they wished. They didn't have to stay in the countryside and work on the land. They could get themselves an education. Girls could be teachers, lawyers, doctors, even engineers if that is what they wanted. They should be encouraged, not discouraged. And boys could pursue more traditionally feminine pursuits if they so wished. And if a child wanted to be a musician or an artist, this too should be nurtured, not disdained; these were noble and worthy pursuits.

However, rather than constantly arguing on the subject, she decided that she would sit down that afternoon and put pen to paper to formulate some of the ideas they had discussed. Even Leonardo had suggested that she should write down her opinions. It would help her to get them clear in her mind.

*

Sometimes, when in a dark mood, Zaira thought being a mother was like being in prison: 'A woman has to be willing to forgo her own self for the sake of her children's well-being.'

And to her mind it was the same for Livietta. She was locked in a loveless marriage for Fabio's sake. As a child Zaira believed that her life was normal because she knew nothing else, but the more she read the more she realised how poor her life was, both materially and spiritually, and that no one's life was ever really 'normal' – there was no such thing. Now, at Bertini, she had many more material benefits, and, of course, she had Leonardo's love, but she still had no power. A woman belonged to her husband, that was the law, and at Bertini both Livietta and Zaira belonged to Leonardo.

That didn't seem right. It was not fair. Zaira did not understand this concept: why did a woman need to sacrifice herself to the so-called prevalent morality of the time?

As Zaira had been brought up motherless, all she had had was some ideal woman to dream about. She had always been told by Bartolomeo how perfect her mother had been, just as Zaira was so imperfect, and so unlike the other girls in her village. Because Zaira's mother had died young, she hadn't had time to develop any faults, and any faults she did have were conveniently forgotten – she *was* perfect.

Maybe this was the reason she felt different, as if she belonged to another time, another morality.

Zaira tried to talk to Livietta about these feelings but found it hard to express herself. Besides, Livietta was indeed a true woman of her time. She had the same moral code as the women in the novels she read. She would rather die than submit to immorality, lust or infidelity. Motherhood was now the only point of her life.

Zaira thought that the peasant class and women especially – even Livietta – were deliberately kept under by the ruling classes, mainly the male politicians and aristocrats. It was in their interests to keep the masses subdued. They didn't want revolution or women fighting for their rights. Leonardo was careful not to sound too strident about women but Zaira had heard some of his friends at dinner parties repeat the standard phrases such as:

'A woman's place is in the home' or 'She is the property of her husband' or 'What on earth does a woman know about government, politics, voting?'

Zaira was annoyed by these attitudes but was never able to express her thoughts on these matters. When she sat at the dinner table with these male acquaintances of Leonardo she had to be courteous and make polite conversation. Her position in the household was precarious. She had no right to have opinions. It made her feel stupid and worthless.

The only person she could express this to was Livietta.

'I would love to say what I think to those men. How dare they talk about women as if we don't exist, as if we don't have brains, as if we are animals?' she cried.

Livietta was calmer about the situation. Although she believed in a woman's right to choose whether to get married and have children, she wasn't so irate about women not being able to vote or their inequality in the workplace, but she admired Zaira's deeply felt opinions on these matters.

When Zaira read books by women from England she realised that the struggle for women's suffrage was long and hard. She and Livietta had attempted to read Mary Wollstonecraft's *Vindication of the Rights of Women* and other treatises by English suffragettes fighting against traditional values and prejudices. Their contemporaries, the Pankhursts – Emmeline, the mother, and her two daughters, Cristobel and Sylvia – were heroines and Zaira imagined herself joining them on marches and in civil disobedience. Livietta, however, said she couldn't imagine herself marching in the street, or chaining herself to railings, let alone throwing herself in front of a racehorse.

Zaira sighed: 'Well, one thing is sure: this kind of thing will never, ever happen in Italy. We seem to be so far behind Britain and the New World. And did you know that women already have the vote in New Zealand and Australia? That really is progress.'

Zaira wondered whether she would ever get the chance to visit places like New Zealand or Australia. She knew she never would in reality, but in her dreams she was still an adventurer, still a traveller to unknown places.

Livietta loved the fact that Zaira had such strongly felt opinions, and besides, they had a lot in common: two mothers sharing a life and house together.

Sometimes she stroked Zaira's hair, almost subconsciously, lost in the sensation of the luxuriant chestnut tresses. If she were completely honest with herself, she longed to fondle Zaira even further. She convinced herself that it was just the same feeling she had when she gingerly stroked one of the semi-wild cats living on the estate. It was out of affection. She was not sure why she had these physical longings and did not wish to explore the reasons. She would never do anything to offend Zaira. Indeed, if she had tried to touch Zaira further, maybe she would react just like one of the cats and get her claws out. That would be mortifying.

Zaira did not guess that Livietta had anything but sisterly feelings for her. She loved Livietta, and was verbally affectionate towards her, but she didn't give her many kisses or hugs. She kept some of herself back and reserved her physical affection for Leonardo and the children. She knew, and even consciously admitted it to herself, that she was much more selfish than Livietta and very unlike her in character. Even though she was now a mother, Zaira was always thinking of herself: her emotions and feelings, her thoughts. And if she never felt completely relaxed in Livietta's presence, she did with Leonardo. She loved to feel physically free and threw off her corsets as often as she could.

Livietta, on the other hand, who had retained her very thin frame, favoured very tight corsets. She enjoyed the feeling of being constrained. And when they ate chocolates together, Livietta was very careful to have only one, while Zaira had to stop herself gobbling up the entire contents of the box. They were like chalk and cheese in many respects, and yet irreversibly linked.

Zaira tried to work out some of her feelings about her life with Leonardo and Livietta but she went round in circles.

*

Zaira and Elena had continued to write the occasional letter to each other, even though they spoke on the telephone as well. Zaira found it easier to write. She tried to put some of her pent-up feelings into her letters. Elena had always been her closest female relative, half sister, half mother to her. In her first letter after she had the twins, she tried to be completely honest with her aunt about her life at Bertini.

Dearest Aunt Elena

Thank you for the presents for the twins. I still can't quite believe what happened. It was such a shock to have two babies. I suppose that is why I had such a terrifyingly long labour. They were so tiny, so vulnerable, I thought they wouldn't survive. I think their lives were in danger for a time, especially Fabio's. He was so fragile, so delicate, but they both seem to be thriving well now. As you know, I only nursed Fabio for a while, and then Livietta found a wet nurse for him. It was strange seeing him nursed by someone else. I could easily have fed them both but the doctor thought otherwise. I have plenty of milk, even now. Still, you must know about this, with your two children.

I'm so pleased that you and Uncle are enjoying such a good life and that your children give you so much joy. The twins are fascinating. Every day they learn to do some new thing, and Alba is teething already. She seems so advanced. Some days I wake up and think this is all a dream – me a mother of two children living in a house like Bertini. I do remember thinking how unfair it was that I had to be born in a place like Torretta. How I wanted to escape! Now, it seems, I have got my wish. But the circumstances aren't exactly how I imagined! I wonder what it would be like if I had not accepted Leonardo's plan. It amazes me how acquiescent Livietta is about our unusual 'life'. She never questions any of it. She seems as fond of me as ever and we are still the greatest of friends. I sometimes feel quite guilty about it all.

As for Leonardo, I do love him, and I think he loves me in return. I still have my doubts, my insecurities, about the situation. I'm not worried about the gossip – people have always gossiped about me, even when I was an innocent virgin – and most people round here seem to have accepted me now. I still have no idea whether the news has reached Torretta yet. I've written to my brothers once, just to say I have had a daughter. I don't know how much they really know, because news travels, even to Torretta, but those two were never interested in gossip. They're so involved in the farm and their own families. They never have time to think about their naughty little sister!

The servants here actually call me 'Signora' now and treat me quite respectfully, so different from when I first arrived. Guerrino has always been a treasure, and protects me against any malicious mutterings. He absolutely adores the children.

Leonardo is constantly trying to reassure me that he couldn't be happier. When we are alone together, I believe him. I can't quite explain it – in our intimate moments, it is always so wonderful. (Please don't show this letter to Uncle!) So different from how I perceived him when we first met, how haughty he seemed then. When we are in public, he corrects my Italian, or laughs at mistakes I make about the name of a wine, or a flower, or if I get a kite and a buzzard muddled up. Once I put some wine in my broth – 'sorbì' (do you remember how my father used to love doing this?) and he was so condescending about my peasant ways. I feel quite angry with him when he's like this. And he never makes mistakes about anything; he's perfect – well that's his opinion anyway. Then, when we are alone, he is so different, so tender. Yet he doesn't seem to understand why I find the situation difficult, even painful sometimes. I am here under his protection. I can tell no one that Fabio is my son and I feel completely beholden to Leonardo. Sometimes I can't decide whether I will always be eternally grateful to him or whether I resent the way he has engineered my life for me. I had so many dreams, I so wanted to be independent, and now I am really just a man's property – but then I am also the mother of two lovely children. I suppose I will never, ever resolve this paradox. I feel so confused.

Leonardo and Livietta seem to get on really well now. It's as if I've saved their lives from disintegrating. And obviously Livietta adores Fabio; she is so happy being a mother. And I am constantly thinking about Fabio. Will I ever be able to tell him that I am his real mother? Will I always have to live this lie?

Oh dear, I shouldn't go on like this. Please forgive me, dear Aunt Elena. You have your own life to lead, without having to worry about me. I will try and telephone you as soon as I can, just to say hello. I really am fine. I know things could be far, far worse.

Your loving Zaira

*

Elena did not write many letters to her niece, but after a while she replied.

Darling Zaira

Thank you for the portraits of Alba and Fabio that I received recently and sorry for this delay. Alba is so like you already! I clearly remember you as a little baby, sucking your fist, your reddish-blonde hair sticking up on your head. And now you're the mother of two babies yourself, just like me! I sometimes wonder what would have happened if you had come to Torino. But then again, it's simply not worth thinking about it. I try not to feel guilty about you – well it's not guilt exactly, but it must have been very difficult for you after I left, then your father dying, and you all alone in Milan. I sometimes wonder why Giovanni and Vittorio let their little sister go away like that. You never told me very much about your time there. It must have been terrible for you.

Still, living in a beautiful place like Bertini must make up for it. I know the situation is not ideal but you have everything you want there. Leonardo obviously loves you and the children. And don't worry about him correcting you. Men are like that – they have to feel superior sometimes, especially when they adore a woman. My husband is just the same, and I used to correct your Italian, too, don't forget! And from your letters to me, I think Leonardo has always done what's best for both you and the children. How else would Fabio inherit the Bertini titles and wealth? I know you thought it was callous of him to take Fabio from you. Yet I wonder how many other people live in families without knowing the real identity of their mother or father. You're not as rare as you think, piccina! And I'm sure in time you will know how and when to tell Fabio the truth. But please be careful. Don't rush into it.

And you must come and visit when the children are slightly bigger. I would love to show you everything in Torino, especially the King's palace in the beautiful royal square. In the heart of the city you can see the Alps one way and then, in the opposite direction, the Apennine hills. I must admit I get a little homesick when I look at the Apennines!

Now I must dash. We are going to attend a recital at the Agnelli house this evening!

With all my love to you and the children,
Elena

21. Alba and Fabio

Zaira did worry about Fabio. She watched him constantly, her child and yet not her child. He called Livietta 'Mama', not her. Yet he was absolutely obsessed with his sister. Alba was a sturdy little girl, and looked so much like Zaira. She had the same wavy chestnut hair, the same grey-green eyes, the same mannerisms, the same speech patterns, and even the same throaty laugh as her Mama.

Alba was learning how to speak in dialect. Zaira didn't want her to forget her roots:

'We say "*ga*", not "*ha*."'

Delicate Fabio was much more highly strung, a mollycoddled boy, treated as the aristocratic heir. Yet Alba was his only passion. Her interests were his interests. He was always trying to kiss her and already talking about marrying her when they were grown up. And he was not even three years old.

'Me, I'm going to marry Alba when I'm big, yes I am,' he constantly said to anyone who'd listen. Everyone always laughed at this as if he'd said it for the first time. Nobody was much worried, except Zaira.

'They don't know they're brother and sister. What would

happen if they did fall in love when they were older? They should be told that they are brother and sister.' She constantly nagged Leonardo about this.

She longed to hug Fabio and caress him like a mother, and tell him the truth. She was affectionate with him, but not in the same way as she was with Alba. She and Alba did everything together: they slept in adjoining rooms, ate together, went shopping and for walks together. Alba could twist her mother round her little finger. There was a game she liked to play:

'Mama, if you say you love me it means you hate me, and if you say you hate me it means you love me, so what do you say?'

'I hate you, *tesoro.*'

'Oh no, Mama hates me,' and Alba would pretend to cry.

'No, I love you!'

'That means you hate me! Boo hoo...'

They played this game a lot and Zaira could never win. And they always ended up laughing and having a cuddle.

Zaira was rather over-protective with her daughter, and quite jealous when Alba went out with Leonardo on her own. Leonardo tried to soothe her:

'Zaira, this is not like you, such a worried mother these days. You must change your attitude. Let me enjoy the girl. She is my daughter as well.'

When the twins were five, Leonardo arranged for a tutor from Parma to come and live at the house.

Alba was very quick to learn, whereas Fabio was always in a dream. He could work if he applied himself, but he found concentration very difficult. He was always prodding Alba, or trying to tickle her, while she shooed him away and told him to be quiet.

'Fabio, Fabio, stop it!'

Alba loved having a tutor. She held her pen in her mouth to

concentrate better, and was fascinated by what the young Signor Manzi told them about how to form letters on a page. Fabio too put his pen in his mouth and tried to listen as intently as his sister, but soon his mind was on other things. Signor Manzi could see that Alba was brighter than her brother and as beautiful as her mother. He had been quietly in love with Zaira from the minute he saw her.

The twins were not always so loving, and like any other normal children they enjoyed playing more violent games together. When there was snow on the ground they engaged in massive snowball fights and Fabio was a surprisingly good shot, always managing to hit Alba straight between the eyes.

Once Fabio locked his sister in the bathroom after a long, complicated argument, and it was only Guerrino who persuaded him to let her out. When Alba got out, she was so mad she chased her brother all over the house. She finally managed to pin Fabio down, and she stuffed his mouth with some soap she had taken from the bathroom. Fabio started to cry hysterically and Alba was filled with remorse. She made him drink and then spit out lots of water, and then she kissed his face all over, and they were friends again.

Alba was very good at making up plays and used to boss Fabio around, making him page to her queen, or patient to her doctor. She was always a doctor, never a nurse, which greatly amused Zaira. Alba had a vivid imagination that was fired by some of the stories Zaira told her, stories she had either read herself or that Elena had narrated. Alba's favourite was about two very poor stepsisters: Rosalba and Rosanna. She used to ask her mother to tell it to her again and again, and then she would discuss the story with Fabio when they played together in the nursery.

'Rosalba is good. I'm Alba, so I will be Rosalba. You can be Rosanna. She's naughty,' she told Fabio. Sometimes the two children would sit at Zaira's knee while she told the old story. She was not sure where she had heard it first, or where the story came from:

Once upon a time there were two stepsisters called Rosalba and Rosanna. Rosalba was industrious and did all the housework, while Rosanna was lazy and always bored. One day Rosalba is walking down the garden and falls down a disused well. When she lands on her feet she sees that she has entered a completely different underground world. It is strange-looking but it has blue sky and green grass and trees just here. In front of her is a yellow-bricked pathway so she walks along it. First she comes to a commonplace-looking stove, but the stove is jumping up and down and can speak. It's saying: 'Help me, help me, take out my cakes, they are burning.' Maybe in this underground world it is normal for stoves to speak, Rosalba thinks to herself. So she runs over to the stove and takes out all the little cakes inside the oven door and stops them from burning.

'Thank you, thank you,' cries the stove.

She carries on walking and comes across a sheep so full of wool she cannot move. 'Please, please, shear off my wool!' So Rosalba, not surprised to hear a sheep talking (if an oven can speak, why not a sheep?), takes up some shears she sees lying in the grass and shears off all the sheep's wool.

'Thank you, thank you,' cries the sheep.

The next thing she sees is a tree laden with golden apples. The tree is so full its branches are bending. She is not surprised when the tree starts crying, 'Please, please shake off my apples. I can't bear the weight of them any longer.' So Rosalba shakes the tree and all the apples fall off.

'Thank you, thank you,' cries the apple tree.

She has now reached the end of the path, and in front of her is a beautiful woman with flowing black hair, dressed in a long white muslin gown. In her hands she is holding two boxes. The woman speaks to Rosalba, 'Thank you so much for helping. Please choose one of these boxes as a thank-you present. Rosalba cannot decide between the plain white cotton box tied with a single white silk ribbon, or the beautifully decorated red box, encrusted with lace and silver threads, and tied with elaborate red silk ribbons. In the end she chooses the white box, because she thinks the other might be a bit too fancy. And when she opens it up it is full of the most wondrous jewels: diamond rings, gold earrings; bracelets made of rubies or sapphires; pearl necklaces and lots of gold and silver chains. When Rosalba returns to her own world above the well, she is covered from head to foot in these beautiful jewels. She is very happy. She can sell the jewels and her family will no longer be poor. But Rosanna is mad with jealousy. She hates her sister's good fortune – she wants the jewels for herself and forces Rosalba to tell her where they came from.

So she too slides down the well. When she comes to the stove screaming for its cakes to be taken out, she tosses her head and ignores it. 'Why take any notice of a stupid stove that talks?' she thinks to herself. When the sheep asks to be sheared, she just laughs. 'Stupid sheep!' she exclaims. And when she hears the apple tree crying, she shrugs her shoulders, as much as to say, 'Too bad.' When she encounters the lady at the end of the pathway holding out the two boxes, she is immediately attracted to the sumptuous red one. She opens it furiously without even waiting to hear what the lady is saying, and inside it is full of writhing snakes and worms, crawling beetles and centipedes and lots of hairy spiders that start to crawl all over her. She screams and falls down dead on the ground.'

Alba started tickling Fabio, pretending he was covered in lots of creepy-crawlies.

'That's enough now, Alba, please,' chided Zaira.

Zaira felt rather sorry for the bad sister, Rosanna.

She tried to explain her interpretation of it to the children:

'Rosanna had to be bad in order for her sister to be seen as good. Good and evil cannot always be separated. It's as if both exist side by side. In life it is difficult always to do the right thing.' But these thoughts were lost on her children. Alba and Fabio just loved the story so much, she told it again and again.

Zaira knew that the children would have to be told that they were twins sooner or later. As she had thought many times, it was possible that Fabio could fall in love with Alba. Then he would have to be told that she was his sister and it would break his heart.

'He's so sensitive, so fragile, he may never recover,' Zaira worried to herself.

She had never properly discussed it with Leonardo – he just wouldn't listen. But the time would come when the children would have to know the truth. She had heard some people calling her a *'puttana'* – prostitute, or *'troia'* – trollop, a couple of times when she was shopping in Tortello market quite soon after she had returned to Bertini. So now would she also be charged with having incestuous sweethearts for children?

22. **The Masked Ball**

However, things continued as usual at Bertini. The three adults and the two children lived in relative harmony and even the servants had accepted the rather unconventional household.

The routine pattern of their daily existence was very well established. Sometimes Zaira would have loved to do something entirely different, but there was so much to do in the house and with the children, she didn't have much spare time. She and Livietta still planned the menus, and generally ran the house together. As a rule, married women had no idea where money came from. And although they did not know much about Leonardo's business affairs, the estate, with careful management by Zaira and Livietta, had now been restored to its former prosperity. The general finances were in relatively good health and the profit and loss accounts always balanced.

It was only in Leonardo's personal business affairs that matters were less than rosy. The car factory was struggling, and when the Contessa died in 1906, Leonardo found it difficult to maintain her interests in the steel industry. He was pouring more and more of his aunt's money into the car business.

Cars were still his main passion, and Leonardo often took

Zaira out in his motor car, a new and faster model every year. She enjoyed the speed as they hurtled through the landscape, the wind blowing in her face, the thrill of going round hairpin bends. Sometimes Alba accompanied them, but Livietta forbade Fabio to go for car rides.

'It's dangerous. He might catch cold. I don't want him to inhale the naphtha fumes.'

Zaira would have liked to tell her she was being silly, but just as Livietta was over-protective with Fabio, she was the same with Alba – emotionally, that was, rather than physically. And she didn't feel she had the right to interfere. She had relinquished that right soon after Fabio was born, when Leonardo had taken her son from her arms.

Zaira was increasingly moody, sometimes lashing out at Leonardo when he was trying to soothe her. Once he told her she was being stupid, and she burst out crying, hitting out at his chest with her fists.

Leonardo could tell that Zaira was not as happy with their life as he was. Strange how things had changed: he who had been so restless was now quite content, and it was she he worried about. Sometimes she was a little sad.

'Darling Zaira, what's the matter with you? You used to be so vivacious once, always laughing and joking.'

He wanted to cheer her up, to make her enjoy herself again. He spontaneously decided to throw a carnival masked ball on the Saturday evening before the start of Lent on Ash Wednesday.

This was something he had never done before. They did entertain occasionally, but not very lavishly. Some of the neighbouring families still came to Bertini, but more usually they had dinner with a few of Leonardo's friends from Milan. This would be different: more ambitious, and more spectacular.

The friends and neighbours who visited Bertini had grown

to accept the *ménage à trois*. It was incredibly civilised and 'that young widow is excruciatingly attractive – who wouldn't be tempted?' was the local gentry's opinion.

Leonardo decided that all the stops should be pulled out for the ball. He ordered champagne from Reims and asked a thrilled Rodolfo to organise the rest of the wine. He was getting caterers in from Milan for the food, and an orchestra from Piacenza. Livietta and Zaira were put in charge of arranging the decorations. The outside of the manor house was going to be lit up with thousands of tiny white candles. They also had to choose their own costumes and had great fun searching through old books in the library. They finally decided what they would wear, and Livietta ordered the relevant materials and was busy sewing up their costumes.

'Zaira, we are going to surprise everybody with our originality!' said Livietta very animatedly.

Zaira was less enthusiastic. 'Do you think my costume will look too daring?'

'No, of course not.'

Leonardo just didn't have the time to think about his costume – the car factory was all-consuming – so he decided to go as Harlequin – *Arlecchino,* as was the family custom. The traditional Harlequin was a nimble and wily servant but Leonardo's version was much more elegant.

On the night of the ball he would be dressed in an all-in-one silvery white and black diamond-patterned costume (rather than multicoloured), a pointed sequinned hat and white stockings with pointed white shoes. With his black mask covering half his face he would be almost unrecognisable.

Livietta had decided that Fabio would stay with her parents for the night at Castellengo. His grandmother Rina was getting over another cold – she had never really recovered from her bout of pleurisy – so she and Rodolfo had decided that they would rather look after their beloved grandson than attend the ball.

They were, however, delighted that Livietta seemed so happy about holding a ball at Bertini. Usually she would have run a mile from attending a dance, let alone organising one. They had been so worried about their daughter in the early months of her marriage but since Fabio had been born, she had changed so much. She was more confident now, and she and Leonardo were getting on quite well together.

Nonetheless, they were more wary of Zaira. They could not make her out and were not quite sure how she fitted into the household. Rodolfo had heard talk of her being a distant relative of theirs, but he had never heard of her before she arrived at Bertini. And her circumstances had changed so much – she was a proper lady now, almost on par with their beloved daughter.

However, they were pleased that she and Livietta were such good friends and, out of loyalty to their daughter, refused to listen to any of the gossip about Zaira.

As far as the ball was concerned, Zaira was enchanted by Leonardo's idea, and that he was doing it for her sake. She was still slightly worried about her costume but was genuinely gratified that he was making so much effort for her.

'It's about time we had a ball here, and I thought it would cheer you up.'

'Thank you, my love.' It was at moments like these that she knew he did really care for her and she loved him for it.

She had promised Alba that she could take a peek at the guests in all their different costumes, 'but you must be very quiet, and you must promise to go to bed when Guerrino and Lili, your nursemaid, tell you it is time.'

On the night of the ball, Alba stood at the top of the marble stairs trying to guess who everybody was, but she could not recognise anybody.

'Where is Mama? She hasn't even come down yet, nor has Aunt Livietta.'

But she thought she recognised Tino, her name for Leonardo. She was sure he was that tall figure in the harlequin suit:

'Yes it must be him!'

Leonardo could see that the ball was a tremendous success and the ground floor of the house was as crowded as the days when Leonardo's parents were alive. People started dancing mazurkas in the ballroom almost as soon as they arrived. Others were getting quite drunk, making the most of it before Lent began. It was rare for such an event to be held at Bertini in recent times, so they were intent on enjoying themselves. Leonardo had invited everyone he could think of, not just the gentry but also the estate workers from both Bertini and Castellengo, and some of the locals who frequented the bars at Tortello. Even his old professor friend from Piacenza, Giorgio Zerbini, had accepted the invitation. He looked so different in his Chinese mandarin outfit, with his long white hair tied in a pigtail at his back.

Livietta had chosen all the music and the orchestra played divinely. The ball had been going on for about an hour and there was still no sign of either Livietta or Zaira.

'Where are they both?' people were beginning to ask and Leonardo himself was glancing up at the stairs wondering what had happened to them.

'Women! It always takes them hours to get ready. Obviously even longer when it's fancy dress!' he remarked to one of his Milanese cronies.

At that moment a masked couple descended the marble staircase, a young man and woman. Professor Giorgio Zerbini gasped: he could not take his eyes off the young man.

The woman was Livietta. She was dressed as a Spanish flamenco dancer in a tight-fitting red silk costume, low-waisted and layered in red ruffles, all trimmed in black. She wore a high, stiff-backed, black mantilla on her head, and red tap shoes on her feet, and held a huge black lace fan to shield her face, even though she was wearing a tiny eye-mask. And Zaira had even persuaded her to wear rouge on her cheeks.

'She looks quite charming,' thought Leonardo, but it was as if he were looking at his sister rather than his wife.

But who was the person holding her arm?

'Is it a young man?' Leonardo peered at the tall, graceful figure, dressed as a Spanish matador, but because of his mask it was difficult to see that well.

Alba looked at the boyish figure and was very pleased with herself when she recognised who it was:

'It's Mama!' she said out loud.

At this point Guerrino decided it was time for her to go to bed.

'My God, it must be Zaira!' Leonardo thought at virtually the same time as his daughter, but he was still not one hundred per cent sure. For a minute he had thought she was indeed a handsome young man.

But no, now he could see her flattened breasts pushing out against her tight jacket. He recognised her as she came towards him down the stairs.

'It is Zaira!'

Her hair was tightly drawn back from her masked face and was hidden by a black shiny matador hat. She was dressed in a sky-blue brocade bolero jacket adorned with gold epaulettes, a white silk shirt and a thin black tie, and her legs were encased in three-quarter-length blue satin trousers and white stockings. On her feet she wore Cuban-heeled black patent leather pumps.

The trousers were very tight and showed off her slender long legs and her boyish but rounded bottom. Livietta had sewn hundreds of dangling glass beads onto the brocaded bolero and the myriad lights from the new electric chandelier hanging from the hall ceiling were all minutely reflected in the jacket as Zaira walked down the stairs.

She looked dazzling. People were simultaneously dazzled by her and the halo of light surrounding her.

'So different from the young country girl who first arrived at the house, and such a slender figure for someone who's given birth to twins,' thought Leonardo as he felt a quickening of his breath, and a movement in his groin.

He walked up to her, grabbed her by the arm and pulled her through the open doors to the ballroom. For a second, Zaira thought he was angry: annoyed by her outrageous costume. They started to dance, a waltz, and she knew he wasn't angry. Far from it. He whispered something she didn't quite hear, but guessed it was something suggestive, and he held her tighter.

It was the first time they had ever danced like this in public. They had danced at night, silently, in Zaira's apartments, just fooling around, but never like this with a full orchestra and with everyone watching them. Even the more drunken members of the crowd in the ballroom stared at them.

'Who are *they*?' Their masks hid their identities well. Some people thought they recognised Leonardo, looking slightly ill at ease in his harlequin suit.

'He's obviously not dancing with his wife.'

'But who is he dancing with?'

'He/she is far too tall for Livietta.'

'Is it male or female?'

'It's the widow, yes it is!'

'No it can't be, not dressed like a man!'

Zaira's jacket shimmered as she danced, the glass beads twinkling from both the electric lights and the multitudinous arrangements of candles glowing in the ballroom.

Livietta had never been jealous of the relationship between Zaira and Leonardo. She was glad they had each other. After all, it had let her off the hook.

And she too was mesmerised by their dancing: she nearly as tall as him, both so graceful, their white-stockinged feet in perfect step, their passion for each other obvious.

Leonardo held Zaira as close to him as he could, not saying anything now, savouring the moment intently, feeling her flattened breasts against his chest. They danced around and around, to the music of Johann Strauss. Zaira felt as if she was floating, but her harlequin was holding her tighter and tighter. His lips were touching hers.

'Leonardo, everyone is watching us!' she whispered.

'I don't care.'

After dinner had been served and the music finally ended, Leonardo bade farewell, rather impatiently it seemed, to all his guests. They left the house either on foot, by horse and carriage, cart, or motor car, all saying what a wonderful ball it had been. One of the old shopkeepers from Tortello muttered on the way out:

Donna bella e vein bon
Fann di amis da rason.
A beautiful woman and good wine
Give you many friends.

Leonardo hurried to Zaira's apartments as quickly as he could. Livietta had already retired but Zaira was awake, waiting for her lover. She knew he would come. She was still dressed in her matador suit. They embraced impatiently as if they hadn't seen each other in months.

Only when they made love did she feel truly his equal, his match. Though she lived in an odd, unconventional set-up, she knew she was fortunate. After all her reservations, he had been right to make her stay here at Bertini.

Zaira had always declared to Leonardo that after the birth of the twins she didn't want any more children. She loved her children dearly. Giving birth to them was a wonderful experience but she had no wish to repeat it. Besides, it would have been impractical.

'How could we explain away further children? Another marriage? Another widowhood?'

Leonardo agreed with her.

Sometimes he got rubber things from Milan, prophylactics they were called. He had also shown Zaira what his actress friends used to do: how they inserted sponges soaked in vinegar deep inside them. But Zaira had found this very unsatisfactory.

Yet somehow she never did become pregnant again.

23. **Livietta**

Every day the children went riding with Leonardo. Alba had a chestnut filly, born of Leonardo's favourite old mare. Fabio too proved to be a competent rider, looking straight and graceful on his dapple-grey mare. There was a ridge they often rode up, beyond Tortello. It went over Monte Ludo, over five hundred metres high, up with the track leading from Tortello to Lunano. One could see the entire Po Valley from here. Leonardo would point out various things to his children: the city of Parma to the south, and Piacenza and beyond to the north; the quartz in the rocks, the broom on the ground, and the swallows flying overhead.

Leonardo was a good father to both his children. Even though he had invested a lot of energy in Fabio, it was Alba who was the most rewarding, most intelligent, most entertaining. It was obvious to everyone that Alba was the more confident of the two, and very like Zaira. The boy and girl were quite different in looks and as Fabio grew older he looked, strangely enough, more and more like Livietta. No one ever doubted that he was her son. He had the same long nose, the same darting look, like a timid deer.

The family spent most of their time in Bertini, but Leonardo now also owned the Contessa's houses in Tortello and Portofino, and an apartment at Salsomaggiore. This was the spa town with its fake-Chinese-design thermal building decorated in the Liberty Style, where the entire family took the waters. At least twice a year they went to the sea, sometimes to Portofino, or occasionally to the nearest town on the Mediterranean coast, Chiavari, or to San Remo further north, or to Rimini on the Adriatic coast to stay at the new Grand Hotel.

Before these trips, Zaira had never swum in the sea, but she now loved it and enthusiastically taught both children to swim. Alba was quite fearless in the water, and even Fabio learnt to dive from quite a great height. Livietta sometimes couldn't bear to watch her son, but Leonardo tried to reassure her:

'Don't worry, *Merlina*, at least now he won't ever drown!'

Sometimes they visited the Dolomites, where Leonardo taught Zaira and the children how to ski. Zaira never did quite master the art, and always felt clumsy with all her winter clothing on and the heavy skis attached to her boots, but she loved tobogganing with the children instead.

She loved speeding down the slopes, especially when they all ended up entwined together. She and her twin babies. This was when she felt closest to Fabio – the thrill of feeling him physically in the snow. She found the snow both comforting and exhilarating. It reminded her of Torretta.

When Fabio was covered in snow, she loved to brush it away from the long, dark hair peeping out of his woolly hat. Once, after she had done this, he stroked her face and said to her:

'Zaira, thank you, my pretty Zaira.' She was deeply touched by this.

Livietta preferred to sit and watch the children at their sporting activities. And after these excursions, they were all quite happy to return to Bertini.

Occasionally, Livietta and Fabio went to stay at Castellengo, where her parents never missed an opportunity to spoil their little grandson as much as they could, something they dared not do in front of their son-in-law.

Leonardo had rather fixed opinions about how to bring up children, and was quite strict with his son. He was trying not to spoil him the way he and Claudio had been spoilt. Fabio was quite whimsical and faint-hearted, so his father often chided him or reminded him of the fact that he would be a man someday.

'Fabio, keep your back straight when you are eating,' or 'Fabio, don't fidget like that.' Then, 'Fabio, your shoelaces are untied. How many times must I tell you to keep your shoelaces tied!'

He taught him fencing, but Fabio had no aptitude for it. He wasn't interested in the things his father thought he should be. He didn't like cars and he cried when he saw the poor dead animals his father had killed after a hunting expedition. He refused to eat rabbit – always.

'I think of them with their fur on, with their bobtails, their timid eyes. How can I eat them?'

Leonardo wanted his son to grow up to be a strong and independent character, but poor little Fabio was not quite sure how to act in front of his father. Whatever he did was never right. He much preferred being with Livietta. So when Livietta and her parents had him to themselves at Castellengo, they liked to overindulge him. They let him pull the rope in the chapel and he did it again, and again, just as Livietta had always done before she got married.

Zaira also liked to fuss over Fabio when she had the chance. One day he got a piece of grit in his eye, and the poor thing was getting very agitated. Livietta was out of the room, and only she and Leonardo were there. Leonardo told him to stop fussing, but Zaira remembered something Leonora, her *Nonna*, used to do a

long time ago in Torretta. She pulled Fabio's eyelid open and shut
a few times, muttering an incantation:

Busca fúra, o indrez'
Che command è San Lorenz
San Lorenz e San Petrocch
Tira búsca fur dall'öcch.

This was a prayer to San Lorenzo. His feast day was 10th
August, when many shooting stars could be seen in the night sky.
The shooting stars were supposed to be the tears running from the
saint's eyes. It was the custom, therefore, to pray to the saint about
eye troubles.

When Leonardo heard her saying this in her rather unmusical
voice, he said in his usual amused way: 'Oh stop it, Zaira, all that
peasant rubbish won't do any good!' But in fact, quite soon after,
Fabio's eye stopped watering and the piece of grit disappeared.

'Thank you, Zaira,' he said rather formally. Zaira longed to
hug him to her but instead she just ruffled his hair.

'I know it's an old wife's tale, but it seems to work,' she said,
making a face at Leonardo.

When Livietta was away, Leonardo, Zaira and Alba quite
naturally adapted to being a little family unit – just the three
of them together. Alba still did not know that Leonardo was her
natural father, but 'Tino' was the only father figure she had, and
he had always treated her like his daughter. Zaira also called him
Tino sometimes, and used to tease him:

'Hello there, you old vat of wine.'

She even remembered it being mentioned in the gospel
somewhere, when she had attended church regularly every
Sunday at Sant'Antonio – something about a father's vines and his
sons who neglected them.

'Tino, *Santo Vino*,' she called him.

When Alba saw her Mama and Tino alone together, she

intuitively guessed there was some great bond between them. He was not like this with her Aunt Livietta. Once, when just the three of them were in the house, Leonardo grabbed Zaira by the arm very tightly. Alba thought he was going to admonish her Mama, but instead he kissed her passionately on the lips. Alba never forgot that moment. It was her first vivid memory of sexual love between two people. When Livietta and Fabio were away, Leonardo frequently slept in Zaira's private apartments. Alba slept next door to her mother and she often climbed into bed with them both. In the mornings, Leonardo tossed her high into the air and caught her on the bed, and then Zaira played the more gentle 'castles' with her, allowing her knees to collapse in a heap with Alba on top of them. Alba loved playing these games, and somehow she knew not to tell Fabio about them. It was her one secret from him. Yet she became used to seeing her Mama and Tino together in bed like this, and because she had never known anything else, she didn't think much about it.

*

With the passing of the years Zaira had grown more accustomed to the family set-up, and was less unhappy, less restless than before. She loved her children, Leonardo, and even dear Livietta, with all her heart. Yet she also feared this complacency. She had learnt that life could be cruel: things did not last for ever. Politically, Italy was quite stable but was still a babe in arms compared to the now-dominant powers of the United States, Japan, France, Russia and Britain. Italy had joined the Triple Alliance with Germany and Austria almost a decade before but its role was becoming increasingly ambiguous.

When the children were ten years of age, Livietta had a very severe attack of influenza. She had always been delicate and she fell seriously ill.

Livietta wanted to ensure primarily that Fabio wouldn't catch the same illness. As his mother she wanted to protect him from all evil, and she refused to let anyone tell him how ill she was. She had never been very strong and the illness was very serious. All her thoughts went towards protecting Fabio.

'Please, please don't let him come near me,' she implored everyone.

She was so intent on preventing his getting ill that she neglected herself, and after five days confined to bed, she died quite suddenly. Because Fabio had never been allowed into her bedroom while she was unwell, when he saw his mother dead the poor boy couldn't understand what had happened.

She was very emaciated, as she had stopped eating as soon as she caught the 'flu. She looked so tiny, like a doll. Her eyes were still open, looking upwards – 'Towards heaven,' Guerrino told him.

'Why has Mama gone?'

Nobody could give him a satisfactory answer.

The family and the servants were bereft. Livietta had always been such a sweet and gentle person. Nobody could ever have wished anything bad to happen to her.

Fabio was inconsolable, and cried and cried for his Mama. Leonardo was also genuinely upset. He had grown to admire Livietta's calm, orderly ways and acceptance of their unusual life together. Zaira had lost a true friend, and she and Leonardo had several Masses said for her and lit many candles. Neither of them were religious and they had not kept up their Catholic faith. It would have been hypocritical of them to go to the church in Tortello, but Livietta had always attended regularly, taking both the children to Mass every Sunday wherever they were. She would have appreciated all the religious rites available at her death, so Leonardo and Livietta did it for her sake.

Livietta's distraught parents arranged for her to be buried at Castellengo and the funeral service was held in her beloved chapel. Zaira remembered Livietta recounting how she used to ring the chapel bell. At the funeral Zaira looked at the simple piece of rope hanging through a hole in the ceiling, and imagined a young Livietta performing her duty so seriously, so lovingly. She knew that Fabio loved to do the same thing.

After the funeral, where Leonardo had dutifully performed his role as widowed husband and bereft son-in-law, he said goodbye to his parents-in-law.

'Dear ones, this is all so sad. But I know Livietta would be distressed if Fabio did not come and see his grandparents at the Azienda. So it will be arranged for him to continue his visits here. Guerrino can accompany him.'

Rodolfo and his wife Rina were extremely happy that Leonardo was being accommodating. They were never quite sure with him: he could have refused to let Fabio come and see them. They knew he might have been difficult and stopped all contact.

And they continued to ignore the rumours about Leonardo and Zaira or, more likely, they refused to believe them. Livietta had always been so fond of Zaira; she had talked about her as if they were sisters. No, the rumours were all lies, and besides, they were too occupied thinking about poor little Fabio.

'How tragic for him, losing his beloved Mama at such a young age,' people whispered. And how tragic for the grief-stricken grandparents to lose their only daughter. Fabio was their only consolation.

Zaira found herself in an intolerable position. As his 'biological' mother she longed to console the boy. She wanted to tell him how she grew up, as a motherless girl, in Torretta where his uncles still lived. She wanted to tell him so much, but poor Fabio had always thought that Livietta was his mother. How could she make him accept anything else?

Leonardo assumed that he and Zaira would marry eventually.

Zaira, after all these years, had never thought about it again. They were married already as far as she was concerned. She knew now that Leonardo really loved her. Why had she ever thought him so cool and calculating? Underneath that exterior he had cultivated, he was so considerate, so loving. He took genuine delight in both his children, was proud of them and proud of their mother. Sometimes he was even jealous. He didn't like the way men, especially the tutor, looked at her. He thought the tutor was besotted with her:

'His dull, watery eyes follow you around like those of a doting puppy,' he teased her.

This was a slight exaggeration but the infatuated young man did admire both her beauty and her mind. She was still full of curiosity about what was happening in Italy, still loved reading, and had made quite good progress working her way through the books in the library. She still wrote a little – poems, short stories – and had an article about women's rights published in the local newspaper, anonymously of course.

Leonardo could see that Zaira was reluctant to talk about marriage.

'Leonardo, marriage is the last thing on my mind just now.' He thought that it was because she was thinking of Livietta, but after some months had passed, he pressed her.

'Zaira, we must discuss the future. We can now be man and wife in the eyes of the world. Isn't this what you have always wanted?'

Zaira looked at him with her eyes half-closed, and remembered those harsh words of his, such a long time ago now. She was a 'silly little peasant', and even if he wasn't married to Livietta, he would never marry her. He had said later that he didn't mean it, but she had never forgotten, nonetheless.

'Leonardo, I don't know. It's too soon. We must respect Livietta's memory, and her parents, and Fabio too,' she murmured.

Leonardo decided to wait another month and then brought it up again. 'It's been ten months. Surely we should discuss getting married now. Everyone is expecting us to, in any case.'

'Leonardo, before we get married we should tell the children the truth. They will have to know sooner or later. It will be their eleventh birthday soon. In no time, they will be reaching puberty. Fabio needs a mother. We have to tell him that I am his mother.'

'No,' replied Leonardo, 'he was very attached to Livietta. It will destroy him, he's so delicate. Why, I don't know what he'd do. We should let things stay as they are for a while. We will tell him after we're married. When he's used to the idea of us being married, he'll come round in the end.'

'But I am his mother. He needs me now – I will console him. We cannot get married until we tell them.'

Leonardo knew how stubborn Zaira could be, so he decided to leave it for a while. But she continued to be insistent. She wanted to tell them the truth on their birthday. Leonardo finally, reluctantly, agreed.

'Leonardo, you must be the one. You must do it. You must talk to both of them together, and I will stand at your side.'

Leonardo was still not sure whether he was doing the right thing or not, but on the morning of their birthdays he called the children down to the main drawing room. The tutor had been given the day off, and the children had been told they were free to do as they wished that day. They were not sure why. Alba knew it was her birthday that day. Fabio, however, had always been told his birthday was one week earlier. Livietta had insisted: she had wanted him to have a birthday all to himself, and people would have gossiped about them having the same birthday. Yet no one ever thought they looked like brother and sister, let alone twins.

Even the gossips that speculated about their relationship admitted:

'They are not physically alike at all – she is quite sturdy and has chestnut hair and green eyes, and he is very dark and thin.'

When the children appeared in the drawing room, they were hand-in-hand, as usual. Alba looked quite grown-up, her chestnut hair drawn back severely in numerous plaits. She was trying to look serious, while beside her the dark-haired Fabio was looking nervous. He couldn't stop fidgeting, and was pulling at Alba's ear. Leonardo started to speak:

'Fabio, stop that and stand still. I want to talk to you both. Zaira and I have something to tell you. It is very difficult to say, but Zaira and, eh, I think now is the time to tell you. As you know, today is the 29th July, Alba's birthday. Well, it's your birthday too, Fabio. Yes, you and Alba were born on the same day, but Mama always insisted that you, Fabio, celebrate your birthday on 22nd July – you know, the feast of St Mary Magdalene.'

He was deliberately not coming to the point. He coughed sheepishly.

'The thing is, Fabio,' Leonardo took his son's hand in his, 'you and Alba are brother and sister. I am the father of you both, and Zaira is the mother of you, eh, both.'

Leonardo, who usually took everything in his stride, had made the most difficult speech of his life. He took a deep breath and exhaled: after all these years, the truth was finally revealed to his children. He also took Alba's hand in his. 'Alba and Fabio, my dear children.'

He looked at Zaira, raising his eyebrows, as much as to say, 'And now what?'

All Zaira's attention was on Fabio, but she knew that Alba would be shocked too. Although Zaira and Alba were extremely close, Zaira had never told her Leonardo was her father. Zaira had kept up the deceit about her dead soldier husband. On the rare occasions that Alba had asked about her father, Zaira had been deliberately vague, saying they hadn't known each other long – it was love at first sight. And then she would say, 'Tino is more like a father to you now.' Zaira and Leonardo had long ago decided that Alba should call him 'Tino', his brother Claudio's nickname for him. Alba had been told that Zaira was a relative of Livietta's. Well, that was true. After all, they must have been fourth or fifth cousins!

Alba had always treated Leonardo like a father, and vice versa, in all but name, so Alba had already accepted him in a paternal role.

'And dearest Fabio and I are brother and sister!' She thought that it was wonderful news.

In the meantime, Zaira tried to join in the family hand-holding but Fabio wouldn't let her. He couldn't face up to the truth that had just been revealed to him.

'No,' he shrieked. He brushed away Zaira's hand and rushed out of the room. Zaira ran out after him. He hurried to his bedroom and lay down on his bed, sobbing hysterically, hitting his fists on the sheets.

'Darling, shush, shush, everything will be all right. I am here, your one true mother.'

'No... it's ... not ... true, it's ... not ... true, my ... mama ... is ... dead.'

He uttered each word between his sobs. Zaira realised now that she may have been too hasty. He was delicate and very highly strung.

'Get out of this room. You're not my mother, you're not my mother, nooohhhh,' he shouted with great determination.

As the days went by, Fabio refused to come down from his bedroom. Zaira knocked on his door constantly but he always shouted at her to go away. He agreed to see Leonardo, albeit reluctantly. He hadn't forgiven his father for his revelations. Leonardo tried to explain what had happened between him and Zaira, but Fabio was still young for his age and could not understand. If his father had been married to Livietta, then why wasn't he her son? It was all so impossible.

'You and Mama were married, so I am your son. How can Zaira be my mother?'

One day, Zaira decided she had to see Fabio. He still hadn't left his room. He wouldn't eat, wouldn't sleep. He was tormenting himself, going over and over it. Even Alba could not console him. The house was gloomy, even worse than when Livietta had died. Zaira was extremely worried about Fabio. A boy like him, with a delicate constitution, could get ill, could die. She entered his room, without knocking this time.

'Fabio, my son, please listen to me.'

'Go away, I tell you, go away. You are not my mother, you are a peasant, a filthy peasant,' he said through gritted teeth. 'How could you be my mother?'

Zaira was astounded; she had never heard him talk like this. She sighed deeply, and realised it was hopeless. She would not be able to reach him, make him understand how much she loved him.

Zaira could not cope with the situation she herself had created. She had ruined everything. She had upset the equilibrium of the once settled and safe atmosphere of the house. If only Livietta had not died. Things would never be the same. Maybe Leonardo had been right – this pretence he had concocted had been the only solution. How else would she have managed to bring up two children on her own, without Leonardo's protection, and now – what now? She couldn't bear to see Fabio suffering so much. She should have continued with the deception. She had been selfish; it was for her own sake that she had wanted the children to know. She had been thinking only of herself, not of Fabio.

She knew Alba would be understanding; she and Leonardo were so close: 'Tino this,' 'Tino that.' It was as if, unconsciously, Alba had known he was her father all along. Mother and daughter had spoken about this in the last few days. 'Well, Mama, Tino has always been like a father to me, so I don't think things have really changed, have they?' Alba said wisely.

'Such mature thoughts for a child of her age,' thought Zaira.

Alba admired her mother, her struggles, and the way she had managed to escape the drudgery of what would have been her life in Torretta. Zaira told her daughter about her time in Milan, the way she had met the Contessa. They laughed about it together. The Contessa was dead now, but Alba still remembered her, how superior she was. 'I can just see her waving her stick around.'

Then, recently, Zaira had recounted her first meeting with Leonardo:

'There was obviously a strong mutual attraction between us which has never been broken,' she now repeated often to her daughter, never quite believing how it had all happened. How, after all these years, that bond between them was still so tangible even Alba noticed it.

'And even the Contessa acknowledged it and accepted it,' thought Alba to herself.

Alba was both shocked and perturbed by Fabio's reaction to the revelations. She was so happy he was her true brother; he had always been like a brother for her. But why did he reject Mama? How could he? She was so worried. What would happen now?

When a sobbing Zaira had fled her son's room, she had rushed to her daughter. She told Alba what Fabio had said to her, and now it was Alba who was the strong one, the daughter consoling the desperate mother.

'Mama, don't cry. He will come round. I'll talk to him.'

But Fabio would not listen even to Alba, his beloved Alba. He didn't want her as a sister. He had even thought that they might get married one day.

Alba did not know this what was Fabio was thinking. She continued to believe that he would change his mind eventually. What a mess it all was! She hoped that when she grew up women would not be put into such positions.

'Why all this pretence? Why couldn't Mama live as she wanted? she said to herself. 'Why do people always have to worry about what the servants think, what the neighbours think? It's all so ridiculous.'

Relations between Leonardo and Zaira were also strained. Leonardo blamed her for the whole unpleasant situation. He reminded her constantly that he hadn't wanted to tell the children the truth. 'You know the truth hurts sometimes, Zaira. We decided on this deception many years ago. I know Fabio was living a lie, but it was a happy lie.'

'But it was you who was so desperate to have a son. You didn't want your daughter, you wanted a male heir. You forced me to give him up, to let him be raised as Livietta's son.'

Zaira tried to throw the blame back to Leonardo, but she was half-hearted in her attack. She was so weary, drained by the way things had turned out, feeling extremely guilty now...

'What else could I have done? I should have divorced Livietta, should I? I know things are changing here in Italy, at long last, but divorce – hah! – that's going to take a while. Do you remember that petition by the Bishop of Piacenza in 1902 when Parliament tried to introduce a new law? The Catholic Church will never allow divorce – the sanctity of marriage is part of our religion, nothing to do with politics.

'Can't you see? This was the best solution. Everyone was

happy. You were able to live here, with both your children, and Livietta and I had a recognised heir. That was the only reason I got married, to have an heir. And now *we* can get married, Zaira.'

He said it almost impatiently and then paused, thinking to himself: 'Fabio, he will have to come round in time – I hope.'

Even Leonardo could not convince himself of this.

Zaira accepted that this intolerable predicament was her fault.

'So you are right as usual. We should have got married first and then told Fabio.'

Fabio would not tolerate his father marrying her now. He was hurt and terribly bitter. He would not accept their marriage.

'I can't marry you now. Our son won't let us,' said Zaira half painfully, half ironically.

And with that she left the room.

Leonardo blew his cheeks out:

'I've got to get out of the house.'

He went for a spin in his motor car, a new model from a company called Alfa (*Anonima Lombarda Fabbrica Automobile*), which his old friend Giuseppe Merosi had joined the year before. He drove as fast as he could. He was speeding so much around a hairpin bend he nearly lost control of the car. Then he suddenly encountered a herd of sheep on the road right in front of him. He tried braking, the car juddered and he swerved into a tree. The whole of the front of the car was ruined. He wasn't hurt himself but the accident stunned him.

'*Accidenti!*'

He banged his fist on the steering wheel. He loved every inch of that car, and look what damage he had done to it. He was surprised how angry he was, and he realised he was still furious … with Zaira. Because of her he had smashed up his car.

'That stupid, obstinate woman!'

There was no more talk of marriage. Fabio finally left his bedroom, and resumed his studies with the tutor. He and Alba gradually became friends again, and within days he was following her around, doing what she asked, taking part in the games she made up. However, with Zaira things had not improved. Relations had deteriorated even further with his mother.

'I hate her, I hate her,' he confided to Alba.

Alba didn't know what she could do. All she knew was her mother and brother would never be reconciled.

Zaira herself came to a decision. She would leave Bertini, maybe for good. She would take Alba back to Torretta. All this time, Zaira had not forgotten her brothers' promise to her about having a house in Torretta one day. She wrote to them to inform them that at long last she wanted to build that house.

At first, the brothers attempted to talk her out of it. Giovanni wrote a badly spelt letter trying to dissuade her, stating that, after all, there had never been a formal contract. But Zaira was insistent.

She wrote back: 'I want to return to Torretta with my daughter, and I want my own house there.' She even enlisted the help of her Uncle Franco, her father's brother in London. He wrote to his nephews saying they must honour what Bartolomeo would have wanted. Yes, it was unusual for a girl to have been left a third share of the land and property, rather than money only, but then again Zaira had nobly given up that third share to them. All she wanted was a house and garden – that was all.

The brothers reluctantly agreed that she could renovate one of the broken-down old farm buildings, rather than build a new house from scratch. Not the place she had wanted originally, near the bread oven, but in a good position nevertheless. The view from it was just as beautiful. She agreed and sent them money to rebuild the old, unused buildings.

When she told Leonardo her plans, he was furious. He

wanted to lash out at her, strike her across the face. Instead he controlled himself and said in his old cold, aloof manner:

'Zaira, you're out of your mind. You don't know what you're saying. You can't go back to your old life. You have changed utterly – you are no longer that young, naïve girl of long ago. You'll be bored to tears in a place like Torretta. And what about Alba? She cannot possibly want to live there.'

But he refused to beg her to stay – he wouldn't demean himself, and in any case he realised it would be useless. However, they would certainly have to come to some arrangement about Alba. No daughter of his would live in such a godforsaken place.

'I want to go back, go back to that simple existence I left so long ago. Deep inside myself I have missed it. Life was so uncomplicated then. I want Alba to see where her ancestors came from. I know Fabio may never see it now, but she must. She is a Crespi after all.'

Leonardo shrugged his shoulders. He would let her go. Maybe they needed some time apart, some space. Time for him and Fabio to re-establish some kind of stability, some routine, as it was before, when Livietta was still alive. He was tired of Zaira's wretchedness – it was exhausting him. He never knew how she would react. She could have married him, but no, she had to have it her way. He could not understand why she wouldn't marry him, but in spite of this he remained in love with her, still feeling her power over him. He had confided to one of his Milanese friends that he loved her because 'She is so different, so contrary. Any woman would have jumped at the chance to marry Leonardo Bertini, but no, not Zaira. Now she can marry me, she won't. Then again, she wanted to marry me when she couldn't!'

He sighed and shrugged again. 'Torretta, humph!

'All right, I will permit Alba to go there for a short stay in the summer, and then we have to decide about her schooling in the autumn.'

He was hoping that after not too long an interval, they could all get back together and start being a family again.

'Zaira, all I want is for us to be together. Your going to Torretta won't solve the problem of Fabio.'

24. **Torretta**

So Zaira and Alba travelled to Torretta. Leonardo had persuaded Zaira to let him take them himself in a horse and trap rather than by car. He didn't want to damage another Alfa on those unmade-up roads.

Alba was enchanted by the place, intrigued by its isolation and lack of modern conveniences. 'Are there really no bathrooms here, Mama?' But she loved the densely tree-covered mountains, the wild flowers, the huge variety of different-coloured butterflies, the songbirds, and at night the brilliant glittering stars and hundreds of fireflies flickering on and off in the darkness.

Alba was to stay for most of the summer in Torretta. After that her parents had finally agreed that she would attend a convent school in Piacenza on a weekly basis, and return to Bertini at weekends. Leonardo had assured Zaira that he would take Alba to Torretta for visits:

'Even though it will be a difficult and tiresome journey for us, I promise to get her there one way or other. But why, oh why, does her mother insist on living in the back of beyond?'

Sometimes he and Alba went on horseback, father and

daughter side by side, either cantering or trotting or, when the road got very steep, their horses treading very gingerly.

Fabio refused to go with them, and while his father and sister were away, he spent his time with Livietta's parents.

Leonardo was hoping that this would not go on for too long, that Zaira would return to her senses and come back down to Tortello.

Zaira was much more frustrated than she had realised she would be when she found herself back in Torretta. The barn/hayloft had been only partially restored. All that money she had sent back to her brothers – what had they done with it? She decided it needed much more work; it had to be thoroughly modernised. Over the months she was there she had electricity and a water closet installed, at great expense, by builders from Tortello. How could Alba live anywhere without facilities? Gradually the barn was transformed into a stonewalled house (the hayloft had been made into three separate bedrooms) and an extension was built for the kitchen and bathroom. Zaira then started to design a beautiful garden on the patch of land surrounding the barn. She was enjoying herself at long last: she loved to see the flowers grow so quickly and to see the trees bearing so much fruit in the now-flourishing old orchard.

This time Zaira was keen to get the converted house and land legally put in her name. Finally, after much cajoling, she persuaded her reluctant brothers that they should go to the notary to draw up a document that would sign everything over to her officially. Her brothers really didn't want to go. On top of everything else, they were now working in a cement factory near Lunano. The farm was barely profitable so they both needed a supplementary income. They rose very early in the morning, worked on the farm, went to the factory in the horse and cart, and returned in the evening to do some more work at home. It was a hard life, but luckily their wives continued to work on the farm as well as bringing up their children, so between them they kept the place going and were not as poor as some of their neighbours.

Zaira kept badgering them about going to the notary. She reminded them that Papa would have wanted it done properly. Her real motive, however, was to give herself some security. She had been beholden to Leonardo for so long, she wanted something that belonged to her, in her own right. Even if they married, she would still be classed as a man's property.

Her brothers were taken aback. She had changed beyond recognition, both physically and in character. She had always been a handful – a little bag of trouble as they used to call her – but now she was so confident, so worldly. They both shook their heads with disbelief when they spoke about her between themselves. But their wives persuaded them they should go to the notary.

'Knowing Zaira,' one sister-in-law said, 'she will make even more trouble if you don't.'

So finally the papers were drawn up and Zaira became the legal owner of her house in Torretta. She planned to spend the autumn months there while Alba was at school in Piacenza. She loved the colours of autumn – the leaves of red, yellow and gold, the temperature high enough to sit outside her house, and feel the sun on her face, and in the evenings the softly-focused pink sunsets. Yet she shuddered to think of the harsh winters she had spent there as a child: the weather so cruel and unforgiving, the storms, winds, rains and then the sleet and snow. Sometimes there was so much snow Torretta became completely cut off and trying to walk anywhere in the deep snow was very fatiguing. In fact, the easiest thing to do was to construct home-made wooden skis. As a child Zaira had tentatively skied over the gently sloping hills but her brothers had become quite fast. Best of all, Zaira had loved tobogganing. Sometimes she and her brothers had all piled on the same plank of wood, an old tray, and raced down the hill, falling into a heap at its foot.

Alba had promised to visit most weekends but there was still Fabio to worry about. Zaira was thinking of going back to Tortello before the end of November. She was too used to the luxuries of a well-heated house; she would find it difficult to survive the bitter cold and snow of a Torretta winter. How she had changed! She had taken it in her stride as a young girl and had hardly noticed the freezing cold and damp winters, with only a couple of wood-burning stoves to keep the entire house warm.

However, she did promise to help her brothers with the wine harvest – the *vendemmia* – in October. She was never quite sure how they decided the grapes were ready. Taste, smell, size, colour, all these things were important. They spent a week pulling bunches of grapes off the vines and collecting them into wooden boxes. Then the horse and cart went back and forth, taking the boxes to the big barn used for wine-making. The grapes were put into long wooden troughs and then all the helpers trod them with their feet. Zaira had never forgotten the sensation of doing this, and found it quite exhilarating. The grape juice was put into huge oak barrels and eventually filtered into big glass containers called demijohns and left to ferment, with any sediment collecting at the bottom.

During Zaira's time in Torretta, Leonardo accompanied Alba on weekend visits, and occasionally stayed himself. In spite of their recent coolness towards each other, Zaira and Leonardo resumed their physical relations. Zaira had missed her lover in her bed – not just their sexual activities, but the way he held her, fitting so neatly against each other's bodies when they slept. Leonardo, too, could not do without his Zaira. They had both been lonely and needed physical comfort and affection.

The local inhabitants didn't know what to make of it all.

Because Leonardo was a Bertini he was tolerated, and they bowed and took their hats off every time he was seen. '*Buongiorno Signore, buongiorno,*' they said, rather than '*Bongiurren*'. They still could not believe there was a Bertini up in Torretta!

'*Chu bell' hum!* – What a handsome man!' they muttered.

Leonardo still thought it was the edge of the world, yet he rather enjoyed the tranquillity of the place, as if nothing had changed for a thousand years. He could relax and lie back, curious about all the peasants' feuds and the tall stories Zaira used to hear as a girl.

Zaira tried not to think too much about Fabio, but nevertheless she did every day. Leonardo had told her that he and Fabio had conducted quite a few reasonable conversations, and sometimes Alba joined in too. Father and daughter both felt that they had made some headway:

'At least Fabio will actually talk about it now,' Leonardo reassured Zaira.

What Fabio had said was: 'Regardless of the real circumstances of my birth, Livietta was always my mother – and her death is too hard to bear.'

If only he could have talked to Zaira, reassured her, sought her opinion, then possibly he could have tried to accept her, but as it was he felt that he would be sullying Livietta's memory if he openly called Zaira his mother. Livietta had been so sweet, so gentle, so understanding with him. She would have shown him how to accept the truth, told him what to do. He missed her so much and could not find any consolation in the fact that Zaira was his mother.

Zaira shrugged. She had to be patient – something she found very difficult.

Leonardo, at the end of each visit, always insisted that Zaira come back down to Tortello:

'Take over my aunt's place in Tortello. I've had it completely refurbished. It would be neutral ground for Fabio. You could ask him to visit you there. You never know, one day you might even be able to talk to him about it all.'

Zaira was finally persuaded. She had already decided not to spend the winter in Torretta. Alba wouldn't be able to visit her if it snowed and became completely cut off, the steep icy tracks impossible to climb. She would stay in Tortello instead. And '*Chi sa?* – Who knows?' she thought. 'Maybe Fabio will slowly come round.'

Leonardo continually tried to soothe her: 'One day we can all live as a family again.'

25. Fabio

Zaira did indeed return to Tortello for the winter. The Contessa's old home had been modernised and all the gloomy old furniture had either been put into storage or distributed amongst the estate workers. The apartment house was now elegantly but simply furnished, and the uncurtained windows let in lots of light. Zaira moved in there as soon as she got back from Torretta.

However, she was desperate to see her son and wanted to go to Bertini. Leonardo told her she could not because Fabio was ill with a bad cold, and maybe she should put off trying to see him.

He had not told her the whole truth: Fabio was extremely ill, possibly dying, the doctors said, of pneumonia. Leonardo knew she would make a fuss and want to visit her son. And then Fabio wouldn't want to see her, and this would make him worse, and oh dear ...

Leonardo was at the end of his tether and didn't know what to do for the best. Finally, when all remedies had failed, and the doctors had all given up hope, Zaira was called to Bertini.

'Fabio is dying,' was all Leonardo said. Zaira hadn't been to the place for four months, and was reminded of that other time she returned to find Livietta nearly dead from childbirth, and her stillborn son in the midwife's arms.

The atmosphere was similarly dark and mournful now. Fabio had lost consciousness and didn't recognise Zaira. She wanted to cry, but could not. She looked at that pale, painfully thin ghost that was her son, and felt numb with shock. The doctor was taking his pulse. She felt a great lump in her throat, and was overcome with guilt. She felt she had hastened his death. It was all her fault for making Leonardo tell him the truth about his origins.

Oh, what torment! She felt so strange: she was weeping inside, but externally it was as if she was in that old trance-like state she had experienced before. This was not happening to her; she was dreaming. Fabio had to recover – he couldn't possibly die. She thought she heard him say something. Was it 'Mama?' She couldn't make it out, but it would be Livietta he was calling, not her.

Leonardo was much more visibly upset. He and Alba were both holding Fabio's hand, on the other side of the bed. When the doctor shook his head and announced that the boy was indeed dead, Leonardo let out great racking sobs. Zaira had never seen him cry like this before. She had to comfort him.

'Poor darling Leonardo.' She rushed over and hugged him as hard as she could. He hugged her back in turn. He needed Zaira more than ever. He had lost his beloved parents, his brother was in America, and now his son was dead.

'Oh Zaira, just hold me, hold me.' Zaira and Alba were all he had left.

He wouldn't permit her to live on her own again. Married or not, they would live together, for ever.

'We must keep together.' He struggled to say the words between his tears.

The funeral took place three days later, and Leonardo and

Zaira got through it as best they could, trying not to let their emotions get the better of them. They wanted it to be over as quickly as possible. Livietta's parents were not so controlled. First their daughter and now their grandson. God had been so cruel to them. He had taken poor Livietta and now Fabio. 'Why, oh why?' they wondered. They, too, felt consumed with guilt. Maybe they had been wrong that long time ago to insist on Livietta marrying Leonardo.

'Oh, how I wish I could turn the clock back to when Livietta was still unmarried, happy and safe at home,' said Rina to her husband, sobbing and wringing her hands, 'and these tragic events would never have happened.'

Rodolfo Ruggieri was a broken man. He had lost all interest in the vineyards and was arranging to lease them out to his steward. He and his wife had insisted that Fabio be buried at Castellengo. Although Zaira was unhappy with this, she hadn't the heart to refuse them, so Fabio was buried alongside Livietta, in the family vault inside the little chapel. Zaira realised that Fabio would have wanted this as well. Fabio, like Livietta, had spent some of his happiest days at the Azienda.

After the funeral was over, Zaira told Leonardo that she would always blame herself for Fabio's death.

'It's all my fault,' she said hysterically. 'If I hadn't insisted on telling him the truth ... He was such a nervous, delicate child ... the truth killed him, it killed him.'

'No, Zaira, the doctors told me he would have died sooner or later.' Leonardo hesitated and swallowed, then continued with a sigh. 'Apparently Fabio was born with a weak heart. When he developed pneumonia, his heart just couldn't take the strain. The doctors were surprised he lived as long as he did. He could quite easily have died when he was a baby.'

He wept quietly, and Zaira held out her arms to him:

'Leonardo, my darling, come to me. Let me hold you.'

She knew she had to be strong. She had been so egotistical, so self-obsessed. She had to think only of him and Alba now.

'I have been so selfish; I should have just left things as they were. Now I just want to look after you and Alba. Ah, my poor darling Fabio, he was so wretched, and he had a weak heart too. And you have suffered so much. Please forgive me.'

It was the first time Zaira had ever been truly contrite in her life.

'Zaira, there is nothing to forgive. We need each other, and we must have the strength to carry on, for Alba's sake. Alba, it is she who matters now.'

Leonardo decided to close Bertini; he could not live there any longer. The last few months after Zaira had left had been so miserable. Fabio was so withdrawn and moody and then there was his illness. He could not bear to remember the boy dying in his room: the heavy drawn curtains excluding the sunlight, the smell of medicines and disinfectant, the moment when the boy died and his still-open eyes glazed over, as if there was nothing behind them, and finally the smell of death itself that lingered even now.

Leonardo moved to the apartment house in Tortello with Zaira. He didn't care about the gossip. Zaira had put up with it all her life; it didn't seem to worry her, so why should it worry him? The house was still very simply furnished and the waxed parquet floors were left bare. The one frivolous item was a fake but fashionable medieval fireplace installed in the drawing room. It was in homage to D'Annunzio who had written *La Figlia di Joreio*. This was the story of a woman who sacrificed her life for her lover, crying:

'*La fiamma è bella!* – The flame is beautiful!' This line became famous throughout Italy and was inscribed in Gothic script along the top of the fireplace. Zaira and Leonardo still enjoyed a private joke about it, and he still called her Rosetta when he was in one of his lighter moods. He wanted to have a portrait painted of her to hang above the fireplace but she always refused.

Alba would return there for weekends from school in Piacenza, but in the summer months Zaira insisted that she and Alba spend some time in Torretta. After all, it was much cooler up in the hills than in Tortello and they could still visit the Mediterranean coast for at least two weeks as well.

Marriage was never mentioned, but one late spring day, just as Zaira was about to prepare to return to Torretta, Leonardo told her to get ready to go out. He wanted to take her to one of the churches in Tortello, a sixteenth-century construction called the Holy Trinity. He had decided against the *Pieve* at the top of Tortello, the stunning Romanesque church that could be seen for miles around, where he and Livietta had married. Leonardo didn't tell her the real reason why they were going to the church. All he said was, 'Zaira, let's go to Santa Trinità today to light some candles for our son Fabio and poor Livietta. This did not surprise Zaira; they now both found these religious rituals quite comforting. They parked the car in the lower part of Tortello and proceeded to walk up the steep road to the top, past the thirteenth-century public wash house, still in use, and up to the red-bricked Town Hall and Podestà, dating back to the fifteenth century.

'I thought we were going to church,' said Zaira.

'We are. I just have to collect some documents from the Town Hall.'

While Zaira waited she looked to the side of the square where there was a path leading to the drawbridge of the castle tower and the castellated battlements, the place where the Visconti of Lombardy and the Scotti had once waged war over Tortello. As Zaira looked round she remembered the story of a virgin, Laura Dellavigna, the daughter of the gaol keeper, who fell in love with a prisoner in the castle. She helped him escape and they attempted to flee but the two lovers were betrayed by some unknown enemy and were brought back, tried and executed in the main square for fornication, of which they were innocent.

'Well, at least that hasn't happened to me ... yet!' mused Zaira.

After a few minutes, Zaira saw Leonardo come out of the Town Hall with some papers in his hand. He quickly took hold of her arm and they walked down the steep cobbled street from the main square and made their way inside the church of Santa Trinità. Zaira could see there was a priest standing at the altar. Leonardo ushered her up the aisle with her elbow in his hand. They were both wearing black, Leonardo in a smart morning suit and Zaira in a tight-waisted tapering silk dress, with a black lace veil hanging from her black bonnet. Leonardo took something out of his pocket and concealed it in his fist. It was a black velvet box. Inside was a gold wedding ring. He twirled it between his fingers. Leonardo had managed to organise the ceremony very quietly, very discreetly, and with special permission from the Town Hall in Tortello. He had told Alba about it but as it was a weekday they both decided it would be better if she stayed at school.

Zaira realised what was happening when she saw Leonardo open the box in his hand and take the ring out. She was just about to say something, to chide him, but the priest after reciting a *Pater Noster* had already started the marriage ceremony. The organist, who had been practising some hymns, and one of the vergers, who had been stacking candles, were the witnesses. Leonardo and Zaira repeated the words of the priest, and he pronounced them husband and wife at long last. Zaira was just 30, and Leonardo was 38. They were quite an elderly couple for that time.

When they left the church, the heat of the sun was fierce on their faces. Zaira looked up at Leonardo, shielding her eyes from the sunlight, and hit him playfully on the arm with her fan. 'You, you ...' She was lost for words. Then they both laughed, and kissed each other gently on the lips.

Zaira, Leonardo and Alba journeyed to Torretta a few days later causing a stir amongst the inhabitants – who had already heard about the wedding. News like this always travelled fast. Somehow a relation of a relation of someone in Torretta had seen the happy couple coming out of the church. It didn't take much to guess they had got married, and the verger proudly confirmed it.

'Zaira, the wife of a Bertini! Who would have thought it possible!'

'*Quella fieula di Barto...* – Barto's daughter, she did well for herself after all, uff!'

When Leonardo was in Torretta, he donned a wide-brimmed straw hat and helped out in the garden, overjoyed to see the vegetables growing so big. He was especially proud of his potatoes that he had grown himself without anybody's help. Zaira teased him that he was turning into an old 'contadino'. He had grown a long black beard and wore a tatty old shirt and corduroy trousers. Zaira said: 'Soon you'll have hair sprouting out of your nostrils and ears, and then your teeth will go black!' The same Leonardo who had once been so fastidious about his appearance and his clothes was now dressed like a peasant. He was a real Tino now.

He and Zaira continued to enjoy good sexual relations, but their relationship was now mainly based on companionship and mutual comfort. They were best friends, rather than passionate lovers. In the back of their minds was always the spectre of Fabio, poor Fabio.

How they had both changed since their first meeting. She had forgotten her ambitions about work, about independence, about travel. She had never even left Italy! Her opinions had become more moderate too, and she was much more considerate of other people. She put all her energies into Alba, her daughter. Alba would do what she had never been able to do herself.

Leonardo had lost all trace of that coldness, that ruthlessness, of his. He was much more aware now of his inner feelings. His car factory had finally failed. They only ever managed to make four cars in ten years. The competition had been too great. The four other car factories in Italy were, between them, producing hundreds of cars a year. Leonardo had been humbled by the failure of his enterprise, and, of course, Fabio's death had made an indelible mark. His son was constantly in his thoughts, but even though he never wanted to admit it to himself, he had realised quite a long time ago that Fabio would have grown up to be weak and vacillating, so very different from Alba.

Zaira and Leonardo knew that Alba was the future. There was hope for Italy and the world. Women like Alba would be properly educated – she would go to university, become a doctor or a lawyer, but only if she wanted to...

26. **Epilogue**

The Great War intervened and lives were changed yet again. Italy was not very fortunate in its colonial ambitions, although it did eventually gain Libya after the war with Turkey. It possibly achieved more respect in the world when, after events in Sarajevo and lots of prevarication, it left the Triple Alliance in 1915 and joined Britain, France and Russia as allies against Germany and the Austro-Hungarian empire.

Leonardo decided to enlist even though he was too old for active service. He persisted in his quest to serve in some position or other. He had always wanted to be a real soldier in a real war, which is why he had suggested a soldier husband for Zaira all that time ago in Piacenza. Zaira tried to dissuade him from going, but he too could be stubborn sometimes.

Finally he was allowed to serve as an infantryman and travelled with the Italian Army to Albania with the rank of captain. Unfortunately the conditions there were dreadful – no proper tents, no hygiene – and he died of malaria in 1916. He was brought back to Bertini and buried with full honours as a war hero, without ever killing a German.

Zaira was heartbroken. She recalled their mutual yet, on her part, reluctant attraction when they first met. They had finally achieved an equal and deeply loving relationship. How she missed that!

She continued to spend her time between Tortello and Torretta, and Alba was with her every weekend.

Zaira smiled to think that she, of all people, was living back in Torretta, when she had been so keen to get away. She and her brothers and their families managed to live in relative harmony together. They had the odd argument about the state of Italy or the goings-on in the village, but everyone had grown accustomed to having Zaira back at home. She already had great nieces and nephews whom she entertained by reading stories or making up her own adventures, pretending she had travelled all over the world, to London, New York, Australia. The entire family adored Alba. Everyone made a fuss of her, even her uncles, which was quite unheard-of for a Crespi.

Alba was keen to do well at school and study hard. Zaira wanted her daughter to attend the University more than anything. She was a Bertini; she could do what she wanted. Zaira, a peasant girl, could never have gone to university, but now, for a girl like Alba, anything was possible. When this terrible war was over, they would start to make plans again for the future. There was lots to plan ... and they might even travel to America to visit Uncle Claudio, or Great-uncle Franco and his family in London.

[They do travel to London, and there Alba meets a boy who will eventually become her husband. They never make it to America, but Claudio returns to Italy after the war is over. He decides to reside at Bertini with Zaira's consent. Leonardo has made sure that Zaira and Alba are comfortably off, but there isn't that much money left. Claudio is already thinking up new money-making ventures. He is involved in setting up a racetrack at Monza, near Milan. He and Zaira become firm friends and it is through her that he finally meets

a young woman, twenty years his junior, who becomes his wife. She
is an acquaintance of Aunt Elena's from Turin.]

Zaira was relatively happy. Tending her garden was her greatest interest. She was still a voracious reader, and interested in politics, and occasionally she wrote an article for the local newspaper, *Libertà*. Life in Torretta was peaceful and relaxing but she enjoyed Tortello as well. There was much more to entertain Alba there.

After the war, the cries for the establishment of a proper organised state and, above all, an honourable nation by the ever-growing illiberal lower middle classes made the rise of Mussolini's National Socialism almost inevitable. 'Oh, who would have thought it, Italy being ruled by such an imbecile?' Zaira couldn't bear to think about it – all the dreams she'd had for Italy, now all shattered.

Zaira was the same age as her father, not even sixty, when she died of a heart attack while at her house in Torretta. It was her wish to be buried at the church of Sant'Antonio, not at Bertini. Torretta was where she came from and where she would return to the earth. Alba, who was now a qualified lawyer, ensured her mother's wishes were obeyed.

[Zaira lies buried in the church of Sant'Antonio at Torretta, but sadly today there is no sign of her grave and no photographs of her were ever found, as if she who was 'born before her time' never existed.]

SD - #0013 - 110425 - C0 - 216/138/17 - PB - 9780992723569 - Matt Lamination